HOT *London* NIGHTS

BOOK 7 IN THE LONDON ROMANCE SERIES

by Clare Lydon

custard
books

First Edition January 2021
Published by Custard Books
Copyright © 2021 Clare Lydon
ISBN: 978-1-912019-48-9

Cover Design: Kevin Pruitt
Editor: Kelli Collins
Typesetting: Adrian McLaughlin

Find out more at: www.clarelydon.co.uk
Follow me on Twitter: @clarelydon
Follow me on Instagram: @clarefic

Also By Clare Lydon

London Romance Series
London Calling (Book One)
This London Love (Book Two)
A Girl Called London (Book Three)
The London Of Us (Book Four)
London, Actually (Book Five)
Made In London (Book Six)
Hot London Nights (Book Seven)
Big London Dreams (Book Eight)
London Ever After (Book Nine)

Standalone Novels
A Taste Of Love
Before You Say I Do
Change Of Heart
Christmas In Mistletoe
Hotshot
It Started With A Kiss
Nothing To Lose: A Lesbian Romance
Once Upon A Princess
One Golden Summer
The Christmas Catch
The Long Weekend
Twice In A Lifetime
You're My Kind

All I Want Series
Two novels and four novellas chart the course
of one relationship over two years.

Boxsets
Available for both the London Romance series and the
All I Want series for ultimate value. Check out my
website for more: www.clarelydon.co.uk/books

Acknowledgements

I'll let you into a secret: book seven in the London Romance series was meant to be about Lib. However, when I wrote the character of India in book six, she jumped off the page and insisted on being the star of this book. I had no choice but to obey. I'd already decided her match was going to be Nagina, and so *Hot London Nights* was born.

One thing I wanted to get spot-on were the details of a Hindu Punjabi family: the names, the culture, the food. Huge thanks to Amisha Jogia for helping me out with that – your guidance was invaluable! Thanks to my wife, Yvonne, and Angela for their first reads and helpful comments. Hugs also to my fantastic advanced reading team for their eagle eyes. You're all ace.

As usual, thanks to my awesome team of talented professionals who make sure my books look and read the best they can. To Kevin Pruitt for the bang-up cover. Kelli Collins for the fab editing. Claire Jarrett for the excellent proofing. Finally, to Adrian McLaughlin for his typesetting magic.

Last but definitely not least, thanks to you for buying this book and supporting this independent author. I hope you love the story of Gina and India, and that this latest London Romance book leaves you hungry for more. I plan to write book eight this year and it's going to be the story of Eunice and Joan, told in present day and flashback. So if you want more from them (I hope you do!), stay tuned.

If you fancy getting in touch, you can do so using one of the methods below. I'm most active on Instagram and Facebook.

Twitter: @ClareLydon
Facebook: www.facebook.com/clare.lydon
Instagram: @clarefic
Find out more at: www.clarelydon.co.uk
Contact: mail@clarelydon.co.uk

Thank you so much for reading!

Just in case you need reminding:
it's never too late.

Chapter One

India Contelli glanced around the third floor of Bloomsbury Set House, scanning the sparse crowd for her brother, Luca. He wasn't here yet. She'd belonged to the private members' club for years, but having been away for three months filming in New York, she hadn't used it for a while.

Now she was back, India hoped London would be more welcoming than when she'd left. She was determined to make it so. Even the wool-grey sky lingering outside the large square windows wasn't putting her off. She pulled back her broad shoulders and straightened her spine.

This was home, and this time, she was going nowhere. Nobody was going to drive her out of her own city again.

A teaspoon clattering to the floor made her turn her head. A waiter bent to retrieve it, apologising to the couple two tables away. The space was only half full at midday in late January, business meetings and lazy coffee breaks taking place on plump, expensive sofas and marble-topped tables. The tall ceilings and ornate stonework lent a sense of grandeur and history to the space. India's parents and grandparents had been members, too. The smell of freshly ground coffee coated the air, along with hot buttered toast.

She glanced out to the roof terrace, empty save for a

solitary pigeon, its grey-and-white belly fat as it strutted across a tabletop. The terrace had the kind of views India wanted in her next pad: in the thick of it, looking at London from the top down. She'd love to move in here, but even she was on a budget.

She sat down on a lush, red velvet couch, then draped her coat over its arm. A waiter appeared in seconds, took her order and delivered her glass of Chablis at speed.

When India looked up, a figure heading her way caught her gaze. Tall, dark hair, aquamarine eyes. They were a carbon copy of each other, and both gay, too. Their parents had been baffled at first, but now, they just wanted grandchildren, and they weren't fussy how it happened.

When her brother reached her, she got up and they embraced. He took a seat beside her, his chiselled jaw prominent, his fake tan perfected. His teeth shone almost as bright as his Cartier watch. They'd grown up rich, and it showed.

But now, India wanted to give something back.

Luca flagged down a waiter and ordered a black coffee. He did it in the way Luca always did, which meant the waiter fluttered his dark eyelashes Luca's way before he left. Her brother had that effect on men. India had the same effect on women. So far though, definitely not the *right* women.

"You really should stop being such a shameless flirt."

Luca ran a hand through his shiny hair and gave her his charming grin. "A little harmless flirtation makes life more interesting. You should try it sometime."

"It normally ends in tears." She didn't want to get into that today. "You look gayer than when I last saw you. Is that possible?"

"I wasn't sure it was possible to squeeze any more gay out

of me, but if you say so. You're a lesbian icon, so I have to believe it."

India rolled her eyes. "Aren't lesbian icons meant to have a stream of women knocking at their door?"

"You need a permanent door for them to knock on."

He had a point. She sipped her Chablis.

"Not doing dry January?" Luca inclined his head towards her wine.

India raised a sardonic eyebrow. "January is hard enough, sweetheart." She paused. "How's Ricardo?"

"So beautiful, I feel like I might get pregnant just looking at him."

"Mother will be pleased."

"We're looking into it more seriously now." Luca twisted the band of his wedding ring. "Surrogacy."

India put a hand on his knee. "A baby Luca or Ricardo will be gorgeous."

"I hope so." He gave her a smile. "Anyway, enough about me, how was New York? Did the filming go well?"

She nodded. "It did. The new series is wrapped, now we wait for it to hit the screens."

India was an accidental semi-TV star, doling out business advice to new shop owners in the UK and now the US in her show, *Shop Wars*. She looked good on camera, and her confidence shone through. When it came to business, India had her shit sorted. Their family biscuit and confectionery company, Stable Foods, was one of the best in the world, and she was its incoming head.

"But now I'm back, I wanted to talk to you about a new project. One I might need your help with to persuade Dad."

Luca sat forward. "He pretty much trusts you now, doesn't he? Isn't he retiring this year?"

He did trust her, to a point. "He's still a little touchy when it comes to gay things."

"Aaaah." Luca thanked the waiter who brought his coffee, added sugar, then stirred.

"We had that whole campaign with the Chocolate Delight spread, and it was a smash hit with the LGBT+ community. This year, I want to get involved with London Pride and do something queer with the business. Make a statement." India had hatched her latest idea on the plane back to the UK. "I want to produce a Pride biscuit. Something rainbow themed and fabulous."

"I'm here for anything fabulous. Let's talk to Dad at our monthly family dinner in a few weeks. You are coming in February, seeing as you haven't been to one since October when you left?"

She nodded. "I am. The lone spinster will be there, among the loved-up couples of my family."

He leaned over and kissed her cheek. "A Pride biscuit is sure to bring all the girls to your yard."

"Thank you, Kelis." India smiled. "Like you say, I need a yard, first. And a door."

"How's that search going?" Luca asked.

"I'm restarting in February. Or maybe March — I'm doing a lot of business travel next month."

"I thought you were back now?"

"I am, but I'm just taking some weight off Dad and doing a few European trips."

"You are the model daughter." Luca smiled. "Good job

I'm giving them a baby, otherwise I'd be well down the pecking order." He paused. "Why don't you ask Dad for his estate agent's number?"

"Because I want to do this myself. I don't want Dad's agent involved. I want this place to be mine, something *I* find."

"I understand that." Luca and Ricardo had done the same with their place in Surrey. Luca had gone one step further and left the family business to pursue his career as a photographer. It's how he'd met the love of his life, Ricardo being a model.

India was yet to meet hers.

Working in the family business had its limitations.

"If we can help in any way with the search, let me know. For what it's worth, Dad will see the PR potential of the Pride biscuits. The Chocolate Delight campaign was a success, right?" They'd run their chocolate spread campaign last year with a lesbian slant, and it had received a terrific reception.

She nodded. "Huge. But he still gets nervous when it comes to alienating any group of people. But I don't see an issue with being the gay food company of choice." She snagged his gaze. "If you could hurry up and get pregnant, it'd give him something else to focus on."

"If it helps you out, we'll kick the process up a notch." Luca leaned forward. "I missed you, by the way."

"You did not."

He drew a cross on his chest with his index finger. "I did! *We* did. Christmas wasn't the same without you."

India shrugged. "After everything that happened with Andi, I needed to get away. The series came along at just the right time."

"I know. But we missed you. London missed you. Even Mum and Dad did. I could kill Andi for doing what she did."

India shook her head. She didn't want to dwell. She'd done enough of that. "It was nice to do something different. I spent Christmas Day walking around Manhattan, and the evening in my hotel bar, sharing love wounds with a gorgeous gay barman. I needed some time." It'd been healing going alone, too. Given her space to focus on what she really wanted.

"Have you heard from her since you got back?"

India shook her head. "Now I'm here, I'm going to focus on growing the business with Dad and making a real difference in the queer community. Give some money to projects, boost our profile."

Luca eyed her. "The lesbian Mother Teresa, is that the look you're going for?"

India smirked, glancing down at her jade-green Armani suit. "I think we can spin it a bit better than that, can't we?"

Chapter Two

Gina Gupta spun around in her office chair, grabbed her stress ball and threw it against the cream-coloured wall. There was a satisfying thud, then she caught it. She did it again. The wall had a grey mark from where she'd been throwing the ball a little too much over the past year. Gina saw it as evidence of keeping her mental health in check.

Her ex, Sara, was certainly testing her boundaries.

She couldn't believe the last two emails she'd received. The first, from a client asking her to up the price of their property by 50k, when she'd told him it was overpriced and a buyer's market. But no, this client knew best. She could hear the tone loud and clear in his email. Having been in the property business a few years, it was nothing new. Neither was the second email from her ex, Sara, despite the fact they'd been split up nearly a year.

The email told Gina that Sara had cleared their joint account "because she had a cashflow issue". Gina didn't recall a time when Sara *didn't* have a cashflow issue. She was a struggling artist, it was in her DNA. Sara's creative side had been appealing when they'd first got together, but Gina soon learned it was a crutch Sara leaned on. It was one of the many reasons they'd split up. Gina would never see that £500 again, but it was a small price to pay. She'd just phoned the bank and shut down the account. She should have done it months ago.

She bounced the ball again and caught it. Sara wasn't going to throw her off track again. Gina was *so* over it. She ran a hand through her short, dark hair.

When they'd first split up, Sara had continually shown up at her office, asking Gina to reconsider. Her business partner, Bernie, had been a saviour, gently coaxing Sara out the door, often taking her back to whoever's sofa she was temporarily staying on.

Gina's life was just getting back on an even keel nine months later, and she was grateful. Sara had been harder to shake than Gina had expected.

She put the ball back into her top drawer, then sat forward and surfed to the Pride in London website. She clicked on the 'Volunteer' tab. They were still looking for people. Should she put herself forward? She might meet some new friends, and she could use some of those, especially queer ones. Plus, she loved the theme of this year's Pride event: 'It's Never Too Late'. It could be the theme of her life.

Gina had been a late bloomer, not coming out until her early 30s. Her late blooming applied to her career, too. The same decade had seen her switch from being an accountant to a successful upmarket estate agent. She'd turned 40 last year, and celebrated by splitting up with Sara. Now she wanted to shake things up. Start a new chapter. Maybe volunteering for Pride was the way forward?

"Good morning!" Her business partner Bernie bustled in, larger than life. She gave Gina a wink as she sank into her pillar-box-red office chair, her phone skittering across her wide oak desk. She patted Connie the cheese plant behind her, Bernie's pride and joy. Although, lately, Gina had been watering Connie because Bernie had been AWOL. It was Wednesday, and this was the first day she'd been in this week. Gina wanted to say something, but she wasn't quite sure what.

"Ask me how much commission I just earned this morning, showing a client around the Tower Bridge apartment?"

Gina glanced right. Okay, maybe her talk wasn't needed if Bernie had actually been working today. "You sold it?"

"On the cusp." Bernie swivelled left, then right, stretching out her long legs. At nearly six feet tall, she had a lot of limbs to contend with. "He's got to consult with his business partner, so he took loads of photos." She shook her head. "I never understand that. We photographed the whole damn flat with fabulous lighting, just show them the website."

"People don't trust websites, you know that. They think it's all smoke and mirrors."

Bernie shook her head. "Look at this face." She cupped her chin with her thumb and index fingers, her close-cropped dark hair not moving an inch. "Is this a face that would lie to you?"

"You did once tell me you were related to Victoria Beckham."

"Yes, but I wouldn't try to sell you a fake flat." Bernie waved a hand. "My mum went to school with Victoria's mum, so it wasn't a lie. I've been in the same car with her when we were kids. She was a sullen child, too."

"She's probably lovely. Don't believe everything you read in the press."

"I know, fake news!" Bernie got up and walked to the

back of the office, grabbing a mug and inserting a pod into the coffee machine. "Do you need a refill?"

Gina shook her head. "I've already had two."

Bernie pressed the button and the coffee machine whirred to life. "It's only 9.45."

"It's been a long morning already."

"Let me guess." She sat on the edge of Gina's desk. The noise of the coffee machine drilled the air. "Shad Thames or Mayfair?"

Gina gave her a smile. She'd been trying to sell the Shad Thames property the whole of January, to no avail. It was gorgeous, but the problem was, it didn't have a direct river view. Rather, it looked out over London rooftops. Gina thought it had a charm, and she was just waiting for the right buyer to appreciate it. But that wasn't her issue today. "Mayfair this morning. He wants to up the price. Can you believe the cheek of the man?"

"There's a reason why these people are rich, always remember that." Bernie pushed herself up and walked over to collect her coffee as the familiar buzzing stopped. "I hope you pushed back?"

Gina nodded. "Of course. He liked it when I did that last time, told me it showed I knew what I was doing. Conversely, Shad Thames man told me to drop the price for the right client today. He's far better to deal with."

"Not all clients are bad."

"They're not," Gina agreed. Even though she was the one who dealt with most of them lately. "Apart from Mayfair man, who's an idiot. As is my ex-girlfriend."

Bernie sat back down in her chair with a groan. She swung

one way, then the other. When she was in her chair, Bernie often treated it like a fairground ride. Gina always knew Bernie was focused when she stayed still for longer than five seconds. Today was not that day.

"What's Sara done this time?" She stilled as she asked.

"Cleared out our joint bank account, claiming cashflow issues." Gina clicked her mouse. The Pride website appeared again. She was going to do it. Put herself out there. She might meet a new friend, or perhaps more. It would restore her faith in women. Prove that not all of them were out to bleed her dry.

"She did?" Bernie frowned, her cheeks flushing the colour of her chair. "I thought you'd cut all contact?"

Gina shrugged like it meant nothing. "I had, but I forgot to shut our joint account. That was our last remaining link. But it's done now."

"She's got some nerve. Stealing money from you after everything you did for her."

"I know, right?" Gina waved a hand. "But she's in the past. Shad Thames is in my future, as is Mayfair. I'm going to sell one of those soon if it kills me."

Chapter Three

India walked into the Sea Containers restaurant and saw Frankie right away. Being tall, sharply dressed and deliciously butch, she was easy to spot.

"Just the woman I need to see on this cold, miserable February lunchtime!" Frankie Stark gave India a firm hug.

India hugged her right back. "Good to see you, too," she replied over Frankie's shoulder, breathing in her aftershave. Always aftershave. Frankie was old school. They parted and settled into their seats.

India hadn't been lying — it really was good to see her old friend. It represented some kind of normality seeping back into her life. Frankie and India were an unlikely pairing, but they'd hit it off as soon as they met. Frankie was a club promoter famous in the queer London scene. India was a business powerhouse turned semi-famous lesbian. They both enjoyed making deals and charming people. Their relationship had started off as a mutually convenient one, but soon blossomed into a full-on lesmance.

When they'd first met, Frankie had been far more brash. She'd needed to be, working in such a male environment. Years in the spotlight had smoothed her rough edges, but her attitude and energy were still punchy, her Yorkshire accent as strong as ever. It was a badge of honour with Frankie. She always told India the day she lost her northern accent was the day she should pack up and leave London.

"Good to have you back in the land of the living after scuttling off to America."

India pressed her thumb into the palm of her opposite hand. "I didn't scuttle anywhere."

Frankie tilted her head. "Nobody would blame you. Andi was a total bitch."

"Ancient history." India didn't want to dwell. She glanced around the restaurant at the bottom of the modern hotel, overlooking the river. The grey of the day was offset by the restaurant's strong lighting, a yellow haze all around the room. "Although did we have to meet on Valentine's Day? Should I have brought you a cuddly toy?"

"I'd have clonked you over the head with it if you had." Frankie gave her a grin. "Are you back for good, now?"

India rolled her head left, then right. "Yes and no. I have a lot of European visits with work, so I'm in and out of the country for the next few weeks. But I'm still based here. No more filming. No more New York." India paused. "How are the Pride preparations going?" Frankie was co-chair of London Pride this year, her third time in a row.

She rolled her eyes. "You know how it is. Same shit, different year."

"I also happen to know you love being in charge, whatever you say. Give you a loudspeaker and you're a hopeless case."

"What can I say? I was born to be a professional shouter."

They ordered the set menu and a bottle of Cabernet Sauvignon, India giving the restaurant the once-over. Nobody appeared to be noticing her, which she was pleased about.

It was only over the past three years, when she'd become a minor TV celebrity, that she'd shot to fame. Suddenly, she'd gone from being mentioned in business pages and the occasional feature in women's magazines, to being papped coming out of a nightclub with a woman on her arm. It'd been quite the adjustment, and one her parents were still coming to terms with. It had also played havoc with her relationships.

"Now that I am back in London, I want to make a splash. Show that the Chocolate Delight campaign wasn't just a one-off to swoop in and take the pink pound for a ride. This year, I want to do a Pride biscuit."

"A Pride biscuit?" Frankie sat forward. "That Chocolate Delight campaign is still causing ripples throughout the lesbian community. The pressure to smear chocolate spread on your lover's lady garden was out of control for a while there."

India snorted. "Lady garden? How is Phyllis and her lady garden, by the way?" Frankie had been with her wife Phyllis for years.

"Good as gold." Frankie glanced over India's shoulder, and her face dropped. "Oh, shit."

India twisted and followed Frankie's gaze until it landed on precisely the person she least wanted to see today. Or any day, for that matter. Andi. Alone at a table on the far side of the restaurant.

India sank down in her chair, a chill working its way through her.

Frankie reached out a hand and put it on her arm. "If she comes over, I can deal with her, okay?"

India winced. "You don't have to, I can cope. But I doubt she's going to come over." She stared out the window in the opposite direction. The Thames sat stony and grey in her eyeline. A river taxi swished by. It was a normal day and they were out for a normal lunch. India could totally handle this.

At the table next to them, a man and a woman sat down, the man presenting the woman with a bouquet of red roses. She kissed him on the lips as she accepted his gift.

India pursed her lips. *Ugh, Valentine's Day.* If Andi was here with a new woman, India might not be able to hold down her lunch. She was not going to look.

"I don't think she's seen us." Frankie eyed India. "Anyway, let's ignore Andi and pretend she's not here." If Frankie was wondering whether Andi's date was going to show up, she was glossing over it like a pro. "I wanted to speak to you today because you said you wanted to do more than donate to Pride this year. We've had a project drop into our laps that I'd love you to be involved in. Would you be up for it?"

Something to focus on other than Andi. India nodded. "Sounds intriguing."

"It is." Frankie reached into her bag and pulled out a large white envelope, handing it over to India as their wine arrived. The waiter went to pour, but Frankie told him she'd do it. He nodded and left.

"Put those in your bag and read them later. Keep them safe. I'll give you the backstory." Frankie poured the wine. "A woman sent us some love letters she found stuffed down the back of an old-fashioned drinks cabinet. They were written by a woman called Eunice back in 1960, and they tell a story of thwarted lesbian love."

India's stomach tightened. Her latest thwarted love affair was sitting mere feet away. "Preaching to the choir," she replied.

Frankie gave her a sad nod before she continued. "The woman who found the letters is called Petra, and she set up an Instagram page to find Eunice. It turns out Eunice is still alive, she lives in Birmingham, and she's just come out, thanks to this."

Frankie drew her hand through the air. "I mean, it's huge. She's got four kids, nine grandchildren and three great grandchildren. But back in the 1950s, before she got married to a man, she fell in love with a woman she worked with. In the letters, she just calls the woman 'H'. She won't give her name. But she's agreed to be interviewed about it and then it's up to the woman to come forward if she sees it. Eunice is coming to Pride as our guest of honour. The theme for Pride this year is 'It's Never Too Late', and Eunice is the perfect example of that." Frankie inclined her head. "Eunice found the one, but then they couldn't be together because of expectations. Quite some story, isn't it?"

"You can say that again." India had only been going out with Andi for six months, but it had been a whirlwind, and she'd briefly thought Andi could be *the one*. It had been short-lived. However, India couldn't imagine finding the *actual one*, but then not being able to be with that person because society didn't approve.

"What does her husband think?"

"He's long gone."

"Leaving Eunice free to spread her wings." India paused.

"How do you want me to be involved?" The letters were hot in her hands. She couldn't wait to read them. A piece of living history. India put them in her bag.

"I want you to be the one to interview her. You're used to the camera and good with people. Plus, you're famous, so it will garner more attention if you do it. I've put our head of special events onto the project, and she's happy to make all the arrangements and go with you to do the interview. You know how to bring out the best in people and make them shine."

Their food arrived and they tucked in. India still hadn't glanced over. "It sounds impossibly romantic and tragic, all rolled into one. Can't we persuade Eunice to say who 'H' is? What if H is still alive and carrying a torch for Eunice?"

"Obviously, I'm secretly hoping you can wheedle that out of Eunice using your special famous-person charms." Frankie's eyes flickered as she peered over India's shoulder. "Just to let you know, Andi is dining with a man. You can look now if you're quick."

India did just that. It wasn't anyone she recognised. Relief swept through her. After such a public fallout from their relationship, at least Andi wasn't here with a date.

Someone approached Andi and asked for a selfie. She agreed right away, posing with her killer smile. She was a much-loved Radio Two DJ. A national treasure. If only they knew.

India blinked then turned back to Frankie, giving her friend her full attention. "I'd love to help, consider me booked," India told her. "Plus, put us down for a float with my Pride biscuits. Do you think Eunice would like to ride on it, too?"

"Depends if you throw in free biscuits for life."

"That's not a bad PR angle." India shook her head. "I can't

wait to read the letters and meet the woman behind them. How old is she now?"

"Seventy-nine. But she's fit, able and looks amazing."

India blew out a breath. "I hope I'm amazing at 79."

Frankie reached over and squeezed India's hand. "You're amazing *now*."

India patted Frankie's hand. "Sweet of you to say." She paused. "I'd be even sweeter if I could find a new place to live. Somewhere of my own. I was just saying to Luca when I saw him recently. Do you know any good estate agents in central London?"

"This is your lucky day," Frankie told her. "I've got a great estate agent. She's got some cracking properties, sorted me and Phyllis out with our place." Frankie picked up her phone and scrolled. "I'll ping you her number. Call her and arrange a meeting. Her name's Gina. Tell her I sent you."

* * *

Frankie had to run to her next meeting right after lunch. She kissed India on the cheek as she left.

Andi was nowhere to be seen, so India relaxed for the first time since she'd arrived, her shoulders falling. She stopped to use the loo, applied more bronze-red lipstick and puckered her lips in the mirror. Maybe Frankie was right. She looked good on the outside. She just had to work on her inside, too.

She could do this.

Fuck Andi.

India ran a brush through her dark, wavy hair just as the bathroom door opened. When she looked up, her stomach sucked itself in like a vortex had just been created in her soul.

"India." Andi walked up beside her, until their reflections were standing side by side in the bathroom mirrors. "Good to see you."

"I wish I could say the same."

The comment pinged off Andi as if it had never been said. "Your hair looks beautiful, by the way, just like always."

Where India was dark-haired, professional and all about business, Andi was blond, calculating and all about making a good impression. Her tapered jeans and fitted blazer with satin lapels screamed for attention. Her long, red fingernails left people guessing. Her laser-beam green eyes drew you in. India knew all about them.

The song on the hotel speaker changed to a tune India had once considered 'theirs'. Now, every time it came on the radio, she switched it off. In fact, she hadn't been listening to the radio a whole lot of late. Not when there was a chance Andi would be on it.

Andi glanced up to the speaker. "They're playing our song."

India's muscles stiffened. Even saying words to Andi took a monumental effort. "There's not an us anymore, so the song isn't ours."

Andi moved her head back. "There will always be an us. We didn't work out, but you can't just erase us from your history. That's not how it works."

India narrowed her gaze. "I decide how things work in my world."

Andi was doing it again, wasn't she? Twisting things, making herself sound reasonable. How did she do it with such ease? India had defended her when they were together, but she knew how Andi operated now. On her own terms, and hers alone.

"I saw you out there with Frankie. Is she still running Pride?" Andi brushed her lapel. "I need to see if I can get on a parade bus this year. I'm guessing I'm not welcome on the Stable Foods double decker?"

"I think you know the answer to that." India crossed her arms, concentrating hard on staying in control and not getting emotional. She didn't want to give Andi the satisfaction.

"It's a shame. Can't we still be friends? We're going to see each other around. We're successful, famous lesbians. People expect us to play nicely."

"I don't want to play nicely, Andi. Nothing about you is nice or playful." India shook her head. Andi had put a severe dent in India's self-esteem, one she wasn't yet fully recovered from. One day they'd been together, the next, nothing. It was too soon to be in the same room as her. Too soon to look into Andi's face, because India could still recall all the lies Andi had told her. The 'I love you' notes scattered around her flat.

Andi put a hand to her chest. "Ouch. I've got feelings, too."

"You sure?" After the callous way Andi had dumped her, India often questioned whether Andi had a heart. It's something she'd only noticed towards the end. Everything about Andi was too perfect. People had flaws, it was what made them interesting. India had realised too late Andi had no layers at all.

Andi put a hand on India's arm. "Are you being too sensitive again? Remember we talked about that, it's an issue of yours."

India saw red, flicking her ex's hand away. "Being sensitive is not a bad thing." Thunder coiled in her stomach.

Andi put on her faux-concerned face. "You need to sort

out your anger issues." She paused. "But it's good we ran into each other, because I've got something to tell you."

"I'm not interested in anything you have to say." India picked up her handbag and turned to Andi for a final time. "I hope whoever you're stringing along right now understands what she's getting into."

Andi's face as India left the toilets was a picture. She wasn't to know that India's heart was hammering in her chest, and beneath her perfect makeup, every nerve ending she had was tingling and red raw.

Chapter Four

Bernie was on the phone to a client, swinging left to right in her red chair. It was her first time in again this week, and it was starting to grate. Gina was thinking about saying something after Bernie got off the phone, and was composing the script in her head.

"You don't seem to have the same enthusiasm for the business as you once did. We're nearly at the end of February, and I can count on my hands the number of times you've been in the office." The only problem was, if Bernie withdrew her money, Gina would have to come up with the shortfall. It would involve going to a bank and that was never fun. Perhaps she could ask her family?

Her stomach turned. She dismissed that idea.

Gina chewed on the inside of her cheek. Perhaps it could wait.

Their buzzer went, breaking Gina's thoughts. She glanced over at the intercom. They weren't expecting anybody this afternoon, and they didn't get many walk-ins off the street because their offices were on the first floor, with no signs in eye-level windows. Most of their clients were appointment-only, word-of-mouth references. The glut of online estate agents hadn't made a dent in their portfolio. Their company, Hot London Properties, dealt in high-end gems that didn't go to the mainstream sites. Customers who came to them wanted something a little different, and usually had bigger budgets to spend. Bigger budgets meant bigger commissions, so it was a win-win for everyone.

Gina pressed the intercom. "If you're looking for SpecStars, it's the next building along." They often got lost customers for the wholesale opticians next door.

"No, it's Hot London Properties I'm looking for. Am I in the right place?"

"You are. Come on up." Gina pressed the buzzer and stood by the door, waiting for the woman with the plush accent to appear.

When she did, Gina had to concentrate on keeping a calm face. Whoever she was, money and class oozed off her. When this woman smiled, flashbulbs went off. She was beautiful, confident and comfortable in her own skin. Gina could tell that within seconds.

She was the kind of woman who made Gina's mother click her tongue on the roof of her mouth.

She was also the kind of woman who made Gina's heart beat that little bit faster. Just like it was now.

Beads the size of gobstoppers hung around her neck with gold, orange and yellow streaked through them. They sat atop a crisp pink shirt, which was matched with a navy-blue suit, tailor-made if Gina had to guess.

When she looked into the woman's eyes, she was struck by their intensity, as well as their colour, a rich, swirling blue.

"India Contelli." She held out a hand, an easy smile gracing her lips. India's fingers were long and slim, adorned with more bling than Gina had seen in a while.

Gina shook it.

India's grip was sure, like she'd never doubted it in her entire life.

"Gina Gupta, pleased to meet you." Gina held India's hand, a flicker of something in her chest, before ushering her to the sofa area opposite. "Can I get you a coffee?"

India shook her head. "No thanks. I'm here because Frankie Stark recommended you. She gave me your details a couple of weeks ago actually, but I've been busy." India glanced over at Bernie, then back at Gina. "Do you have time for a quick chat?"

Gina settled beside India. "Sure. Any friend of Frankie's is a friend of mine." Gina's brain processed this new information, trying to make sense of it. A friend of Frankie's. Did that mean India was gay? That put a whole new spin on India Contelli. Her face rang a bell, but that was probably because Gina would have seen her at one of the myriad of gay women's networking events she attended. Gina turned up at them religiously, as they were good for seeking out potential clients. Plus, she lived in hope she might meet someone interesting, someone who got her. She'd met Sara at one such event on the South Bank, but that hadn't panned out quite as she'd hoped.

"Are you looking to buy a property?"

"Yes. I want—"

"India Contelli?" Bernie interrupted their conversation, walking up and extending a hand.

India looked up, frowning.

"It is you! I was just over there wondering, but I thought I'd come and say hi. Wow, a real-life celebrity in our midst."

India stood up and shook hands with Bernie, her height matching Gina's partner's. Gina glanced down at India's feet — she was wearing impressive heels. Not many people matched Bernie.

"You know each other?" Gina was confused.

"We do not, but I watch India's TV show. *Shop Wars*, right?" Bernie glanced at Gina. "India visits failing retail empires and tells them what to do to get back on track."

India sat down. "Guilty as charged."

"I love your show!" Bernie gushed.

Gina gave her a look.

"Anyway, I'll let you get back to your chat. Are you after a property?"

"I am," India replied.

"Wonderful!" Bernie raised an eyebrow. "You're in perfect hands with Gina."

Gina waited until Bernie was back at her desk before she began talking again. "I don't watch much telly, so sorry, I don't know who you are."

"Believe it or not, I prefer that. Most people get a bit intimidated by TV stars. I see myself as more of a business person who's occasionally on TV."

"What line of business are you in?"

"I run a company called Stable Foods, and we're most famous for our biscuits. That's my day job. Celebrity kind of punched me in the face when I wasn't looking."

"Sounds painful." Gina should watch more TV. Her mum would probably know who India was. Her favourite pastime outside cooking and gossiping was watching TV. Being Indian, she'd also think her name was ridiculous. "Which do you prefer? Biscuits or fame?"

India gave her a look. "Biscuits, of course."

Gina smiled. "The only sane answer." She sat up. "So, what are you looking for?"

"That's a big question." India quirked an eyebrow.

"In a property," Gina clarified with a smile. "Flat? House?"

"Probably a flat. Two bedrooms, light and airy. I love rooftops, so if it's got a rooftop view, I'm sold. Also, I work fairly often in Southwark, so not too far from there. It's where I'm living right now."

The Shad Thames flat sprinted to the front of Gina's brain. It could be the perfect solution. India must have money, and the price had just come down after two months on the market. Gina had failed to sell it during February, despite her best efforts. Perhaps next month would prove more fruitful. "I have just the place. It's only a five-minute walk from here, it's got a balcony with views and a roof terrace. It all depends on your budget."

"My budget's flexible for the right property." India paused. "I'd love to see whatever you've got with that criteria. I want to be in zone one, near the river. This area is great." India gave her a smile, showing off rows of perfect teeth.

Her budget was flexible. How Gina would love to be able to say that. However, an accidental TV star had fallen into her lap and might be able to take the Shad Thames property off her hands and, in the process, make her a handsome profit.

Gina was going to do everything in her power to make sure India Contelli liked what she had to offer.

Chapter Five

"**A** Pride biscuit? What are you going to call it?" India's mum, Vanessa, held out her wine glass to Luca. Her brother duly poured the white Rioja.

"I hadn't thought that far ahead." India helped herself to some roast potatoes, having to stand to get them. Her parents' dining table had eight chairs, but in reality, it could probably seat 12. Today, as usual, Luca and Ricardo were on one side, India on the other, her parents at either end.

"Sapphic Snaps?"

"Rainbow Raiders?"

"Dyke Dunkers?"

Luca and Ricardo were enjoying this, weren't they?

"I think it's a great idea." Dad passed her the roast beef, his smile encouraging. He was Italian in heritage, but his accent was pure London.

India gave him a look. "You do?" Even though he was semi-retired, Dad always had an opinion on her decisions. This was the first time he'd agreed right away.

"You're not dying, are you?"

He frowned. "What are you talking about?"

"It's just, you normally have an opinion on my ideas. Especially the gay ones."

He poured gravy on his Yorkshire pudding and gave her a smile. "I grilled you about the Chocolate Delight campaign when you wanted a lesbian couple in the ad purely for business reasons. Coming down on one side of the fence can harm your bottom line. But you were right to take a stand — it proved a winner. I trust you, India. I need to if I'm retiring soon, don't I?"

This was a turn-up for the books. "I guess you do." She glanced at her brother. "We'll do some gay biscuits and we'll be on top of a float being gay, too. It's going to be the best Pride ever."

"Can we come on the float with you?" Ricardo asked.

"Only if you wear your sparkly disco shorts." He looked fantastic in them. Being a model, and Brazilian, Ricardo looked fantastic in practically everything.

Ricardo gave her a look. "It's Pride. An alarm goes off in our house if I don't wear those."

"Perfect. Luca can take photographs and you can look pretty. Plus, we've got a 70-something granny who's just come out and is looking for her long-lost love. The photo opps are going to be huge."

"Goodness me. I'm 67, there's hope for me yet."

"Mother!" Luca said.

Mum gave him a mischievous grin. "You're so easy to rile sometimes." She turned to India, changing tack. "How was New York?" Her mum used a tone like New York was a fragile, cut-glass decanter she didn't want to break.

"Fine. The filming went well, and the show should be on US TV in the autumn."

"But you're back here and ready to work again?" Dad asked. "Because we need to discuss timelines and transitioning of the business into your hands. John knows all about it, so he's keen to chat, too." John was her dad's number two, and he knew everything there was to know about Stable Foods. India knew a fair bit after 12 years in the business, too.

"I am. I just need to sort out a flat, then I'll have my life almost sorted."

"Good. We're both proud of you." Mum was using her soft tone again. India waited for the follow-up. Why did she feel the need to duck?

"Especially after Andi. Luca filled us in while you were gone. She turned out to be quite the piece of work, didn't she?"

* * *

India was hiding in her old room a few hours later. She'd gone up on the pretence she was looking at what she wanted to take when she finally found her flat, but really she'd just had to get away from the surrogacy talk. Luca and Ricardo had told her parents they had a meeting soon, and her mum had responded by getting out baby photos of Luca. India was happy for her brother, but being older by three years, she'd always thought it would be her to have kids first, not him. Life didn't always work out how you expected, did it?

She opened the drawer of her bedside table and got out some old passport photos from her youth. The one with the thickest eyebrows, aged 18. The one with the big, puffy coat, aged 21. The one with the massive sunglasses that the passport office had refused because you couldn't see her face.

A knock on the door made her look up. She put the photos back and shut the drawer just as Luca poked his head inside.

"Can I come in?"

She gave her brother a nod, sweeping her hair from her face. She should have it cut. Draw a line in the sand. Pre- and post-Andi.

Luca sat on the bed next to her, the floral duvet cover one she didn't recognise. Nobody ever slept in the bed, so it was all for show. Her parents didn't need the room. They had a guest wing on the other side of the house.

"I thought you were going half an hour ago?"

"We were, but then Mum made more tea. Ricardo's entertaining her." He paused, eyeing her. "You're okay with our plans?"

India felt a blush rise to her cheeks. She thought she'd been stealthier, but Luca knew her. "I'm thrilled about your plans." And she *was*. "I'm less thrilled that you filled Mum and Dad in about Andi." She hadn't meant to bring it up, but now it was out there.

Luca made a face. "You ran off to New York at a rate of knots. They needed an explanation. I just told them the truth, that Andi ghosted you after six months together. Better they found out from me rather than reading it in the papers."

India winced. "Did the press speculate much?"

He shook his head. "A week or so. Then they lost interest when you weren't here." He paused, taking a deep breath before continuing. "Talking about Andi." Another pause. "I saw her at a work function on Friday."

India controlled her nerves. "I saw her a couple of weeks ago. She was her usual charming self."

Luca's face became drawn. "Did you hear her news, though?"

India's jaw tightened. She shook her head, pressing her

back molars together. "What news?" A dark cloud passed over her mind. News was never good, was it?

"I wanted you to hear this from me, and nobody else." Luca winced. "There's no easy way to say this. Andi's engaged."

The words seeped into India's brain in slow motion, invading her head like hot lava. Andi was engaged when they'd only split up five months ago? Heat spilled down her, and every part of her skin flushed red. "She's what?"

"She met someone recently, and they're getting married in the summer." Luca twisted his wedding ring again, as if guilty by association. "I know you're done, and it's been a while since you split up, but still. I can see how it would smart."

He wasn't wrong. It did. Andi had cut her open again and she wasn't even there.

India twisted her mouth one way, then the other. She thought back to meeting Andi in the restaurant recently. Andi had told her she had some news, and India had cut her off. Thank goodness she'd done that. If Andi had dropped that bombshell on her, India might have crumbled. Better to hear it from her brother than her scheming ex.

"I just wish I'd never brought her home to meet Mum and Dad. It's going to take a few more trips before the association is washed away."

Luca leaned in and wrapped a solid arm around her. "You know what? Andi did far more damage to my strong, independent sister than I would have ever deemed likely. But you'll get through this, and you'll meet someone who eclipses anything Andi ever had."

A year ago, India would have believed Luca's words.

Now, she wasn't so sure.

Chapter Six

"Thanks for fitting me in today, I appreciate it." India's long limbs were crammed into the front of Gina's blue Citroën.

"No problem. You want to buy a flat. I have one to sell. I'm just glad you finally managed to find the time. It's been more than a month since you turned up at my office."

Plus, Gina's car had never smelled so good. Ninety per cent of the rich people she dealt with were men, and none smelled like India Contelli. They didn't look like her, either. Gina concentrated on the road as she drove along the back streets of south London. When they stopped at a traffic light, she turned her head.

"I'm glad the rooftop pad is still available."

"Me, too," Gina replied. "How do you know Frankie? I really like her and her wife, Phyllis."

India nodded. "They're great. We met at a drunken club night and I haven't been able to shake her since."

The lights went green and Gina eased them into the traffic. They weren't going anywhere fast on this brisk early April afternoon that felt more like February. Gina's navy-blue coat was slung across the back seat, but India was all wrapped up in her long cashmere number, a cream scarf wound artfully around her neck.

"That's everyone's Frankie backstory apart from mine. I met her by selling her a flat, and her gaydar pinged. It's because of her that I became involved in all the female-focused networking events, and they've been invaluable. But I feel like I've missed out by not getting drunk with Frankie at least once."

India's warm laugh coated the car. "It's never too late, just like this year's Pride slogan says. Frankie doesn't need much persuading to have a drink." There was that laugh again. "There have been quite a few nights where we've watched the sun come up across London on a rooftop somewhere. Normally wrapped in three different coats, because we live in London and not Rome, right? London can be romantic, but it's not a swelteringly hot European city."

Gina leaned forward and stared up into the white-cloud sky, the sun an infrequent visitor. "It's certainly not sweltering today. As for romance, it doesn't come under my remit, I'm afraid." She twisted her head left. "Are you a romantic, then?"

India let out a strangled laugh. "Depends which paper you read. Most think I'm a player, that every woman I'm seen with is my latest shag." India glanced at Gina. "We should be okay, seeing as your car is estate-agent branded, but who knows? If some paparazzi sees us, they could spin it any way they want."

"I wouldn't want to live like that. I prefer the shade to the sun." Gina clutched the steering wheel that bit tighter. India had just answered her burning question. She liked women. Now Gina was really going to have to concentrate on not saying something stupid.

"I wouldn't recommend a career in TV, then." India paused. "What about you. Are you romantic?"

"Me?" Gina searched her head for an answer.

India put her hands on her knees. "Uh-huh."

"I've no idea." It was truthful, at least.

India gave her a look. "You don't know if you're romantic? That's a bad sign. What happens if you go on a date, or to a bar to meet women?" She paused. "Or men. I'm not presuming you like one or the other."

Gina scanned her mind once more, but could only come up with the truth. "I don't go to that many bars or on that many dates. With women, for the record."

"You don't?" India sat up.

Gina shook her head. "I work long hours and I'm not a huge drinker. My mother thinks I should get out more and at least try to meet someone."

"Mothers always think they know best, but the world was a simpler place for them, wasn't it?"

"One I'm glad I wasn't in, as I'd have been married to a man back then. It took all my strength to hold it off for as long as I did before I came out." Why was she telling a total stranger her life story? *Shut up, Gina.*

"I get that. But I'm imagining coming out in Asian culture is different than coming out for me."

Gina nodded. "My parents aren't devout Hindus by any stretch of the imagination, but they didn't expect a gay daughter." She shook her head. "Anyway, I'm selling you a flat, not telling you my woes."

India drummed her fingers on the dashboard for a second, then seemed to remember it wasn't her car, pulling her fingers away. "I'm nosy, so feel free to tell me your woes any day."

"Be careful what you wish for," Gina replied, turning her head and meeting India's pure blue gaze and dazzling smile. Dammit, her smile should be illegal.

"Where's this one you're taking me to now?"

Gina flicked on the indicator and turned the corner. It was taking every muscle she had to stay this cool, calm and collected. "Have you ruled out the one we've just seen?" Gina had taken India to a flat in Bermondsey, with the space she'd wanted, but no large terrace. India had made all the right noises, but Gina knew people, and she'd been in this job long enough. It was a no-go, but she needed to hear it from India.

India moved her head from side to side, before finally shaking it. "It wasn't for me. Lack of light."

They pulled up outside the Shad Thames apartment. "That's something you're not going to accuse this flat of. This is the rooftop property I told you about when we last met. It's got bags of soul and it's been fully refurbished. A developer has come in and done all the work. All you need to decide is, can you see yourself living there?"

* * *

"Wow."

Gina knew what India meant. Wow was exactly what she'd uttered when she'd first walked through the front door of the Shad Thames flat. She followed India over to the living room's showpiece, the floor-to-ceiling arched windows leading out to a huge terrace overlooking the rooftops a few streets back from the Thames.

"I wanted rooftops, and you've given me rooftops." India spun on one foot and gave Gina a look that made her smile. Happy clients made Gina's life rosy, too.

"I aim to please."

Everyone else who'd seen this flat had loved it, but they usually turned it down because it was too far from the river, and so lacked uninterrupted views. If you stood on a chair, there were definite river glimpses. But this flat was all about living in the middle of London and being among the ripple of life. Just what India had wanted.

India's gaze settled on her for a moment. "I've only just walked in here, but I love it. And yes, I know I'm meant to be holding back so I can negotiate on the price, but fuck it!" India covered her mouth. "You don't really drink, but you do swear, right?"

Gina raised an eyebrow. "It's been fucking known."

India let out a bark of laughter. "I like you." She held Gina's gaze a beat longer, before turning back to the view. "Can we go outside?" She pointed to the terrace.

"Help yourself."

India stepped through the double doors and walked to the farthest point of the terrace, before turning back and facing the wall of glass, shaped like the front of a ship. "This is honestly incredible. I can't believe you took me somewhere else first." She snagged Gina's gaze. "Were you chuckling internally when you showed me around flat number one?"

Gina shook her head. "I don't always know what clients want. Sometimes they tell me one thing, but they mean another. I have to show them a breadth of options."

India took in the view again. "But this." She swept her

hand around the array of rooftops. "It's like a scene from an arthouse movie. Exactly what I want." She turned, putting a hand over her heart. "Rooftops are such special places to me. They're somewhere you can hide, but also allow such a different perspective on life. A river view is cool, but this is just exceptional. Like you've dropped me in the middle of *Mary Poppins*. All it needs is some loungers and a hot tub. Which I very much intend to get." She paused. "How much is it?"

"Not what Mary Poppins paid."

"She didn't pay a penny, she was magic."

"So I've heard," Gina replied. "It's on the details."

India took the sheet Gina held out to her, then nodded, sucking on her top lip. "It's doable. Especially if we knock them down a bit, right?" She turned, taking a deep breath, as if sucking in the view. "Although I have to have it. But don't tell your client that." She turned again. "Is there any other interest?"

Gina shook her head. To another client, she might have told a little white lie. But not to India. "When the river is so close you can almost touch it, people want a clear view. Especially when they're paying this price."

India grinned. When she did, her face lit up. "Exactly what I wanted to hear." She walked over to Gina, pausing inches from her. "I've been looking for a flat for over a year with no luck. Then I meet you, and my luck finally changes. I don't know you, Gina, but I could kiss you."

India might as well have sucked the breath right out of Gina.

India put a hand on her arm. "There's no need to look so aghast." She smiled again, taking a step back, assessing the flat. "It's just, life hasn't been that kind to me of late, so finding this is like an upturn. A change of fortune, you know? I needed it." Her gaze met Gina's. "But that's just between you and me, right?"

Gina nodded. "Of course. What happens in any of our properties stays right there." Gina was pretty sure whatever had happened to India was fairly minor in the grand scheme of things. She had money, fame and adulation. But everything was relative.

"I'm not sure what to do now. I feel a bit giddy." India fixed Gina with her stare again. One Gina found hard to wriggle out of. "I know this is a little weird, but do you fancy a drink to celebrate?" She held up a finger. "I know you don't drink much, but neither does my brother, and I take him to places that do amazing mocktails. I know the best in town. Plus, I feel like I owe you. Getting this flat is a massive thing off my plate. What do you say?"

It wasn't the first time Gina had been asked to go for a drink with a client after showing them a great property. However, it was the first time the person asking was an attractive lesbian. A *famous*, attractive lesbian.

The only thing holding Gina back was she didn't fancy getting in any papers. She was an introvert. Plus, her parents had only just accepted that she was gay. She couldn't risk them or their friends seeing her out and about with India Contelli. They might put two and two together and come up with nine.

"I'm happy to have a drink with you, but how about we do it at a low-key bar?" A thought struck her. "Or we could pick up a bottle of something and take it to another rooftop in London, if you like? I have keys." What was she saying? This wasn't the done thing. Especially not by rule-abiding Gina.

However, something in India's enthusiasm for rooftops had awakened her own.

She couldn't backtrack now. Particularly not after seeing India's excited face. "You've been holding out other rooftops on me?"

Gina laughed. "The one I'm about to take you to costs twice what this flat does, so not exactly holding out. Plus, it's only available for rental. But if you pretend to be a potential rental client, who's going to know? Plus, it has loungers set up already and an outdoor heater we could use."

Gina ignored the alarm bells going off in her head. Who was this brave, bold woman with the keys to the kingdom? This was not what Gina normally did with clients. Gina showed the flat, was professional and sealed the deal.

She was trying to impress India Contelli, wasn't she?

If that was the case, by the look on India's face, she may have succeeded.

"Take me to the lounger rooftop, oh wise one," India replied.

Chapter Seven

"Yikes, this flat is equally impressive." India stepped into the double-height living room, then stopped and stared.

Gina followed her in, checking the front door was locked before replying. "Good to see the cleaners have done their job. The tenants moved out last week."

"It's definitely shiny. Plus, it smells like lemon zest." India took a deep breath. "I've often wondered what these flats in the new area of London Bridge look like, and here we are." She swept a hand over the kitchen island, marvelling at the copper fixtures and fittings, along with the granite worktops. "Whoever's done this knows what they're doing."

"They certainly do." Gina pointed a finger. "Those tiles on the wall were shipped from Italy." She stamped her foot. "The marble on the floor, too." She walked to the bifold doors and unlocked those, before sliding them back.

India stepped out onto the terrace and breathed in the city. Below them, the River Thames sparkled under the early evening dusk. Car horns blasted intermittently, and commuters crawled across London Bridge on their way home, coats wrapped tight. But up here, they were cocooned. Like they had a box seat at a grand West End production. It was why she loved rooftops.

Could she afford this flat? Possibly, but it was a bit showy. Having a river view always added to the price tag, too. Plus, it didn't pull on her heart strings the way the last one had.

Gina grabbed a stripey tea towel from the kitchen and dusted off the metal loungers, then produced two glasses as India opened the bottle of Pinot.

"Will you have a glass, or do you want to stick to water?" India didn't want to be a wine pusher.

But Gina's face softened. "Pour me a small one. I want to like red wine. It's my aim this year to drink more. Plus, it's warming, right?"

"I like your style," India said. "Most Londoners are trying to give up."

Gina shivered, glancing at the freestanding patio heater. "I'm not most Londoners."

India was getting that. "The only thing that would have made this better was if I'd have brought biscuits."

"It would. Do better next time." Gina dragged the heater in between the two loungers, then fiddled with the switch, frowning as she did so.

India put the drinks on the wooden side table, then went to stand beside Gina. She smelled divine, like citrus and basil. "Having trouble?"

Gina glanced up, nodding. "Apparently I am. I'm flipping the switch but nothing's happening."

India reached out to help, and their fingers touched.

A zap of electricity travelled up India's arm, catching her by surprise. It landed in her chest and made her gulp. She steadied her breathing, then lifted her gaze to Gina's. The hairs on the back of India's neck stood up. Time paused for a couple of seconds.

Gina's tongue skated along her bottom lip.

India dragged her eyes from it. She didn't know about the heater, but a switch inside her had been flipped.

India shook her head and removed her hand, bending down. "Perhaps there's something down here that needs to be switched on?" India peered around the base, happy to have something to focus on. She found the switch, pressed it and stood back up.

Gina greeted her with a warm smile. "Well done. A TV star, and practical as well."

The blood rushed to India's cheeks. "I do my best." She settled onto her lounger, trying to regain her equilibrium. She handed Gina her glass of wine, careful not to touch her hand again. Then she refocused on the view, and the fact it was Friday. A time to relax.

India raised her glass. "Here's to me hopefully securing the *Mary Poppins* flat."

Gina inclined her head. "To Mary Poppins and hot tubs." She sipped the wine. "This tastes like Ribena."

"Is that a good thing?"

"Probably not, as I love Ribena. I could develop a taste for it." Gina sipped again, then put her glass down. "Can't drink too much, though, as I'm driving."

India screwed the cap back on the wine. "I'll take whatever we don't drink home." She paused. "You said you're not a big drinker. Is that a cultural thing, or just a 'you' thing?"

Gina gave her a slow smile. "It's a 'me' thing. Most of my family like to drink. You should see our family weddings. But it's just never been my thing."

"But now you're trying to broaden your booze horizons?"

"I guess I am."

India nodded. "One other thing I wanted to ask about was your partner, Bernie. Does she go to business events? I feel like I know her face from somewhere." India couldn't quite pinpoint it.

Gina nodded. "She does. We met at one, actually. I went along with a proposal for Hot London Properties, and she was looking to diversify and sink her teeth into a new venture. Bernie has fingers in many pies."

"I'm sure there's a lesbian joke there somewhere, but my brain's too fried after this week to dig it out."

Gina smiled. "Without her, I'd never have got the business up and running. She put up nearly half the cash to invest in the first place. We share client relationships, but I steer the ship. Although Bernie deals with our accountant and sets out budgets and goals. I used to be an accountant, and I'm a bit allergic to it now."

A waft of biting air brushed India's face. "Are you in accountant recovery?"

"Something like that, much to my parents' chagrin. They were baffled enough when I gave up a sure-fire career to set up my own estate agency." Gina stretched out on her chair. "But it's worked out. Plus, it means I get access to some of the best views in London."

"You're not wrong." India unfurled her scarf as she spoke. "Who rents this place?" She ran a hand through her hair as she settled back into her seat. Was this the first time she'd truly relaxed all week? It felt like it.

"Very rich people."

"People like me?" India glanced across; she'd love to know what Gina was thinking. Did Gina like her? People often liked the TV version of India, or the business version. The real-life India — the human version — wasn't to everyone's taste. As she'd found out with Andi.

But she wasn't going to think about Andi.

She sipped her wine, swallowing down any negative thoughts.

"I don't generally drink with them, so not exactly." Gina paused, as if she was choosing the right words. "We're the sole agent for this particular flat. I've come up here a couple of times alone when I shouldn't. The owner lives in Dubai, and they come back very occasionally to check on all their properties. This one has only just come back on the market — it was rented out to some brokers for six months. When I came to inspect it, the flat looked like they'd never even been here. I know they work long hours and probably ate out, but that seemed like a crying shame."

"Criminal." India tipped her head back, staring at the patchwork sky, myriad shades of grey. "Do you have a rooftop view where you live?"

Gina shook her head. "No, but I have a water view. I live in Canary Wharf. No rooftops, just high-rises. You said you were renting at the moment?"

"Not so much renting, more living at one of my parents' flats." India held up a hand. "Before you say it, I know I'm privileged to do so, but I want my own place. Scrap that, I *need* my own place. My parents have keys, my brother's got keys, it's where everyone stays when they come to London overnight. I want somewhere where nobody has keys but me."

"I have that. I recommend it." Gina paused, assessing her. "There's not a Mrs India to be given a second set of keys?"

India pressed her head into her chair, then shook it. "No, there is not."

"I'm surprised."

India turned her head. "You are?"

Gina nodded. "You're India Contelli." She blushed. "I might have googled you after we saw each other in the office the other day. I do it with all my clients. You're not the first famous one I've had."

"Semi-famous."

"You've got a Wikipedia page, that means you're famous."

India frowned. "I did have a partner for a while. But we split up seven months ago. It was part of the reason I went to New York last year and pursued a filming project I'd been offered. It came at the right time. It was a messy break-up, so leaving the country was perfect. My friends and family told me I was running away, but sometimes you need to do that."

Gina gave her a knowing smile. "I know I've wished I could run away from my love life in the past."

India raised an eyebrow, her gaze resting on Gina's heart-shaped face. Something about her made India not want to look away. "Yours was messy, too?"

"It was. My ex and I drifted apart, we didn't really want the same things. But she took months to move out. We split up when I turned 40, and I'm 41 next month."

India knew all about messy. "People think it's different

because I'm famous, but it's not. It's still just two people trying to get along, trying to fall in love and stay there, which is no easy task. I'm 38 years old, but I haven't managed it once. I've never lived with anyone."

"I've never truly been in love, even though I thought I was at the time." Gina put a hand to her lips. "I can't believe that just came out of my mouth."

India sat up. "Maybe there's a truth forcefield on this rooftop." She swung her legs around and sat facing Gina. "Maybe I haven't either. What a pair we are." She paused. "Is your ex still in the picture?"

Gina shook her head. "She cleared out our joint account a few months ago, and that was our last link. I shut it down the same day, so there's no way she can access me anymore. She wasn't that bothered about doing so, anyway. She'll miss the money, though."

India stood up and walked to the other side of the balcony. "Mine was just a straight-up bitch. She messed with my head, told me she loved me, then left without a word." She paused. "To top it off, I recently found out she's marrying someone else this summer. She met her three months ago, which tells you everything you need to know about her sincerity and my stupidity." India still wasn't okay with that. "But I have to keep going. Pretend it doesn't sting. Pretend I'm superhuman."

Gina stood up and walked over to India. "You don't have to pretend anything up here. You can be who you are. Human." She reached out and squeezed India's arm.

Goosebumps broke out along it. India squeezed her toes tight inside her heels. It'd been some time since a woman had touched her who wasn't Andi.

India held her gaze. Where had this woman come from? A few weeks ago, they were strangers. Now, Gina had some kind of weird hold on India. A hold India very much wanted to lean into.

"Thank you."

Gina's gaze burrowed into her, making India look away. She stared out into the chilly gloom, wondering when the sunshine would arrive in the world and in her love life. "Thanks for bringing me here. If you've got any other rooftops you need to stake out, I'm your woman. I promise to provide a new wine every time to further your education, and good cheer."

Gina's hazelnut stare snagged her once more. "You've got yourself a deal."

Chapter Eight

Gina smashed the tiny black ball against the wall in front of her.

Her sister, Neeta, did the same. This time, though, the ball rebounded towards Gina. Before she could move her feet, it hit her in the face, knocking her backwards.

"What the fuck!" Gina let out a groan, then doubled over, hand to her eye, her white squash racket clattering to the ground. Her face throbbed and the world became dark.

"You okay? Your eye still in place?"

"No thanks to you!" It was a carbon copy of their childhood. When Gina came up for air, satisfied her eye was still in its socket, Neeta's arm was around her.

"You'll live, that's my professional medical opinion." Neeta gave her a squeeze.

"You haven't even seen the damage yet." Gina peeled her hand away, cracking open her good eye.

Neeta put her face right into Gina's. "I can confirm your eye is still in place." She paused. "Is this just your way of stopping the game because I'm winning?"

Gina's eye watered and she closed it again. "Seeing as I still can't open my right eye, maybe." She tried again, but it was still smarting. She knew it was too much to expect sympathy from a doctor. It just didn't happen.

Neeta sighed. "Come on, then. Take my arm, I'll lead you out. Only, don't tell Mum I hit you. You know what she's like when it comes to you, Saint Nagina."

That made Gina snort. "I think your status in the family went up the minute I told them I was a lesbian." She inched open her eye.

"Yes, but now they're coming round, I'm dropping like a stone."

"I hardly think they're coming round." From weekly phone calls, her communication with her parents had dwindled over the past few years to once a month.

"They're thawing. Mum asks about your life. They acknowledged Sara just before you split up. It's only a matter of time. I know I'm a doctor, but I married a white boy. Until I give them grandchildren, she's not interested."

They packed up their gear and got in the lift to Gina's flat, the squash court being a perk of their building. The sisters played whenever they got the chance, Neeta living in the same block with her husband Neil. Both Neil and Neeta were A&E doctors, so squash was played according to their rotas. Gina spent time with her sister whenever she could get it. Despite their differences they'd always got on, with similar outlooks on life and the common denominator of their parents.

Gina put a bag of frozen peas on her eye when she got in, her sister putting the kettle on. When Gina took the peas away, Neeta gawped.

"Shit, you actually do have the beginnings of a black eye."

She walked over and pressed the peas back to Gina's face. "Keep it there."

"Great." Gina sat on her cream sofa with a thump. "Bernie and I have got meetings with some prospective new clients tomorrow. A black eye was not in the preparation."

"A bit of makeup and you'll be fine." Neeta stared at her. "You've got makeup, right?"

Gina tried to raise an eyebrow, but wasn't able. "Just because I'm a lesbian does not mean I don't own makeup."

"You've just forgotten to wear it for the past year."

"We were playing squash."

"I'm not talking about today. I'm talking about the past however long. You falling out of love with Sara. Taking less care of yourself. Almost like you were trying to make her fall out of love with you, too."

Gina sat up. It wasn't something she'd done on purpose, but Neeta might have a point. "I can put makeup on."

"Good." The kettle boiled. Gina went to get up, but Neeta made her sit, tipped her head back and pressed the peas to her face. Only when she came back with tea did she take the peas away. "Don't want them to defrost totally. Waste of good peas. Unless you were planning on making a pea surprise later?"

"It wasn't top of my list." Gina blinked. "My face hurts."

"It still looks pretty. At least it will be, when you've got some makeup on."

"You've made your point."

Neeta sipped her tea before she spoke again. "Have you heard from you-know-who?"

Gina filled her in.

Neeta whistled. "At least she's gone." She paused. "Do you think she's living with a friend, or found a new sucker to hitch her wagon to?"

Gina blew out a long breath. "Who knows? But if I had to lay bets, the ease with which she finally left would suggest she's found someone new. But I'm not an expert on women, as we've gathered over the past few years. A stuttering coming out, a couple of mediocre shags, and then my first long-term relationship with gold-digging Sara. The only way is up, right?"

"Exactly. Good riddance to dead wood. Now you can focus on you, and getting back up and out there."

"It won't be for a while. I need some 'me' time first."

"You had that when you were with Sara. Every time I saw the pair of you, you were leading different lives."

"Says the doctor married to a doctor and they barely see each other."

"Yes, but we signed up to that. Nothing's changed since we got together. We met on the job, and we're going to die on the job."

"So romantic."

"I know. It's why Neil married me." Neeta got up. "Have you got any biscuits?" It was a rhetorical question. Neeta always made sure Gina had biscuits. Neeta returned with the tin, taking a Chocolate Rocket first. She bit into its salted caramel centre and sighed. "Sometimes I wonder if it would be wrong to want to marry one of these. 'I take thee, salted caramel biscuit thing, to be my lawfully wedded spouse'. We almost have more of a relationship than me and Neil."

Talk of biscuits turned Gina's mind back to India and

their biscuit chat on the rooftop. She'd managed to negotiate a good deal for her on the flat, and the next stage was sorting out the paperwork with her in-house solicitors. Gina didn't normally take a hands-on approach when the process reached this stage, but she'd made an exception for India. They'd shared a drink, a connection. She still wasn't sure what it was, but it was something. She didn't want to let it go.

"Have you heard of India Contelli?" The words were out of Gina's mouth before she could process them.

Her sister nodded. "Course. From that TV show? Tells shops how to sort out their businesses to make money." She held up her Chocolate Rocket. "She makes these, doesn't she?"

Maybe Gina was the only person to *not* know who India was. "I just sold her a flat."

Now she had Neeta's interest. "You did? That must have been a tasty commission."

Gina nodded. "When it goes through, I'll buy you a box of Chocolate Rockets, how's that?"

"Makes a change from me buying them for you." But Neeta wasn't to be thrown off that easily. "She's gay, isn't she?"

Another nod. "She is."

"Just come out of a relationship with Andi Patten last year. The Radio Two DJ."

That made Gina sit up. India's ex was a national radio DJ? No wonder she'd been hesitant about sharing information with Gina. And yet, India had. A subtle warmth flowed through her.

"You should invite yourself round for a celebratory drink. You two could bond over your single status."

If only Neeta knew. "Unlikely. I just sold her a flat, that's all. Plus, I'm an estate agent, and she's on TV. I don't think those two things go together, do they?"

"Imagine if they did." Neeta's face went all dreamy. "If you made her my sister-in-law, I could have free biscuits for life."

Gina's phone ringing snagged her gaze. Her mother. Gina's heart sank. It wasn't that they didn't get on. It was just that, ever since she'd come out, things had been stilted. They still were. Every time she mentioned another woman to her mum, there was an intake of breath. Her mum thought Gina slept with every woman she met. If only she knew the truth of her chaste existence.

Gina clicked the green button. "Hi, Mum."

As soon as the words were out of her mouth, Neeta was on her feet. She stuffed the rest of the biscuit in her mouth, then pointed at the door and slunk away.

Traitor.

"There you are. I tried you twice the other day and no answer. What's the point of a mobile if you don't take it with you?"

That was the other thing with her mum. She expected Gina to be at her beck and call, no matter what. That Gina refused was a constant source of irritation.

"I was working." That excuse was always acceptable.

The line went still, as it always did. Gina had spent the first year after she came out filling in the silences. She was done with that now. If her mum wanted to talk to her, she'd have to do just that. In the background, she could hear Zee TV burbling away, probably screening one of her mum's beloved Indian soaps.

"Did I tell you what your uncle's done?" Ah, the standby family chat.

"You didn't."

"Converted his shed into a gym. At his age. Says he wants to get fit and build muscles. I told him he's more likely to keel over and die, but he didn't listen. I think he's having a midlife crisis at 50."

Deepak was her mum's baby brother. Whatever he did was a constant thorn in her mum's side, because he was still their parents' unashamed favourite. Gina had never come right out and said he was her favourite uncle, but she was pretty sure her mum knew. Deepak didn't have a lot of competition. Her mum's other brother was a jerk.

"He can do what he likes, he's a grown man."

"He should start acting like one, then."

More silence.

"How's dad?" Gina cursed herself for caving.

"Good. Still tinkering in the garage. He's made some shelves for the spare room." Her dad was a DIY enthusiast. "How are you?"

She could almost hear the strain in her mum's words. As if she was asking her, "please don't tell me too much, I don't want to know".

"Good. Work's busy. I just played squash with Neeta."

"She's off work? I'll call her after this." Gina would get shit for that, but it wasn't her fault. She needed safe topics of conversation and Neeta was just that.

"Any plans to come and visit? Your dad and I would love to see you. Both of you."

There it was. The guilt, laid on thick. Gina had last been back to visit in December. She was overdue, she knew.

"I'll check with Neeta to see when she's off work and we'll

54

let you know." Gina had to take backup. The thought of going alone made her feel sick.

"Don't leave it too long. Your father and I aren't getting any younger."

"I know."

Gina hung up, then went to the bathroom to check her eye. It was swollen, but hopefully, it'd look better by the morning.

She got out her makeup to have a practice run.

Chapter Nine

"I hear it's full steam ahead for your new pad?" Frankie sat in the main meeting room at Stable Foods, eating cheese-and-onion crisps and crunching way too loudly.

India tried not to focus on it. She'd offered the venue when Frankie said she needed somewhere. The Pride board was volunteer-run, so their meetings were held in whatever central space could be found.

"It is. A price has been agreed, just waiting on an exchange date." India couldn't wait.

"I told you Gina would sort you out."

"She did. I like her." India had thought about Gina many times since their rooftop liaison two weeks ago. She'd been trying to think of a reason to get back in touch with her, but it hadn't hit her yet.

Frankie nodded. "You know she's family, right?"

"I do. We chatted a bit, traded war stories."

Frankie did a double take. "You told her about Andi?" Her friend's tone spelt surprise.

She nodded. What's more, she hadn't worried once that Gina might share her personal details with the world like India would with other people. She had no idea how she knew

Gina wouldn't share her secrets; she just felt it in her bones.

"How are you feeling about Andi now? Getting married to the heir of a retail giant. It's like she had you in the palm of her hand, decided she didn't want you, and then got a ready-made replacement."

"The new one's got blond hair."

"You know what I mean." Frankie shook her head. "Plus, what the fuck is it with retail heirs that they're all lesbians? What gives? If she wasn't with Andi, I'd make it my business to tap her up for a Pride donation."

"You could do that anyway. In fact, I'd encourage it. It would annoy the shit out of Andi."

Frankie smirked. "Good point." She got out her phone and tapped a note. "Consider it done."

India let her gaze glide around the room. Mint-green walls, and a dark green carpet, plus the white oval table they were sat at, surrounded by ten ergonomic chairs. She'd sat at the other end of the table last year when her dad had told her his plans to ease out of the business. She recalled the joint feelings of terror and excitement. She'd felt alive. She was looking forward to finally getting stuck in this year.

"I'm also making you the first bus on the Pride parade, seeing as you gave a whacking donation." Frankie paused. "How are the new biscuits coming along?"

"Great. We're calling them Rainbow Rings, and they're going to be a cinnamon biscuit sandwiched with a vanilla cream, covered in rainbow icing. I've got a meeting with the PR team next week. We're going to be giving snack-packs away from our bus on the day. My aim is to get the whole parade eating Rainbow Rings all day long."

"Let me know if you need volunteers to give them out, or if you've got enough help from your employees."

India nodded. "Will do."

A woman walked into the meeting, greeting Frankie right away. When she clocked India, she paused, her eyes widening.

India was used to it. She stood up. "I'm India." She held out a hand and the woman shook it.

"I know." Her cheeks coloured pink. "Sorry, I meant I'm Lucy." She grimaced, then pulled out a chair the other side of Frankie. "I wasn't expecting you at the planning meetings, I thought you'd be far too busy."

Frankie leaned forward. "We are in her office building."

Lucy's blush turned crimson.

Frankie gave Lucy a grin. "This is perfect, actually." She turned to India. "Lucy is the one in contact with Eunice, our 79-year-old late bloomer." She glanced at Lucy. "India will be doing the interview with Eunice. I was going to put you in touch with each other, but here you are!"

"Here I am." Lucy gave them both a grin. "I spoke to Eunice for the first time last week, and she's so great. Really on the ball, and remembers everything like it was yesterday. She was so thrilled to be reunited with the letters, but reticent to talk about it still. It was another time back then."

India nodded. "I bet. Which is why her agreeing to be the centre of this is so brilliant. I hope she knows what she's getting into. Are her family supportive?"

"They are. Otherwise, she wouldn't have done it. They want to know if this mystery woman is still out there, just like we all do. Eunice doesn't want to upset the applecart, though."

"We have to respect her wishes," India replied. "But maybe

she could be persuaded by a visit from me prior to the official interview. Go to her house, just to let her know she can trust me. I wouldn't record anything. I'd like to give it a go if we could."

Lucy nodded. "Got to be worth a try. The story is gold in itself. But just imagine if we reunited them, too."

Frankie rubbed her hands together. "Let's make it happen."

India turned to Lucy, breathing her in. "Are you wearing Bright Crystal perfume?"

Lucy blinked before nodding. "I am. Good nose."

"My ex used to wear it." India had been trying not to react the whole time they'd been chatting. But it was hard. Like Andi was in the room.

"Oh dear." Lucy's face told India she was calculating if that ex was Andi. "I hope it's got good associations for you."

"I can make new ones."

"Actually, we have friends in common via the lesbian grapevine."

India tilted her head. "We do?"

"Eden Price? And her partner, Heidi?"

India leaned back in her chair. Eden Price was her PR guru, and someone India had a lot of respect for. She'd asked her out a year or so ago, but Eden had been pursuing Heidi at the time, so she'd turned India down. Thankfully, it hadn't affected their relationship and they were still friends, as well as business colleagues.

"I love Eden and Heidi. I'm meeting Eden next week about Pride and the biscuits." India shook her head. "The lesbian world, eh?"

"Heidi's the official Pride photographer, too. She might

even be involved in this project we're doing with Eunice." Lucy gave her a grin. "You know what they say: if you haven't slept with the woman you're chatting to, the likelihood is that someone you know has."

"Never a truer word spoken." India smiled at Lucy. She liked her.

India agreeing to come along tonight and do this project had been a good thing. Putting herself out there again, running the risk of bumping into Andi at fundraisers. It was going to happen, just like Andi had told her. India just had to grow a thicker skin and have a few more people on her side. Frankie was definitely in that category, as was Eden, and perhaps now Lucy. Allies were always good to have. She was pretty sure she could count Gina in that band, too.

"By the way, I know I shouldn't say this and I should act all cool, but I love your *Shop Wars* show. Your advice is stellar. I actually used the one about window decorations and the website marketing tips for my opticians, and it worked a treat. So, thank you."

India's shoulders relaxed. "Good to know my strategies still work."

"My friend Kate helped me out with the graphics for the website, and it's doing so much better now. She's actually helping out with the graphics for Pride, too." Lucy indicated all around the room at this year's logo and theme. "She did all of these."

"I look forward to meeting her." India paused. "If you and any of your friends aren't working the actual parade, you should come onto the Stable Foods parade bus. We're going to have special Pride biscuits and Eunice. It's the place to be."

Lucy's face lit up. "That would be amazing! Count us in."

Chapter Ten

When Gina walked into the office, Bernie spun around in her chair, phone to her ear. Her eyes went wide. She swivelled back the way she came and finished her call quickly. Then she spun back around, her grin wide, clearing her throat.

What just happened? Gina had no idea. She strolled over to the coffee machine and flicked it on. "You okay? Did I come back at an inopportune time?"

Bernie walked her way, shaking her head. When she grabbed a cup from the cupboard above the machine, she left it to dangle from her little finger. "Course not. Just didn't expect you back so soon." She peered closer. "Your squash injury is still showing."

Gina frowned. "Stop changing the subject. Are you plotting my downfall?" She was keeping it light. She knew Bernie had her own life, but she wasn't normally secretive.

"I love that you go there first." Bernie shook her head. "It's your birthday in May. Maybe I was planning a big cake to arrive with a scantily clad woman inside."

"If you were, I'm walking out the door again, and please carry on with your ordering."

Bernie gave her a grin. "I knew this whole 'I'm taking time for me' was all just an act."

"If a woman jumps out of a cake and wants to seduce me, I'm not going to stand in her way. I'm only human." Gina thought back to telling India she was only human on the rooftop a few weeks ago. She hadn't seen her since, just exchanging a few emails after the price was agreed on for her new flat. Somehow, it wasn't quite enough.

India was different to anybody she'd met of late. She was vulnerable, which was the last thing Gina had expected. She'd opened up. That wasn't new. Gina had one of those faces, but it hadn't happened in a while. India had lifted the lid on herself slightly. Now, Gina wanted to know more.

Gina retrieved her coffee from the machine. She waited for Bernie to get hers, then they walked back to their desks together. Bernie still had half a tuna baguette on it from lunchtime. Gina's stomach rumbled. She hadn't eaten lunch yet and it was already 2.30pm.

"Anything new come in today?"

Bernie nodded. "Something for you. I forwarded you the email. A new flat along the river in Rotherhithe, with a roof terrace and a log burner. Something for every season."

"Are you meeting with those investors in the Tyler project today, too?"

"Yep." She checked her watch. "Meeting them at five, could be a long one." Bernie's phone beeped. When she picked it up, she frowned. "Shit."

"What's up? Cake lady fallen through?"

Bernie gave her a forced smile. "Something like that." She bolted her coffee, then winced. "That was hot." She glugged some water, then stuck her tongue out, panting like a dog. "I gotta run. See you tomorrow."

Gina clicked on the email about the new flat and glanced through the dodgy photos of the place. She'd have to get them redone before she listed the property. She squinted at them more closely. The kitchen looked like it might need to be ripped out, but she guessed the owner might be leaving that for the buyers to do. However, Gina was pleased to see her virtual assistant had already arranged for the deep clean of the flat to happen tomorrow. She'd no idea how she managed before she'd employed Amy.

Gina clicked through the photos again. The terrace looked out over rooftops. India would love it. She glanced around, but her office was internal, with no windows. She checked the weather on her phone. Fourteen degrees and cloudy. However, with coats, another terrace visit could be possible.

Gina scrolled to India's number in her phone, then hesitated. Calling her would mean their relationship had progressed to another level. A friendship. She couldn't be sure that was what India wanted, but she was compelled to try. Plus, hadn't India said to call her for any rooftop action? Before her brain could stop her, her finger made the decision.

India answered after three rings. "Hello, stranger. More flat news?"

Gina's cheeks burned. Was this a mistake? She glanced up at the photos and ploughed on. "Sort of, but not about yours. I've just been sent through the details of a place that's getting all spruced up tomorrow, and I thought of you. It's got a rooftop view and a log burner on the terrace."

"Oh my god, I'm in. Should I buy this one, too?"

Gina paused. India could probably afford it.

"That was a joke, by the way."

"Right." Gina clicked back into her email inbox on-screen. "It's probably silly, but I'm free tonight, and I wondered if you fancied coming with me to see it. We could have a drink on the roof terrace, compare our weeks." Now that the words were coming out of her mouth, they sounded beyond ridiculous.

Or perhaps loaded.

Like she was asking India out on a date.

Which she totally wasn't.

However, India immediately shut down Gina's brain chatter. "I'd love to. Best offer I've had all week."

Relief washed over Gina. "Great." She tapped her fingers on her desk. "Shall I message you the address and we can meet there at seven?"

"Sounds perfect. I'll bring a bottle."

Something kicked in Gina's chest. "See you there."

She hung up and stared at her phone. They'd just strayed beyond a client relationship for sure. They'd dipped a toe with their last rooftop soirée. But this time, they were definitely venturing onto a different playing field. It felt good.

A message came in from her VA, entitled 'Strange Withdrawals'. Gina clicked on it. Amy had listed a series of withdrawals from their business account that were a little out of character. She was hot on that sort of thing, something else Gina appreciated.

Gina studied them. Twelve withdrawals of around £100. Nothing to break the bank, but then again, a steady depletion of funds. She made a note to ask Bernie what she was withdrawing the money for. She'd deal with it tomorrow.

Tonight, she had other plans.

* * *

India was standing slouched against her cherry-red Audi, hands pushed into her pockets when Gina pulled up. She cut the engine and took a moment just to stare. She was such a striking woman. Someone who looked like they knew what they wanted and went after it. Which is why knowing she had a softer side made Gina feel so connected. Let in. Special.

Special? She really needed to get a grip and be a little more professional before she launched herself into this evening.

Gina pulled down the driver-side mirror and dug out her makeup from her handbag. She'd taken her sister's advice and added lipstick and foundation before she left. She touched up her lipstick now, then took a deep breath. It was just a flat check-up with a friend along for the ride. Nothing more.

Gina grabbed her black bag from the passenger seat, then slammed her car door. She retrieved her coat from the back seat, then walked over to India, shivering.

When she saw her, India's face broke into a smile. "You should put your coat on and not just hold it over your arm. It's fairly common practice."

Gina smiled. "I know. Let's get inside and see if I need it. Some of these flats are ovens once you're over the threshold."

"Lead the way."

They got into the private lift allocated to the penthouse of this apartment block, and were soon spat out into the sprawling flat. Gina's eye was immediately drawn to the terrace, but the flat itself was in need of some love. The kitchen needed an update, its surfaces scratched. The sofa in the lounge sagged in the middle. It wouldn't take much to make it sparkle again, but flats were like people — they needed love and attention, otherwise they went stale.

"This could be lovely." India walked around the open-plan wide expanse. "The space is brilliant, but it's like a time capsule from 1996. If the Spice Girls are on the terrace, I'll know I've been punked."

"I'm pretty sure you're safe, but let's look." Gina unlocked the doors and they walked out. Across the river, old brown-brick warehouses had been turned into flats and hotels. To their left, Tower Bridge was small in the distance. Gina poked her head around the corner of the wrap-around terrace. "No Spice Girls, you're safe."

India pulled her coat tight as the wind whipped around their faces. "I would have been quite excited if it had been Geri. She was always my favourite." She glanced at Gina. "You want to get your coat?"

Gina did, then reappeared, buttoning it up.

When she glanced up, India was giving her a soft smile.

"What?" Gina looked down. Had she done her buttons up wrong?

India shook her head. "Nothing. You just look…" She left the sentence hanging.

Gina narrowed her eyes. What was India trying but failing to say? Her ears tingled as warmth spread through her. Was India trying to give her a compliment? She had no idea.

"What do you think of this terrace?"

India blinked, then cleared her throat. "It's wonderful. The terrace that time forgot." She indicated to the lounge chairs. "Shall we pull them over to the edge? I brought coffee and biscuits. I figured we're both driving, and you don't want wine all the time." India produced a shiny metal flask, some proper camping mugs and a packet of Chocolate Rockets.

Gina was touched. She pulled a chair over before she replied, "I can't imagine you stopping off at Starbucks on your way here."

India looked a little sheepish. "My assistant did the coffee, but I grabbed the biscuits from my stash." She poured the coffee and handed Gina a mug.

She held it up. "Proper tin mugs, too." Gina tilted her head. "Don't tell me you're a camping lesbian. You don't look the type. My campdar isn't that far off, is it?"

India cackled. "Your campdar — if that is a real word — is safe where it is. I've never camped, but my assistant clearly knows what she's doing."

Gina held up her mug, steam coming out the top. "Here's to assistants everywhere. I don't know what I'd do without mine, either." They touched mugs, and took a sip. "By the way, my sister loves these biscuits." Gina pointed at the packet on the table between them. "When she heard I'd met you, she was begging me to set up a hotline so she could order direct." Gina decided not to tell India that Neeta had also wanted Gina to marry India. This was only their third meeting, after all.

"She's not the only one. They're our top seller. I'm hoping the Pride biscuits will be as big a hit, too. We're calling them Rainbow Rings. What do you think?"

"They sound pretty gay to me." Gina paused, staring across the river at Dryden Wharf. They fell into silence for a few moments, but it didn't feel heavy at all. In fact, the opposite. As Gina stretched out in her lazy chair, all the stresses of the day seeped out of her. She should have started rooftop surfing a long time ago. "Do you know what the word 'wharf' stands for?"

India turned to her. "I don't."

"Warehouse at river front."

India raised an eyebrow her way. "You are full of knowledge and surprises."

"Blame my sister, Neeta. She's a wealth of useless information."

"Let me know her address. I'll send her some biscuits."

"She lives three floors below me."

"Perhaps I can drop them off to you one day."

Gina held India's stare, the intention in the words leaping from her. Was India inviting herself to Gina's? Gina was trying not to read too much into it, but she wasn't doing too well. Her ears, which had tingled with heat earlier, were now roasting.

"Did I tell you I'm taking part in Pride this year?" India licked her lips as she spoke.

"You didn't. I love their theme of 'It's Never Too Late'. I'm a walking example of that. I was thinking about volunteering, but I keep forgetting to sign up."

India tilted her head in Gina's direction. "I need volunteers for the Stable Foods bus if you want to do that? Bring your sister, too. It involves biscuits."

Neeta would freak. "I'd love to."

India gave her a sure smile, and something wobbled inside Gina.

"Good," India replied. A few moments passed before she spoke again. "Have you heard about the long-lost love story this year? The 79-year-old whose letters have been found?"

Gina nodded. "Pretty incredible stuff."

"I read them the other night. They're so coded, so heart-breaking. I'm meeting the woman at the centre of the story soon. She's called Eunice. I'm going to try to convince her she should appeal to see if her mysterious love, H, is still alive. What has she got to lose? If H doesn't want to come forward, she doesn't have to."

Gina's stomach rolled. "Coming out is never easy, though, is it? I only did it in my early 30s, and it was traumatic, wondering what everyone's reactions would be, and how work would react. It was one of the reasons I wanted to run my own business. If I'm my own boss, I have none of those worries."

India nodded. "I get that."

"If I put myself in Eunice's shoes… Coming out and then searching for a long-lost love after all this time… I can't imagine how it would feel, even if the life she lived was happy." Would she be kicking herself? Be embarrassed? Ashamed? A mix of all three? "If I saw this campaign, though, it would spur me to come out if I hadn't already. Her story is romantic and hopeful, but it also serves as a warning to live your best life. Your *true* life." Gina paused. "Going to meet her is exciting, though. Where does she live?"

"Birmingham."

A punch to the gut. "My hometown." Gina shivered, but not from the cold.

"Really? You're a Brummie? You don't sound like a Brummie."

"I've lived in London far too long. That's what my mum would tell you, anyway." Gina rolled her eyes. "She constantly moans that my sister and I don't visit enough. She's right, but that's how it is with family, isn't it?"

"I wouldn't know. I work with mine, and we see each other far too much." But India's grin told Gina she didn't mind that one bit.

"I couldn't imagine that. My parents, being first-generation Indian, aren't so keen on me being gay. They're slowly coming around to the idea, but it's like moving an oil tanker. The fact I turned 40 and nothing's changed might have influenced their decision."

"Mine were a little flummoxed when both my brother and I came out, but they're fine with it now. They have to be. There's no other choice." India gave a small laugh. "Did your parents meet your ex-girlfriend?"

Before Gina had a chance to reply, India shook her head. "What is it about us and rooftops? We start pouring out our life stories to each other. Just wait until I move into my flat. Although, perhaps that'll get it out of our systems, then we can just have light-hearted chats and drink coffee and wine."

Now it was Gina's turn to laugh. "And biscuits I hope." She paused. "But no, Sara never met my family, she was never that interested."

India furrowed her brow. "You were going out for how long?"

"Eighteen months."

"That's a statement."

"I never pushed it, but yes, you're right. I think if my parents met someone, it might crystallise it in their heads, make it more real. Right now, my being gay is imaginary if I don't have someone to be gay with."

India shook her head. "Straight people never have to go through this, do they? It annoys the fuck out of me."

"I gave up being annoyed at things I can't change a while ago."

India held Gina with her gaze. "I'm getting that about you. You have good energy." She smiled. "If you're ever pressed by a reporter, don't tell them I said that. It sounds a bit woo-woo. They'll paint me as a hippy."

"There are worse things."

"Not for a CEO of a multinational company. I work in a strait-laced world."

"A shame for someone who's not so straight."

"Exactly."

Gina glanced at her. "Do you get that a lot? Hassled by reporters? I'd hate that. I'm a very private person."

India shook her head. "Not as much as some. I don't live my life in the spotlight, so it's not that difficult. If you're not falling out of bars in the early hours or having public fights with your other half, they tend to leave you alone." She paused. "It happened a lot more when I was with my ex, but now we've split up, it turned out it's her they're more interested in. She's more in the public eye, being on the radio every day. I'm just a woman who makes biscuits and tells shop owners off. We're not on the same level."

"Sounds like your life's simpler without her." Gina couldn't lie. She was also glad there was nobody else in India's life. Not when it was just the two of them on a rooftop.

India stared, then nodded. "You're right. It is."

"I know since Sara and I parted, a weight's been lifted." Gina snagged India's gaze. "Bernie told me Sara wasn't right for me at the start, but I didn't listen. She never liked her."

"Sounds like Bernie is a smart cookie," India replied.

"I wish someone had told me that about Andi, but I probably wouldn't have listened, just like you. We're all stubborn, aren't we? But I still believe there's someone out there who's perfect for me. All those love songs and sappy films can't be lying, can they?"

Gina's heart thumped in her chest as their gazes connected. It took everything she had to press it down and appear normal. India's words were so open and honest. Gina wanted to reach out and run her fingers down India's smooth cheek, and tell her it was going to be okay. That there was someone just for her. It might be in the last place she looked. Or it might be right under her nose.

Gina gulped at the thought. *Right under her nose.*

"I hope you're right, for my sake, too," she replied. "I'm pinning all my hopes on it."

Chapter Eleven

India peered in the window of the specialist whisky shop on Old Compton Street. Her eye was drawn to the bottle of Laphroaig in the window. It was Andi's favourite. India could never get on board with the taste. It was too peaty for her. In fact, she wasn't really much of a whisky drinker, full stop. So why was she looking in the window of a whisky shop?

She shook her head and carried on walking. When she got to the cafe by Eden's offices, Eden was already sat in the window, peering at her phone. She glanced up and gave India a wave. Then, when India was close enough, she followed it up with a hug. They didn't have a typical business relationship. India would almost class them as friends. Although she hadn't poured out her heart to Eden recently, in the same way she had to Gina.

India's heart picked up pace as she recalled their second rooftop liaison last week. They were an unlikely pair, and she wasn't sure where it was going, but every time her phone lit up, she hoped it was Gina asking her for another rooftop date. Not that they were dates in the strictest sense. But having that pressure off her was probably the reason India had been able to open up to Gina. At least, that's what she was telling herself for now. She wasn't ready to go down any other route just yet.

"Good to see you. You're still impossibly tall, you know that, right?" Eden gave India her usual grin.

"You're still impossibly good at doing PR, if those campaigns for Rainbow Rings I saw are anything to go by." Eden was also impossibly well dressed. She was the only other person India knew whose love of primary-coloured trouser suits rivalled her own.

"I like to do a good job. It's a terrible habit of mine."

They settled down, India ordering a flat white, and Eden getting another espresso.

"You like the boards we sent over?"

India nodded. Eden's company, Quote Media, had offices on this very street in central Soho. India never minded meeting here. She loved the bustle of central London, the crackle of energy zipping around the pavements, the queer vibe of every other person on the street. She was sure Eden was used to it. India didn't come across it so much in the stuffed-shirt world of fast-moving consumer goods. Public relations was the glamorous end of the business. The biscuit factory was essential, but there wasn't much glamour when you had to wear a hairnet.

"I loved them. Also, your suggestion of getting a real-life young lesbian couple for the campaign, I loved that, too. I want it to be real, and I want the ad played on the big screens on Piccadilly Circus on Pride day. We're going to have a big bus and give out the biscuits to everyone who wants one."

"Sounds like a bus I can get onboard for."

India laughed. "You *have* to be on the bus. Bring your

mates, plus Heidi and Maya, of course. I met a friend of yours at a Pride meeting recently. Lucy?"

Eden nodded. "She's more Heidi's friend, but we've met a few times. She's lovely."

"How are your wonderful family?"

Eden gave her a wide, genuine smile. "They're fabulous. I'm selling my place and moving in with Heidi, did I tell you? It's about time. We spend most of the time at hers anyway, because Maya's nursery is that way. Makes sense for me to move in. My place has already had an offer, so it's all systems go."

"Congratulations!" India was thrilled for her. "It only seems like yesterday you were getting together, and now you're moving in."

"I'm in the family photo this year, so it seemed like the time to do it." She leaned forward. "I'm planning on proposing to Heidi, too." Eden's face went pale. "I don't know why I just told you that, as I haven't even bought the ring yet. Please forget I told you!"

Eden's stricken face made India smile. "Relax." She put a hand on Eden's arm. "We're living parallel lives at the moment. I just bought a flat, too. Plus, I keep spilling my guts to someone, saying stuff I never normally would."

Eden still wasn't relaxed. "Seriously, don't say a word. *Especially* not to Lucy, then the whole lesbian world will know."

"I won't, I promise." India crossed her heart. "You can trust me."

Eden nodded. "I know. Anyway, enough about me. You wanted to chat about the Pride business campaign you're setting up, too? Giving ten bursaries to LGBT+ companies is very generous."

"This year is all about me giving back. I want good karma coming my way, and I reckon this is how to get it."

"Hello, ladies." India looked up to see Johan, Eden's colleague, standing with a takeaway coffee in his hand. "I'm not staying," he said, pulling up a chair.

Eden frowned. "But?"

He shook his head. "I'm really not. Just thought I'd come and say hi to our favourite client." He grinned at India. "I love that suit, by the way. You look radiant."

"Thank you, Johan, you're as charming as ever." India smoothed down her orange trouser suit.

"It's my USP." He turned to Eden. "While I remember, Lib called. She's going to be late tonight. Something about an interview at an estate agent's?"

"Okay," Eden replied. "Anything else?" Her tone told him to bugger off.

Johan took the hint, giving her a sweet grin. "See you later. Bye, India!"

"Is Lib your estate agent? I've got a fab one." An image of Gina appeared in India's mind, her styled hair swept to one side, Gina's brown eyes beckoning India to her.

India blinked. She refocused on Eden, tuning out everything else.

Eden shook her head. "No, Lib's my best friend. She's having a career change and becoming an estate agent. Her life took some turns this past year, but she's decided to go with the flow. Change is the one constant in life, isn't it? Look at us, both moving house."

"You can say that again."

"Fancy meeting you here."

India picked up her distinct scent at the same time she heard her. What the actual fuck? The slow drawl of Andi's words scraped the edges of her brain. India stood to face her ex.

Her shoulders stiffened. "Andi." India held out a hand. "This is Eden, my PR expert."

"Pleasure," Andi said, giving Eden a handshake, before dismissing her with the blink of an eye. "Your PR expert. I did wonder if I'd been replaced by a newer model."

"Would it be any of your business if you had?" This was the problem with London. People thought it was a big city, but Andi's radio studios were within a five-minute walk. Still, it was sod's law they'd be in the same cafe.

Andi tipped her head back, giving India a smirk. "Still prickly. You need to let it go, Inds. Like Elsa the *Frozen* princess says."

"Goodbye, Andi." India practised slow, controlled breathing just like her meditation app told her. Even though her fists were balled by her side.

Andi held up both palms. "I'm going. My coffee should be ready now." She glanced at Eden. "Good to meet you." She waltzed off, leaving the scent of Bright Crystal in her wake. It was one of India's most hated smells now.

India bit her lip, then sat down.

"Remind me never to get on the wrong side of you."

India shook her head. "You could never hope to be as much of a bitch as her. What I ever saw in her, I still don't know."

"We all make mistakes. I know I have. I just got lucky with Heidi, which is why I want to make it official."

India nodded. "I get that."

A banging on the window made India jump. "For fuck's sake, what now?" When she turned, Luca was on the other side of the glass, making faces at the back of a retreating Andi. Ricardo was beside him, his eyes wide. They were inside within five seconds, using the chair that Johan had left and pulling up another.

"What the hell is this, my life passing through one cafe in half an hour? Is the woman I lost my virginity with going to show up in a minute, too?"

Luca looked confused. "I don't know, what's her name?"

"Very funny. But Andi was just here, and now you." India's mind was all over the place.

"You're clearly sending out a bat signal for people to come and find you."

India rolled her eyes. "Clearly."

"What did Andi want, anyway? I can still feel the sharp spikes in the air." Luca turned to Eden. "Luca, India's brother. My husband, Ricardo."

Everyone shook hands and Eden introduced herself.

"The famous Eden! India only has good things to say about you, as does my dad."

"Then I'm doing my job well," Eden replied.

Luca put a hand on India's arm. "It looks like Andi did a number on you before she took off on her broom. You look stressed and pink. Like an overripe peach." He looked around. "Do you want some water?"

India shook her head. "I'll be fine. I just didn't expect to see her, that's all."

"She works around the corner."

"I know that." She gave her brother an icy stare.

He shut up.

Regret gnawed at her skin. It wasn't Luca's fault Andi had showed up, and she was taking it out on him.

"Sorry," India said. "It's just, she knows which buttons to press."

Luca nodded. "I lived through your relationship and watched her press them one by one."

"Hmmm," India replied. "What are you doing here, anyway? Andi is understandable. But you two live in Surrey." She leaned back. "Plus, you both look like you're going to a wedding. Or perhaps to a joint job interview." Both Luca and Ricardo had starched trousers, shirts and blazers on. "What gives?"

They grinned at each other, then kissed.

"Do you want to tell her?" Luca's cheeks blushed bright red and he tugged at the collar of his white shirt.

Ricardo shook his head. "You do it."

Luca shook his. "No, *you*."

India's eyes widened, and she let out an exasperated sigh. "Will somebody tell me *something*, please?"

"Okay." Luca took India's hands in his, giving Eden a wide grin before jigging in his chair. "We're in London because this is where our surrogacy agency is." His jigging went up a notch. "We've just had our third meeting, and it took first time." His grin got even wider. "We're pregnant, and you're going to be an auntie!"

India stood up and pulled her brother into a hug, quickly followed by Ricardo. "I'm so thrilled for you both! I knew you said you were thinking about it, but I didn't know it was going to be so quick."

Luca looked bashful. "We didn't want to say until it was confirmed. It could have taken months, even years, but we were lucky."

"Congratulations, even though I just met you," Eden said. "Having welcomed a toddler into my life in the past couple of years, I'll just say, having children changes your life irrevocably."

"That's what we're hoping for," Ricardo told her.

India raised her coffee. "Here's to you and your baby." Suddenly Andi didn't seem as important. This definitely was. "What were we just saying, Eden? The only thing constant in life is change?"

Eden nodded. "Death, taxes and change."

India was going to be an auntie.

She had a sudden urge to share the news with Gina.

Chapter Twelve

India's survey had shown up some damp on the front windows of her proposed new flat. Gina had been in touch with the owner's UK representative, and he was coming to meet her there to discuss what needed to be done. When she arrived, Barry greeted her warmly, chatting about his day. Gina had a lot of time for him.

They walked out onto the balcony together, Barry pushing up the sleeves of his mint-green jumper, tilting his head to the May sunshine. She recalled India doing the same into the gathering dusk when she'd first seen the flat. How her face changed from pinched to relaxed when she saw the rooftops. Barry was clearly experiencing the same reaction.

"This is one of those flats, isn't it?" He turned to her, his close-cropped hair not moving in the wind. Rooftops were breezy, that was another universal truth. Even in May. "The kind you have in your management portfolio, but would love to live in. I remember it being built and thinking the same. But my wife doesn't want to live in central London with three children, so what can you do." He gave Gina a shrug. "In another life, where I was a carefree bachelor, this would be my pad."

"Mine, too, but my bank account disagrees," Gina replied.

Barry laughed. "That's also a consideration." He stared out

across the city. "You know what, I'm feeling good this morning. Plus, it's India Contelli buying, and she seems lovely on the telly. Tell her I'll get all the damp issues seen to asap if we can exchange by the end of this month. Okay?"

Gina nodded. "That sounds reasonable, I think she'll be happy with that."

Barry walked over and shook Gina's hand. "Then we have a deal." He swung his head back around to the view. "I know we could have done this over the phone, but I wanted to come and see this view one last time. Shame we don't have a bottle of something to toast this sale, isn't it?"

Gina laughed. What was it about rooftops that made people want to crack open booze?

Barry strolled back into the flat, waiting for Gina to lock up. "And you know what? I also wanted to say thank you for all you've done. You're a great agent."

Gina stopped in her tracks. "Thank you. It's not often we get thanked."

"I've been meaning to let you know."

Gina waved him off, then got into her car, checking her phone. No reply from her sister yet. They had been due to have dinner later at their favourite restaurant in Canary Wharf, but Neeta hadn't confirmed. Given her job, Gina was used to her sister cancelling plans at the last minute, but she desperately hoped tonight wasn't one of those nights. Gina needed some good food cooked by someone else, in the company of somebody who got her.

If Neeta couldn't be there, maybe Bernie would be able to? Although she'd been leaving work on time and seemingly had a never-ending stream of social engagements of late.

It flashed through Gina's mind that India might want to have a rooftop date. But they hadn't been in contact for a couple of weeks, so maybe that friendship was dying. Gina hoped not.

Gina's phone bleeped with a message from Amy, letting her know there had been another two withdrawals from their business account this morning for the same couple of amounts. Also, one of just over £80 for something at TK Maxx.

Gina's stomach sank. TK Maxx was Sara's favourite shop, so Gina had always hated it irrationally. Nothing in their business needed to be bought at TK Maxx. What the hell was Bernie doing shopping there? Gina had asked Bernie about the withdrawals, but she had said it was a few lunches out, plus some last-minute client gifts. But something was off, she could feel it in her bones.

Gina needed to have a bigger chat with Bernie. She flicked through her phone to her calendar app. Perhaps Bernie had been buying her a present for her upcoming birthday? If she'd done it on the company account, Gina would be less than impressed.

Her phone flashed again, this time a message from India. Gina couldn't stop the smile from invading her face. The message read: 'Let me know about the flat when you hear. Would be lovely to meet up for a rooftop chat soon. x'

She'd signed it off with a kiss. Plus, India Contelli still wanted to meet her on a rooftop. That almost erased the fact mystery transactions were happening on the company's business account. Almost. Gina sucked on her bottom lip, then checked her calendar again. Her next appointment wasn't until this afternoon, and she was pretty sure Bernie was in the office this morning. No better time to confront her than now. Plus, their coffee machine did far better drinks than their local coffee shop on the corner.

Gina put on her seatbelt and started the engine.

* * *

Gina waved at Ranj from SpecStars as she parked up her car, then keyed in the code and walked up the beige-carpeted two flights to their office. Their building was ten years old, but somehow, it managed to retain that 'new' smell, as if it had just been pulled out of its wrapper. Gina approached their office, a plush branded sign proclaiming they were 'Hot London Properties'. She tried the door, expecting it to be on the latch, but it wasn't budging. Perhaps Bernie was still in TK Maxx. She used her key, smiling as she walked into their office.

However, what she saw next wiped the smile from her face in an instant.

Gina's brain couldn't quite compute what was happening in front of her. She gripped the door handle, her eyebrows knitted together in confusion.

Bernie was on the couch, her face stuck to someone else's. Someone with familiar hair. Familiar clothes. A scent that took Gina back to the 18 months she'd spent with her.

Gina shook her head. Her stomach plunged. Her vision swayed, like she was on a particularly vomit-inducing ride at Alton Towers. She wanted to lean against the wall to steady herself. Her brain was having trouble accepting that Bernie was on their office couch with a woman.

The fact that woman was her ex, Sara, was enough to send Gina over the edge.

Gina let go of the door handle and advanced towards the

pair, wanting to look away, but being inadvertently drawn to them, like watching a car crash.

Bernie and Sara? It made no sense at all. Bernie despised Sara. Had told Gina on many occasions how she'd done the right thing getting rid of her 'dead wood'. But now Bernie was in their office, kissing Sara like this definitely wasn't the first time it had happened. Kissing Sara so deeply, it took Gina clearing her throat for them to spring apart, and for Bernie to jump up, eyes wide, staring madly at Gina.

"Fucking hell, you scared the shit out of me!"

Gina didn't even know what to say to that.

Bernie straightened herself up, pulling down her shirt, running a hand through her hair, wiping her mouth with the other. Sadly, it couldn't erase the image from Gina's mind. Bernie's lips had just been kissing Sara's.

"I don't really care if I scared you." Disbelief ebbed away, replaced by anger. "What the hell are you doing? You and *Sara*? Since when?"

Gina glanced at Sara, who wouldn't meet her eye. Instead, she gripped the bottom of her denim skirt, intentionally not looking up.

"It's not what it looks like," Bernie told her.

Gina scoffed. "What is it exactly then, Bernie? What the fuck is this other than you snogging my ex?" Gina glanced at Sara. "I thought she was 'dead wood'? I thought it was good that I'd got rid of her?"

Bernie spun around to Sara, shaking her head. "I never said that."

Wow. At least Gina knew where she stood. Her business partner was putting Sara over her.

"You fucking did, Bernie." Her anger heated up. It swirled in her veins, hot to the touch. She shook her head. "What is this? Are you together now?" Gina's mind wound back to the strange payments that had been leaving their business account for the past few months. She began to join the dots. She'd lay bets they had something to do with Sara.

Bernie held up a hand. "I was going to tell you, there just never seemed to be an opportune time."

"So you thought a public display of affection in our workplace would be the best way? I've got news for you, it's not."

Bernie shook her head, then took a step towards her. She went to touch Gina's arm.

Gina shook her head. "Don't touch me, not now." She balled a fist at her side. "How long have you been fucking my ex?"

Bernie dropped her hand. "We've been seeing each other for a few months, and we were going to tell you."

"*A few months?*" Gina's voice was elevated as she scanned through what had happened in the past few months. The conversations she might have had with Bernie that had been relayed back to Sara. All the while, Bernie was sleeping with her.

Gina couldn't quite believe it.

"Have you both been having a good laugh at my expense? When I say my expense, I mean it, literally. Amy's been telling me there have been some payments coming from our business account that she couldn't account for. Strange payments, but persistent. Including £80 spent at TK Maxx today." Gina put a hand on her hip. "It wouldn't have anything to do with Sara and you, would it?"

"It's not Bernie's fault, Gina." Sara was wading in now. Just what Gina needed. "Bernie gave me money when I needed it. I took the wrong card to TK Maxx on Saturday. Bernie was going to replace the money."

"Oh, was she?" Gina couldn't quite believe her ears. "What about all the other money that's disappeared, wrapped up as 'client gifts'?"

Bernie shook her head. "Some of those were client gifts. A couple of times I took the money from our account by mistake, too. I was going to reimburse you. Sara is my problem now, not yours."

Sara's face fell. "I wouldn't exactly say I'm a problem."

Gina fully recognised the entitlement in Sara's voice. She'd been on the end of it so many times.

Bernie's cheeks flushed. "I meant responsibility." She paused. "Or rather, my girlfriend."

"Girlfriend?" Gina spat. "Are you joking with me?" Bernie had been with Gina through all the trials associated with Sara. How no job was suitable for Sara. How she always wanted the best, but could never pay for it. How she was a financial drain, then an emotional drain. Bernie had been with Gina the whole way. Now they were a couple?

"Gina, I was going to tell you, I promise. I was going to the other day, but I just couldn't find the words."

"I understand why." Gina still couldn't move. She was rooted to the spot.

"But Sara is my girlfriend now. We were just talking about telling you before you walked in. If I want to give her money, I can. But it should be my money, from my account. I know that."

"You're damn right it should. I've given her far too much money. I don't want to give her another penny."

Sara went to speak.

Gina held up a hand. "Please don't chime in about being an artist and having cashflow issues. I've heard it all before." She turned back to Bernie. "As have you, which is why none of this makes any sense."

Gina needed to get away from this madness. Plus, she wasn't ready to contemplate the consequences. How her business partner and friend had lied to her. Had compromised their business. Not to mention betrayed her confidence.

Gina took a deep breath. "I can't even deal with this right now."

Bernie closed her eyes, and went to say something.

"Whatever you're going to say, save it. I'm going. Please don't be here when I get back." Tears pricked the back of Gina's eyes. "I thought I meant more to you than this, I really did."

Gina turned and fled down the stairs. There was a ringing in her ears. Lead in her stomach. A searing pain in her head.

She pushed open the main door, shielding her eyes against the lunchtime sun.

She had no idea where she was going.

Chapter Thirteen

There were other cars on the road, and Gina wasn't sure how she was avoiding them. She was on autopilot.

Words, sounds and colours splashed around her brain.

Bernie. *Red*.

Sara. *Double-red*.

Together. Kissing. Having sex. Having a relationship. *Sound-the-alarm-blazing-red*.

None of it made *any* sense.

She stopped at some traffic lights, peering out at the lunchtime queue outside the local Italian deli. Her stomach rumbled, but there was no way she could eat.

Five minutes later, she pulled up outside a primary school in Southwark, the screech of children audible even inside her car. She clutched the steering wheel as the engine purred. She switched it off, but didn't take her finger from the ignition. She was in a trance.

Gina took some calming breaths, holding in the tears. The movie kept flashing in her mind of Bernie and Sara on the couch. Bernie saying that word 'girlfriend'. Had Bernie lost her mind?

Suddenly, the car was too hot. She needed air. Gina threw

her tissue in the footwell, grabbed her bag, got out and locked the door. She stumbled onto the pavement.

She began walking, bumping into a woman heading in the opposite direction, who gave her an evil glare.

"Sorry," Gina muttered.

The woman shook her head as she passed.

It was another dent in Gina's fragile day. The euphoria of sorting India's flat with Barry, and getting that text from India, seemed very far away.

Gina slowed her pace. A man behind walked into her, swearing lightly.

Gina rubbed the back of her leg, staring after him.

Emotion bubbled up through her, and then she stopped completely. She couldn't walk another step.

The world lurched one way, then the other. A tomato-red postbox a few feet away became her destination. Gina reached it, leaned against it, then began to sob gently, as the pain of what had just happened reached every part of her body. Her legs ached. Her heart broke when she thought about Bernie's deceit. She wanted somebody to come and make it better. This was when it was nice to have someone to call on.

Someone like Bernie. Or at one time, Sara.

More sobs, as Gina's body shook.

People passing by gave her a wide berth. Gina didn't blame them. She'd do the same.

She reached into her bag and retrieved her phone. She pressed Neeta's number.

Voicemail.

Damn her and her job that meant she never answered her phone.

Gina steadied herself, blew her nose and started to walk again. Steady breath in, steady breath out. She was just getting into a rhythm, managing to avoid passing pedestrians, when her foot caught on a wonky paving slab. Gina glanced down, her heart rate accelerating as she stumbled forward. Bile hit her throat. She put her hands out to stop herself, eyes half shut, bracing herself for the impact of her fall.

Only, it never came. Instead, firm hands gripped her shoulders, and another body broke her fall.

Gina was so relieved, she clung to the warmth of this stranger, the red material of their clothing. It was only when she dared to open her eyes and peek out to thank her saviour that she saw who it was.

India. What was she doing here?

Also, *damn it*.

Her new friend had just stopped her from falling. Gina leaned against her, tears running down her face. As fourth impressions went, Gina had done better.

In response to what Gina imagined was a wild look, India pulled her closer, concern shining in her eyes.

That was Gina's undoing. She broke down into sobs, burying her head into India's shoulder.

To her credit, India said nothing. Instead, she put an arm around Gina, and led her across the street to a bench. She sat her down with all the gentleness of someone putting a baby to bed.

Gina hung her head, trying to get a grip on her emotions. It wasn't going to be easy.

A tissue hovered into view. Gina took it and blew her nose.

Eventually, she glanced over at India.

There was no judgement in her eyes. Just questions.

Gina took a deep breath. "Can you stop looking at me with such kindness? It's killing me."

India gave a gentle laugh. "Sorry." She gave Gina a stern frown. "Is that better?"

Gina sighed. "Much." Then she put her face in her hands. "Thank you for saving me, by the way. I was convinced I was going to face-plant into the pavement before you stepped in."

"You would have, so you're welcome."

Gina blew her nose again. "What are you doing here, anyway?"

India pointed to the shiny metal office block opposite, the morning sunshine dappling its windows. "Stable Foods has an office in that building. I quite often work from there, which is why the flat you showed me is perfect. I can walk to work. I can also save damsels in distress, it turns out." India paused. "You don't have to tell me why you're wandering the streets sobbing in the middle of the day, but can I take you somewhere if it would help to talk?"

Gina shook her head. "That's very kind, but I'm sure you have things to do." Gina searched her mind for what India might have to do. "Biscuits. You're the head of biscuits, right?"

India gave a loud laugh. "Biscuits can wait if they need to."

Gina got up, put the tissue in a nearby black metal bin, then sat down again. When she looked up, India's sapphire stare was trying to work her out. Heat rushed through Gina. "I don't know where I was going. I was driving, then I needed air. The car was too stuffy."

"Okay." India stroked her shoulder. "Listen, I live close to here. How about you come back there and I'll make you a cup of tea? You can see my terrible rooftop-less flat, and we can forget this ever happened, if you like." India's gaze penetrated her defences.

It was the best offer Gina'd had all day by a country mile. "I just need to put a parking ticket on my car. After that, tea would be lovely. Thank you."

* * *

They arrived back at India's flat, and Gina stared out the window at the shops and the main road four floors below. India was right. The views from her new place were a definite upgrade, even though the inside still looked like it came direct from an interior design magazine. However, this flat was a little more twee, more country-style than Gina would have imagined for India. Her personal style said bold colours, larger than life. Here, the curtain pelmets, embroidered cushions and old-fashioned rugs told Gina this was somebody else's style entirely.

She clutched her phone, staring at the screen. No apology from Bernie yet. No reply from her sister. Thank goodness for India.

Her saviour came out of the kitchen with two mugs of tea. She put them on the wooden coffee table, then disappeared again, reappearing moments later with biscuits. Of *course* she did. Biscuits were India's thing. Her smile lit up her face as she sat on her white sofa.

Gina sat on the sofa opposite. She stared at her tea and the biscuits. They were rainbow coloured. Gay biscuits. Gina put her phone beside them. She must look a state. If she'd somehow been appealing to India before, she was pretty sure that ship had now sailed. Still, India was being beyond kind, and Gina appreciated it.

"Here's to today getting better. The only way is up." India raised her mug. "Try a Rainbow Ring, our Pride biscuits. Fresh off the production line!"

Gina shook her head. "I'm not hungry." She wasn't risking crumbs or hot liquids on India's white sofa. Not when her heart was racing at 100mph, so who knew what her body might do given half the chance. "Thanks, though. For the tea and the rescue." She ground her teeth together. She owed India an explanation. However, Gina was convinced an explanation was going to expose her for being weak and stupid. She should have seen what had been going on over the past few months, shouldn't she?

She had no idea about anything anymore.

Her phone lit up with a message from her sister. Neeta couldn't make tonight.

Gina's face fell. She grabbed a pink velvet cushion and hugged it.

"What now?"

Gina shook her head. "Just my sister cancelling plans for dinner tonight. She's a doctor. It happens."

India frowned. "You're not having the best day."

"You could say that. I just walked in on Bernie snogging my ex in the office. Turns out, they got together a few months ago and have been struggling to work out how to tell me. This method was a little too real for my liking, but hey." So much for keeping it all in. But that hadn't been her pattern with India, had it? With India, she was a blurter. A blurter for Britain.

"Your business partner and your ex?"

94

Gina nodded. "It sounds worse when you say it out loud."

"You've had quite the morning." India shook her head, her black hair shimmering, looking almost dark green in the light. "Between you and me, we have ex issues, don't we?"

Gina smiled for the first time since the office showdown. She put the cushion on the sofa beside her. She missed its comfort immediately. "You could say that. On the plus side, your seller has agreed to fix the damp for the price you offered, so I was going to let you know later. But now I can tell you in person."

India gave her a grin. "That's brilliant news." She eyed Gina. "But in the meantime, what can we do to cheer you up today?"

Gina was fairly sure the answer was "not much", but she raised an eyebrow like she was thinking about it anyway. "Rewind and start again?"

India shook her head. "But then I don't get to be gallant. You've done me a favour today. Being gallant is my most favourite thing."

Gina smiled. "Glad I could help."

India checked her watch, then winced. "Listen, I have to go for a quick meeting with Frankie, but you stay here and relax. I was on my way when we met, but I won't be long."

Gina shook her head, standing up. She didn't want to be a burden to anyone, least of all India. She straightened her jacket and rolled her shoulders. "I'll go, you've got stuff to do."

But India walked over, put a hand on either side of Gina's shoulders and pushed her back onto the sofa.

The action was soothing but also exhilarating. Gina recalled their hands touching on the rooftop when they'd last met. How it had jolted her senses then. Today was no different.

Her body reclined as India's hands pressed into her shoulders. She looked up, and India's face was inches from hers. When their eyes met, Gina's heart reared up like a startled horse.

India went to say something, but stopped.

The moment sat between them, pulsing. It would have been so easy for Gina to reach up and press her lips to India's, but she was pretty sure it wouldn't be that welcome. Gina was a sobbing mess. Hardly a catch in anyone's language.

A few more beats went by before India pulled back, picked up the remote control and put it in Gina's hand.

Another zap as their hands touched. Gina's heart thudded.

India stepped back, her eyes wide. She cleared her throat. "I'll be back in an hour, so help yourself to whatever you want. Seriously. Eat some Rainbow Rings, just relax."

Gina leaned back into the sofa. It was a tempting offer and she had nowhere better to go. "I've still got a couple of hours until my parking ticket runs out, so okay."

Chapter Fourteen

Frankie favoured walking lunches in her daily routine, as she said she spent far too much of her life sitting and chatting. India was behind her sentiment totally, and was now used to grabbing a coffee and walking the Southbank with her friend. On a day like today, with summer just over the horizon, it was the best remedy ever. Particularly when her mind kept jumping back to a forlorn Gina on her sofa. India hoped she stayed where she was.

"You okay? You seem miles away." Frankie didn't look at India as she walked. To their right, the River Thames rushed as a water taxi went by, swiftly followed by a tourist cruise jam-packed with eager travellers.

India nodded, the coffee too hot in her hand. She should have got one of those cardboard holders. She stopped, got a tissue from her bag and wrapped it around the cup. "I forgot my reusable cup today. Bad me, killing the planet." India paused, taking in the row of restaurants to their left, their outdoor patios full of tourists and locals alike. "I'm a bit distracted. Remember Gina, your estate agent and now mine?" *Also, someone who just made me walk out of my flat all flushed and disorientated.*

Frankie nodded, sipping her water.

"I just ran into her, and she was quite upset. She's back at my flat, having a cup of tea while I meet you."

Frankie stopped walking. "She's back at your flat? What's she doing there?"

India shrugged like it was nothing. "She was upset. She'd just walked in on her business partner snogging her ex. I guess I know what it's like to have an ex who doesn't really give a shit about you. I wanted to make sure she was okay." Somehow, in the short space of time they'd known each other, Gina's happiness had climbed higher on India's list of priorities.

"But she's at your flat and you're not there." Frankie crinkled her face. "Has something happened? Are you seeing her?"

India felt the blush spring to her cheeks. "No! I'm not in the market for a girlfriend. I'm just being compassionate to a fellow human being."

"Or you fancy her." Frankie's gruff laugh coated the air around them.

India wanted to deny it, but knew that would only fuel Frankie's fire. "I do *like* her. She seems genuine. Plus, she had no idea who the hell I was, which makes a refreshing change."

They walked on for a few moments, walking around the stalls selling dog-eared paperbacks on the riverside. India usually stopped to browse, but never with Frankie in tow, who skipped around the stalls like they held poison. Frankie was not a reader.

"Hang on, her business partner. You mean Bernie?"

India nodded. "Yes. Do you know her? I met her once. Didn't get a good vibe."

Frankie nodded. "Unfortunately, yes. I had bad dealings with her once, so it doesn't surprise me what you're saying. She's in it for herself and nobody else. She's always seemed to have more money than she should to me, too. I know her business, how it works. I don't understand how she's got her fingers in so many pies." She wagged a finger at India. "Tell Gina to get out while she can."

"Not easy when they're tied up financially."

"She can borrow money. Gina and Bernie were always a strange match. Maybe Bernie's only showing her true colours now."

"I'll let Gina know." For now, Gina was probably more concerned with Bernie sleeping with her ex than business issues. But India would remind her to see the whole picture.

They navigated around the queues for the London Eye, past the London Aquarium. India was stopped twice for selfies, and graciously posed for them, having learned early on it was easier and quicker to do them than to disappoint fans and feel guilty for the rest of the day. Plus, it didn't happen that often, despite what her family thought.

Frankie steered them away from the river, down into some gardens where they got onto a path and began walking in a long, slow loop. India breathed in the freshly cut grass, loving how green it was.

"I wanted to let you know the committee approved Rainbow Rings as the official Pride biscuit, so you can use the logo on the packaging if you like."

"Fabulous news." India gave Frankie a grin. "Wait until you taste them, they're delicious."

Frankie patted her stomach. "Me and biscuits don't mix at

the moment. I had too many of them on holiday, I'm trying to regulate my intake."

"I shouldn't send you a box for free, then?"

"Don't you dare."

"I'm sending a box of Chocolate Rockets to Gina's sister. Apparently, she's a big fan."

Frankie gave her a look as they passed a gorgeous bed of yellow and white roses. "No, you don't fancy Gina at all. Not one bit."

India nudged her friend with her elbow. "What's wrong with carrying out a nice gesture for someone? Plus, I'm a grown woman. I don't *fancy* people anymore. I admire them. Respect them."

Frankie let out a strangled yelp. "You want to jump her bones, you don't fool me. I've known you too long, remember?" She nudged India back. "The other reason I wanted to talk to you was about Eunice. You're still on for meeting her in Birmingham on Sunday?"

India nodded. "It's in my diary, especially after I read the letters. So much longing and so many things unsaid."

Frankie nodded. "I know. They broke my heart. I so want us to find H and reunite them, which is your job to make happen. But on that, I have bad news about Lucy going, too. She was on the list for a minor operation, and they've moved it forward to that week, so she can't make it. Will you be okay to go alone?" She paused. "Or you could ask Gina, even though you don't fancy her one bit."

India rolled her eyes. "I'm not rising to your bait." She pictured Gina's face on the bench earlier. She'd looked so defeated. India wanted to put a smile back on her face today.

"Although, a trip away might take her mind off her troubles. Plus, I think she said her family lives there." Bright plans rolled through India's mind like a summer showreel.

"You do what you have to do. So long as you try to coax Eunice into finding the mysterious H, okay?"

"Got it."

* * *

India let herself back into her flat, not quite sure what she was walking into. After all, she didn't know Gina that well. She'd left a virtual stranger in her flat alone, which is something she'd never normally do. Only, Gina wasn't a stranger, was she? She was someone India felt at home with. Like she hadn't with anyone else in quite a while.

'*You fancy her,*' Frankie had said. India hadn't let her mind go there before. Not totally. She enjoyed Gina's company. Her body tingled when she was around. But did she fancy her? Did she want to jump her bones? She wasn't sure she was ready.

Maybe India shouldn't invite her on the trip to Birmingham. "Or maybe you should!" said the devil on India's shoulder. She glanced at her reflection in the hallway mirror, but the devil was nowhere to be seen.

"Only me!" India shouted, like this was something she did every day. It wasn't. There was normally nobody waiting in her flat.

"I hoped it was you." Gina turned her head. "Burglars don't normally have keys."

India stood in the doorway, staring at Gina in a new way. Gina's pain was still evident in the crease of her brow. However, after speaking to Frankie, and thinking about asking Gina to come away with her, it was like India had allowed herself to think beyond what she had before. Now, she really took in Gina's sparkling eyes. Her elegant nose. Her kissable lips.

Heat slid down her body. Maybe Frankie had a point.

Although, India wasn't acting the way she normally did when she liked someone. In those circumstances, she was normally bold and brash. But with Gina, it hadn't happened that way. She'd edged into her life, mainly on rooftops. Now, Gina was on her sofa, an empty mug on her coffee table, and she looked like she belonged there. That thought hit India harder than she ever expected.

Gina moved her feet from where they were buried under her, and sat up straight. "How was your meeting, and Frankie?"

"Both good. We walked the Southbank and marvelled at all the people queueing for the London Eye."

Gina smiled. "You're not a fan?"

"It's the most hyped big wheel in the world, and you have to share your carriage with a bunch of other people." India sat in the armchair to the right of Gina. "So no, not a fan."

"I went up on it with my family when they came to London. The very first time after I came out to them. I was grateful for those other people. It lessened the awkwardness we were all feeling."

India gazed at her. "I get that." Maybe Gina wouldn't want to come to Birmingham, after all. Disappointment pooled in her stomach. She was already counting on Gina coming, wasn't she?

"Any word from Bernie or your ex in the hour or so I've been gone?" A change of subject. Patience personified.

Gina's face clouded over. "Nothing. Which says a lot. They

probably started shagging on the sofa the minute I left. Or went on a TK Maxx shopping spree." She gave India a shrug.

"TK Maxx? That's very specific."

Gina waved a hand. "It's a long story, I'll tell you another time." She paused. "Anyway, is Pride going to plan? I never did sign up as a volunteer."

"You're helping out on my bus, so you're good." India sat forward. "Plus, there's another way you can contribute, too. I have a Pride proposal for you." Heat hit India's cheeks as soon as the words left her mouth.

Gina spluttered. "If you're asking me to marry you, I'm going to turn you down. Call me old-fashioned, but I like at least one date first."

India put her head in her hands before looking up at Gina. "Okay, I'm going to try this again. You know the 'It's Never Too Late' campaign where I'm going to Birmingham to meet the author of the love letters?"

Gina nodded. "I remember you spoke about it."

"The organiser, Lucy, can't make it now." India made sure she had Gina's eye contact. She did. "The trip is to meet Eunice, put her at ease and get her onside, nothing documented. I actually think just me going to meet her the first time makes more sense, so you don't even have to come to the meeting. However, you said you wanted to help, and this is a way you can. I'd love the company, and you know your way around the city, so you'd be doing me a favour."

Gina narrowed her eyes. "You know that going back to my home city isn't a natural fit for me? The lesbian Indian girl. There won't be any bunting in the street."

"Don't tell your family you're coming. It's only going to

be overnight. You don't have to see them if you don't want to." India let that realisation sink in.

Gina's brows knitted together. "I suppose I could do that, although I always think they'll just know anyway. My mum has a sixth sense when it comes to her children. I usually avoid going, full stop. But that idea is revolutionary." She pursed her lips. "You're opening my mind to new possibilities."

India knew exactly what she meant. "Ditto."

Her phone beeped in her handbag, but India ignored it. She didn't want to break this moment, break the spell that was thick in the room. It would go in seconds, but for now, it was perfect. "What do you think about the weekend?"

Gina moved her mouth left, then right. "Possibly yes. A weekend away from London and my life sounds good. When are you going?" Gina's gaze burned India's skin.

"This coming Saturday. I'm meeting Eunice on Sunday."

India's phone beeped again. And then again. She got up and retrieved it. "Sorry, I'd better take a look." Her hand shook as she clicked her home screen. Was Gina feeling this, too? This charge in the room between them? Whatever it was, it crackled with fresh energy as India grabbed her phone from her bag.

"Let me just check who needs me." Two emails from her operations manager. One from her dad. But also, two text messages from Andi.

What the hell did she want? India was determined to stay in the room, keep the vibe. But her fingers had other ideas, clicking on the texts.

Andi wanted to meet up. She had something she wanted to tell her. Was India available this week? Annoyance rose in her. Could she never escape Andi's clutches?

She could if she ignored her. India threw the phone back into her bag, then focused all her energy back on Gina. On the way her hand rested on her thigh. The arch of her neck. Particularly on Gina's lips.

"Do you need to get going?" Gina moved to the edge of the sofa. "I need to rescue my car anyway. The ticket only lasts until three."

India stood up, shaking her head. "Stay there. I'll put the kettle on. You need to eat a Rainbow Ring before you go, and you can't do that without fresh tea."

Everything else could wait.

Especially Andi.

Chapter Fifteen

Over the following few days, Gina cleared her inbox, chased invoices, signed up three new properties and had lunch with two potential new clients. She even cleaned the coffee machine, being mildly nauseated at the green mould in the drip tray. When was the last time anybody had cleaned it? It looked like the answer was never. Gina thought Bernie was the most toxic thing in their office, but it turned out she was wrong.

Amy confirmed there had been no more strange transactions from their business account, and Gina had sent Bernie a message telling her to meet on Friday to discuss next steps. Gina wasn't sure Bernie was going to show, but she'd run it past India when she'd told her she was coming to Birmingham, and India had told her it was the right course of action. Gina couldn't stand around waiting for Bernie to contact her. She was taking back control.

She peered up at the clock on their office wall. White with large black numbers. She and Bernie had chosen the classic style together, one of their first purchases when they'd opened three years ago. Gina had met Sara not long after, and she'd been a fixture on the office sofa for months afterwards.

Gina racked her brain for memories of those interactions.

Had there been a frisson between Sara and Bernie then? Was anything going on when she'd still been with Sara? She made a face. She didn't want Sara anymore, but she couldn't think about she and Bernie sharing the same woman at the same time. Bernie had said it had only been going on for a couple of months, but Bernie had lied to her this whole time. How could Gina trust her now? The plain fact was, she couldn't.

The clock ticked around to midday. At two minutes past, Bernie walked in.

Gina clenched her buttocks. She almost expected Sara to follow. When she didn't, Gina's shoulders relaxed. Then she remembered what Bernie had done. She had to keep control in this situation and not fly off the handle. That would get her nowhere. This was about her future, not her past.

"Thanks for inviting me." Bernie stopped short of Gina's desk, seemingly not sure where she should stand. Eventually, she moved towards the coffee machine. "You want one?"

Gina shook her head. She sat while the machine whirred.

Bernie brought it over to her desk and walked up to her cheese plant. She touched the soil, then looked up. "You've been watering Connie?"

Gina nodded. "She shouldn't suffer in our divorce."

Bernie said nothing, just swivelled her chair to face Gina, sucking on her top lip. She looked up, but couldn't hold Gina's eye for long.

Gina sighed before she spoke. "You know what, I've been thinking about this ever since we last spoke. After I left you the other day, I drove, I burst into tears, I wasn't sure what the fuck was happening. But now, I'm just tired. Of your lies." She stood up and walked around her desk, before settling her bum against the edge of it. "It's not even that you're seeing Sara. We've been broken up a year." Gina pressed a finger to her chest. "It's more that you lied to me. That you allowed her to take the company card and spend on it. That you stole money for her."

"I didn't steal, it was a genuine mistake."

Gina shook her head. "Cut the crap, Bernie. Give me some credit. Once is a mistake. Twice maybe. There are 13 instances of cash being withdrawn. That's not a mistake."

"They're not all Sara. Some were client gifts."

Gina gave her a steely stare. "You really need to stop defending yourself. It's not a good look."

Finally, Bernie hung her head. If she'd come here for a fight, it was the wrong tactic.

"I'm sorry I didn't tell you about Sara." Bernie spoke to the floor.

Gina held up her hands. "You can see who you want. Why you would *want* to is a different matter, as you've seen the inside track. But who am I to judge? I fell for it." She stood up. "That's not what I want to discuss." She paused, holding Bernie in place with her stare. "But honestly, what the fuck are you thinking?"

Shut up, Gina. This is not what you agreed to talk about.

Bernie looked up but didn't reply, so Gina pressed on. "I want to buy you out of the business. I've got Amy to print out all of our assets and I've got our accountant to prepare what we need. There's a figure in it I think is fair. I knocked off what you owe me for all the Sara expenditure. Plus, a little more. I'm pretty sure the swell in client dinners and gifts over the past two months haven't all been legit."

Bernie dropped her gaze. That was confirmation enough.

"Like I said, you can fuck who you want, but I can't be in business with someone who's going to let Sara anywhere near our money. Nor can I be in business with someone who lies to me."

"What if I don't want to sell? Because I don't. I love working with you. We make a great team, you know that."

"We did, past tense. You should have thought about that before you started fucking my ex behind my back."

"How long does she stay your ex for? You said it yourself, you split up a year ago." Bernie got up and leaned on the edge of her desk, facing Gina.

She was close enough for Gina to lean over and punch her. She wasn't a violent person, but after that last comment, Gina was seriously considering it.

"I can't trust you anymore, Bernie. That's the crux of it. Look at the figure and get back to me. I emailed you all the information. There's no going back." Gina was surer of that final sentence than she had been of anything in her life. It was time to branch out on her own. She wasn't sure where she would get the money to give to Bernie, but perhaps she could ask her parents? They had the money. Would they lend it to her? If she went with India to Birmingham, she could ask them in person.

Maybe the Birmingham trip was a sign.

Chapter Sixteen

India looked over her shoulder as she steered her car onto the M1, trying to ignore the jiggle of Gina's leg beside her. She kept intermittently doing it, then stopping, aware of herself, then starting again when she forgot. India didn't want to ask what was on her mind. It had, after all, been quite some week. On the dashboard, the satnav had a red flashing light focused on the road ahead. That was never good.

"Traffic ahead on the M1 in around three miles," said the woman's alluring automated voice.

"Is it wrong to be attracted to your satnav?" India asked, foot on the accelerator. She was going to take these three miles at speed while she could. "She sounds like she'd be cool to go on a night out with. Like she'd be a good kisser. What do you think?"

That broke through whatever thoughts were clouding Gina's brain. She gave India a laugh. "It's probably only an issue if you attempt to mount the dashboard. Then I'd be worried."

India grinned. "It's purely a voice thing, I promise you."

To her left, green fields stretched out to the distance. To her right, the incoming lane yawned with cars and lorries. They sat in pillowy silence for a few minutes before Gina spoke.

"What time are you meeting Eunice in the morning?" Gina had a hand on her knee to keep it still.

"Eleven o'clock at her house. I offered to take her out, but she insisted on hosting." India glanced in her rear-view mirror as the traffic ahead ground to a halt.

"I'd take the offer of going out, but I know my parents would be the same. They'd want to show you hospitality, not the other way around."

India nodded. They hadn't discussed Gina's family plans this weekend yet. Now was as good a time as any. "Are you seeing your family while we're there?"

Gina turned her head, then nodded. "It's why I was asking about tomorrow. I'm not going to tell them I'm coming until tonight though, maybe not even then. I don't want a fuss, or a round-up of every relative under the sun for a huge dinner. I just want to drop in. Just a small chat with a cup of tea and some samosas. Maybe some biscuits, too."

"If you tell them, it'll be a big deal?"

She sighed. "Maybe if I visited more often, it wouldn't be. My sister and I normally go together, so it's a bigger deal then, too. But no fuss suits me. Plus, I want to ask them if they might consider investing in my business when I buy Bernie out." Gina began jiggling her leg again. "I know they have the money, and they invested in my brother's side business. It's just, they might not want to give their money to set up a gay business."

"Hot London Properties is not a gay business. It's a profitable, smart, well-run business." India couldn't imagine a parent using that as an excuse, but she knew she was lucky.

Gina smiled. "Thank you."

"I mean it. Plus, you're still their daughter."

Gina snorted. "In name, yes." She shook her head. "My dad might be willing. My mum, not so much. She'll have some excuse. 'It's not the right time, Nagina'."

"Nagina? That's your full name?"

Gina nodded. "It got shortened to Gina at school. Plus, if you pronounce Nagina wrong, it means 'conniving bitch'. I learned early on that Gina works better." She shut up for a few minutes, before leaning forward. "Do you mind if we have some music?"

"Go ahead."

Gina pressed the button and Radio 2 lit up.

India's stomach clenched. Why was it set to Radio 2? Then she remembered. Her dad had borrowed her car yesterday while his was in for a service. She checked the car clock, then remembered it was Saturday. Andi was a weekday DJ. She wouldn't be on now. If this was the station Gina wanted, India could cope.

"That was Laura Marling with her haunting new track," Andi said.

India flinched in her seat, as every hair on her body stood on end. Heartburn roared in her chest. *What the fuck?* Andi should be tucked up in bed with her fiancée, not talking at them in the car.

"This is Andi Patten sitting in for Ramona on a Saturday."

Gina turned her head right as the words sank into her brain. "Is that…?" she asked, pointing her index finger at the radio.

"Uh-huh." India sucked in a breath. "My ex."

They both reached over to change the station at the same time, but not before Andi said, "This next one is going out to a very special person in my life. Someone who means the world to me. Someone who, if she's listening, I hope she knows it." The first bars of the same tune that had played in the toilets at the Sea Containers when she'd run into Andi floated into the car, slamming into India as if she'd just hit a wall.

"Jesus Christ," India muttered, the enormity of what Andi had just said reaching her brain. What the hell was she playing at saying stuff like that? Unless she had the same song for her fiancée? India shook her head. *That is precisely something Andi would do.* Have the same song for every girlfriend so she could keep track.

Gina hit the scanner button, and Magic FM came up on the dial. Old-school Take That seeped into the car. They were on much safer ground.

"Was that dedicated to you?" Gina's eyebrows couldn't get much closer together.

"It sounded like it, but who knows? Andi likes to stir. I'm just glad to be shot of her." India shivered. Andi had sent her a couple more texts, too, asking to meet up. After ignoring her hadn't worked, India had replied with a firm no. She had no idea what Andi was playing at.

India pulled on the handbrake as the traffic stopped again. "How did things go with Bernie yesterday?"

Gina leaned back into her headrest. "About as well as I'd imagined. She's stubborn and doesn't like to be told what to do. I hope she sees sense."

"If you need to run anything else by me, just let me know."

"I will. Thanks for helping me the other day."

India smiled. "It's what friends do, right?" She paused. "While I think about it, my friend Eden has a friend who's looking for work in property if you need help. Shall I see if she's still looking?"

Gina nodded. "Sure, pass her details on. I'm still a bit at sixes and sevens with it all, but I will need someone eventually."

"Of course, no rush. Tell you what, shall we make a pact for this weekend: no more talk about our exes or business?" The traffic eased forward, the flashing roadwork signs disappearing. India put her foot on the accelerator as the traffic lanes opened up.

"I'm in," Gina replied, perking up. "How about we talk about the fact that your flat paperwork should be through this month, which means you'll have the keys in June, in time to be in for London Pride. If you weren't in the parade, you could almost smell it from your rooftop."

India snorted. "What does Pride smell like?"

"Rainbows and unicorns, of course." Gina paused. "Are you going to throw a moving-in party?"

"Definitely. And you're invited. Guest of honour." India gave her a grin, and their gazes locked. India couldn't pull her eyes away, and the car slid sideways. Her heart picked up speed as something passed between them. It was only when she refocused, and the car slid onto the hard shoulder, vibrating as the wheels hit the rougher road, that she remembered she was driving. She needed to get them to Birmingham in one piece. Not stare into Gina's eyes like a lovestruck puppy.

India hauled the wheel right, centred the car and gripped the wheel.

They were okay. Nobody was hurt. Just her emotions were getting a workout in this car today.

India's phone beeped in the phone tray.

They both looked down at it.

It beeped again.

She glanced at Gina, then back at the road. "I meant to put it on silent, otherwise it drives me mad. Can you put it on silent? It's probably my dad, or my brother posting me baby memes."

"Sure." Gina picked up the phone, then paused, shaking her head. "Sorry, I didn't mean to see, but it's from Andi. The shorter message is on your screen."

India's heart sank. "For fuck's sake." Andi was texting while she was on air? She'd never done that even when they were together.

"Are you back in touch?"

"We're not. At least, I'm not." India's tone was clear. "But Andi hears what Andi wants. Right now, she wants to get in contact with me, and she's using any means possible. I'm sure a lot of my friends heard what she said on the radio. The *Daily Mail* will probably pick it over, too, and dig out a photo of the pair of us in happier times if it's a slow news day." She blew out a raspberry. "Modern celebrity ain't all it's cracked up to be."

"You should block her."

"I've thought about it, but it seems a bit much?"

Gina gave her a look. "It depends if she's getting too much, doesn't it?"

She had a point. India slammed the steering wheel with her palm. "Anyway, we said no more talk of exes. When we eventually get to Birmingham, we'll check in to the hotel, have a lovely dinner and relax. Deal?"

Chapter Seventeen

Gina leaned in to the mirror and nearly poked her eye out on her toothbrush. She took a step backwards, moved her toothbrush from the shelf, opened her eyelid and applied her dark eyeliner, followed by some lipstick. Her sister would be proud. A light knock on her door made her turn her head. She wasn't quite ready. She opened it, and then ran back to the bathroom. "Make yourself at home, I won't be a sec!"

India's gorgeous, musky perfume sailed around her nose. It always announced India way before she actually appeared.

"Okay!" India shouted back.

Gina would lay bets India hadn't changed her outfit three times today. Or scrubbed her eye shadow off once and redone it, deeming it too sparkly. Gina was going to dinner with another woman, something that hadn't happened in over a year. While it wasn't strictly a date — this was business, of sorts — they were going out to eat in a public place. That was reason enough to make Gina nervous. Plus, India was famous. What if someone snapped a photo and it got back to Gina's family? She'd have a lot of explaining to do.

Five minutes later, she strolled out to the room. India's sleek silhouette was visible through the glass doors to the balcony. India hadn't stinted on accommodation. She'd got them both deluxe rooms side by side with spacious balconies. The sun was setting over Birmingham, and Gina was grateful it wasn't raining or grey. For some reason, making India like her hometown was important. This was where she'd been born. Birmingham was a part of her.

It was only when she got out to the balcony that she saw her mistake. She'd left her birthday card from her sister on the table. Neeta had put it in her bag as a surprise when she stopped by her flat the night before. Now India was holding it in her hand.

"When were you going to tell me it's your birthday?" India's face wore a glittering smile.

Gina's stomach flipped. "It's not until tomorrow."

India's mouth opened, then closed. "Which makes it all the more important to celebrate. It's your birthday weekend and we're at a hotel! We're going all out tonight with dinner and drinks." She paused. "Was that why you didn't want to tell your family?"

Gina glanced over the view, then back to India. "Not really. It'll just be awkward, whatever. It'll be nice to see them on my birthday. Or it won't be. I don't know until it happens. It's the first time I've seen them in their space on my own since I came out. What I do know is that I don't want to build it up into something big." She shook her head. "Can we add my family to the list of things we're not talking about tonight?"

"Of course we can." India put the card down. "Seriously, though. Is dinner tonight what you want to do? Would you rather go birthday clubbing in Birmingham's gay quarter?

I hear it's quite the scene." India was dressed in black trousers and a silver top, cut low to expose her smooth, tanned skin.

Gina's eye was immediately drawn to her strong collarbone, which she could already imagine touching, licking. She blinked, then dragged her gaze upwards.

When she did, she met India's interested, rich stare.

She'd been caught.

She styled it out the best she could and refocused on India's question. Spend the night in Birmingham's gay quarter? She knew the answer to that one right away. "No thank you. Been there, done that. Dinner here would be great. Maybe we could have a cocktail in the rooftop bar, too? I think you're partial to a rooftop, if memory serves?"

A smile played around India's lips. "Okay. But dinner's on me. No arguments. As a thank you for coming and a birthday present. Okay?"

* * *

The rooftop bar was elegant and stylish, just like India. Encased in glass, it had fairy lights all around, an abundance of greenery and plush velvet upholstery everywhere Gina looked. A pianist played cocktail bar classics in the corner, his soothing tones currently crooning Barry Manilow. It smelled of success and money, although smells, like looks, could be deceiving. Gina knew that. The one thing Gina was certain of was that she was the only Asian in the room. Birmingham had its fair share of first- and second-generation migrants, but not many were staying at The Formula Hotel.

Beside her, India swept to the bar like she was on a magic carpet. That's what growing up rich did for you. Gina would never have that particular superpower. India ordered a gin martini with a twist, then turned to Gina. "What can I get you?"

"I'll have the same."

India's eyes widened. "You sure? It's not for the faint-hearted."

"It's my birthday and I've never had one. Now's as good a time as any."

India placed the order, and they found a table. Beyond them, the city spread out through the floor-to-ceiling glass windows, a patchwork of light and dark.

"I've never really been to this city, only the outskirts where our factory is. Should I come back?" India's gaze settled on Gina.

Gina's insides glowed amber. "I was happy growing up here." She glanced to her left, then back. "But the view's stunning from where I'm sitting." Gina gulped. She'd got through dinner without embarrassing herself, but now she'd drunk some wine, was that all about to change?

The drinks arrived just in time, and Gina took a sip, then froze. The alcohol slithered through her veins. "Wow, that's strong and cold."

India gave her a grin. "The perfect gin martini, some might say." She narrowed her eyes. "You've never even tasted one before?"

Gina shook her head. "I don't drink much, but when I do, gin is what I like. Although normally with tonic, not neat. The word 'gin' is in my name, so I feel obliged to do so."

"I like that." India made a face. "We should come back here in June or July, when the rooftop patio is more doable. You might even be able to bring your parents by then." She raised an eyebrow. "It might happen, you need to give them a chance. Plus, now I know you drink gin, I'll make you a gin and tonic on my rooftop when I move in."

"I'll hold you to that." A fire long forgotten roared inside Gina. She stared at India. Something had shifted between them this trip. Was it coming away, being out of their usual environment? Even though this was Gina's hometown, it didn't feel like it tonight. When she visited, she saw family, and that was it. She didn't stay in hotels. She *definitely* didn't stay in hotels with hot women. Gina was breaking new ground.

Up in this bar, with this gorgeous woman opposite her, she was above everything. She was invincible. Anything felt possible. Even, perhaps, her family taking her seriously tomorrow. Gina almost laughed at that thought. She certainly didn't want to get her hopes up. Her parents still didn't get why she'd walked away from a steady job to start her own business.

Gina gulped, her breathing scattered. Her eyes dropped to India's collarbone and below. She blinked, searching for a topic that didn't involve leaning over the table and kissing India Contelli.

None immediately sprang to mind.

Think, Gina. Think.

"Is everything on track for tomorrow with Eunice?" If in doubt, fall back on the reason they were there. Eunice. Not the two of them working out what was happening between them right now.

Do not focus on that.

India gave a nod of the head. Even that sent a shiver down Gina's spine.

Not helpful.

"I spoke to her granddaughter. She gave me her address

and told me she'd be there, too, which is fair enough. I could be anyone."

"But you've been on telly."

"Precisely. Never trust anyone who's been on the telly." India gave her a rueful smile.

"I wonder how Eunice is feeling tonight?" Gina took another sip of her martini. She tried hard not to make a face. "She's got to talk about such a personal thing to a stranger tomorrow. After that, have the spotlight shone on her. It's no small thing."

"I imagine she's nervous. But I'm going to make her feel as much at ease as I possibly can." India snagged Gina's gaze. "It's been lovely sharing tonight with you, so thanks for coming with me. I know we've only recently met, but it's been a real highlight of my year. I was nervous about asking you along, but you've made *me* feel at ease."

Longing slid down Gina's skin. India had been nervous about asking her? She took a steadying breath. Their eye contact over dinner, the pregnant pauses, the ache that kept catching in her chest…

Maybe Gina could believe that India was feeling something for her, too. Perhaps she'd been pushing it away because she wasn't sure what to do with it.

She still wasn't.

India looked at her, lips parted, waiting for a reply.

All Gina could do was stare at her lips.

Say something.

"You're very welcome. Plus, you're not the only one who was nervous tonight. It's been a while since I went out for dinner with a beautiful woman." She said the words with as much intent as she could muster. Her words came out strong and true, even though she was feeling anything but. Fake it til you make it. It was a motto she lived by in the business world. There was no reason it couldn't work in romance, too. Even if her heart was about to explode through her chest, and her lips longed to press themselves to India's.

Maybe. Just maybe…

India sat up straighter, a glimmer of a smile gracing her lips. "I was just thinking the same. You look gorgeous tonight. I almost dropped your birthday card when you walked onto the terrace earlier. You were radiating something magical. You might not like your hometown, but I think it likes you."

Gina put her gaze anywhere but India. Anywhere but on the face of this woman, with compliments about Gina dropping from her divine lips. What the hell was happening here? She'd come on a trip to find love for someone else. She hadn't been expecting a side order for herself.

"I know you haven't had much luck in love, but do you believe in it?" India's eyes were brimming with emotion.

Gina gave a slow nod. "There's not much else worth believing in, is there?"

India's smile was dazzling. The most dazzling Gina had ever seen it. She breathed deep, hoping to frame this moment in her mind, just in case it slipped away.

"It's what I'm hoping Eunice says tomorrow. That she'd like to find this woman. That she'd like to give love one more try. It's got to be worth it, right?"

"I'd say so. But I'm not 79, with a life behind me."

"How old are you tomorrow? Did you say 41 when we spoke on the roof?"

Gina nodded. "Yep, I'll be 41. I came out when I was 33. I'm still young, in gay terms."

"We're all still young in gay terms, still trying to unlearn the lies we're told growing up. That we're not worthy, not good enough. Look at Eunice. You're way ahead of her."

"Am I?" Gina stared at India. "I don't know. My sister's married. My brother is too, and he's got three kids. I always thought by the time I was 41 I'd be more settled. Not necessarily married or with kids, but at least with someone I connected with. Someone who got me. It hasn't happened yet."

India gave her a mesmerising smile once more. "You said yet. I like your hope. Remember this year's Pride slogan: 'It's Never Too Late'. Maybe it's not for you, either." India paused, staring into Gina's eyes, then back to her drink. "Shall we take this back to the room?" She checked her watch. "We could have it on your terrace. It's almost a rooftop. We could toast your almost birthday."

Gina's heart thudded in her chest. "I'd love to."

* * *

If Gina had thought their exchanges were charged on the balcony earlier, it was nothing compared to what was happening now. The earlier chat had flavoured the air with something daring and exciting. Now, a magnetic forcefield had settled on them, meaning they couldn't be more than a few feet apart. Even walking back from the bar, their elbows and hands kept touching.

India followed Gina into her room and put their martinis on the balcony table. Before them, the inky Birmingham night spread out like a lit canvas.

India breathed it in, as she always did on rooftops. Gina hadn't known her long, but she already knew this. It was as if rooftops helped India to breathe, like she needed the space. Balconies served the same purpose. When India turned back from the view and their gazes met, Gina stilled. India had a way of looking at her, as if she saw the whole way through, right to Gina's core. It was unsettling, but impossible to ignore. It made Gina want to open up, share what made her tick. They'd done a fair bit of that already.

India sat opposite, pulling her black plastic chair a little closer. She raised her martini, never taking her eyes from Gina. "Happy birthday to you, my new friend. Here's to a successful weekend for both of us. Me with Eunice, and you with your parents. They're going to be surprised when you show up on their doorstep on your birthday."

Gina put a finger to her lips. "No parent talk, let's not kill the mood."

The corners of India's mouth turned upwards.

That smile.

"Sorry," she whispered. She moved her chair a little closer still. "Am I allowed to ask what you're hoping this year brings? I mean, apart from a gorgeous new friend, but that's already happened." India gave Gina a small bow before continuing. "Any big plans for the next 12 months of your life?"

Gina smiled. "One thing I've learned in my 41 years on this planet is that you can plan all you like, but those plans might never happen. For this coming year, I'll just say if I can buy my business back and be happy, that'll do. I don't want to stress out the universe, or it might kick me in the arse when I'm not looking."

"What about love? We were talking about it in the bar." India's gaze was scorching.

Gina stared at her. "Wasn't that the martinis talking?" When she pressed her thumb to her palm, it was hot.

"Maybe. But sometimes you need martinis for a little courage." India pushed her drink away. "I won't finish this one, I want to be fresh for the morning. Eunice deserves the best of me." She paused. "Luckily, you're here, and you bring out the best in me." India frowned, then shook her head. "Maybe one martini and a glass of wine have muddled my thinking. I keep saying things that sound a little corny." She raised her eyes to meet Gina's. "Maybe a lot corny. I'm sorry."

"There's no need to apologise." Gina's skin prickled as she stared at her. India thought she was saying too much? Quite the opposite. It had been some time since any woman had given Gina so many compliments in one go. She had no intention of turning off the tap.

She cleared her throat. "Plus, you know what I think about love. That I hope to experience it with a woman who truly gets me." The words were hot in Gina's throat. But she'd started down this path now, so she was determined to finish. "With a woman who listens and really wants to know me." She paused. "And if that someone dresses with such style they make my knees weak, so be it."

A surprised smile crossed India's face. She went to say something, but the words seemed to catch in her throat.

The moment pulsed in the air, so much so, Gina got up and leaned on the balcony wall.

Deep breaths. Fresh air. That's what she needed.

Behind her, the scrape of chair legs pierced the air, and in moments, India was beside her, their elbows touching.

Gina drew in her deepest breath yet.

"The rooftops in Birmingham seem smaller than in London." India's voice was low, gravelly. It reached into Gina's soul.

She smiled. "That's because we're on the 35th floor."

India nudged Gina's hip with her own.

Gina turned, and when their eyes met, the world stopped. Suddenly, what they'd been dancing around all evening seemed inevitable.

Gina straightened up, turning her body towards India.

India did the same. Her gaze dropped to Gina's lips, then skated back up to her eyes. It didn't stay long.

As if driven by some invisible emboldened force, Gina reached out a hand and snaked it around India's waist.

India stilled at her touch. "You're not who I expected to meet this year, Gina Gupta. Not by a long shot." India licked her lips. "But you've walked into my life and changed it. Now, I want you to change it some more."

Gina felt the words in every part of her body. They boomed in her heart, they made her eyelids flutter, her toes tingle.

"That's a big ask. But the last 41 years has also taught me it's best not to think about the past or the future. It's best to live in the moment. If you do that, the future normally takes care of itself."

Right at that moment, somewhere in the city, a bell tolled. India pulled Gina closer, until their mouths were inches away from each other.

India's lips were full and inviting. The kind of lips Gina

could get lost in for days. The kind she *wanted* to get lost in for days.

"Happy birthday, Gina," India said.

The low drag of her voice vibrated through Gina with some effect.

India cupped her face. She brushed the pads of her thumbs across Gina's lips.

An insistent pulse began between Gina's legs as she leaned closer still. Her hands tightened around India's hips.

Finally, India closed the gap between them and pressed her lips to Gina's. When Gina tasted her, she floated away.

Whatever fantasies or daydreams she'd had about what India's mouth might feel like paled in comparison to the real thing. Her lips were soft, yet firm. Her musky scent was even stronger close up, and Gina breathed her in. Her kisses were unhurried, as if she were easing into Gina.

Gina had no complaints.

A few moments later, India ran her tongue along the front of Gina's teeth, before sliding it into her mouth.

Gina swooned. In response, she moved her hand to India's pert backside and squeezed. Damn, that felt good.

India dropped kisses on her jawline and up to her ear.

Gina closed her eyes, all her concentration going towards staying upright and in the moment.

Then India brought her mouth back to Gina's lips and stared into her eyes. "I've been wanting to kiss you all night long." Her tone was a growl. Then her lips were back on Gina's, sliding across them, showing Gina just how much she wanted her.

The feeling was mutual. Gina's body told her so.

Eventually, they pulled apart.

Gina's vision returned, her breath scattered, her thoughts, too. However, she knew with some certainty they couldn't go any further. Tomorrow was too important. India had to meet Eunice. She had to meet her parents. The last thing Gina wanted to do was turn up having had no sleep, looking sex-ravaged.

Even if that is *exactly* what she wanted to do.

She took a deep breath, then pulled India back close and kissed her lips.

Damn, she was delicious. Gina never wanted to let India go.

When she opened her eyes again, their noses were still touching, as were their foreheads.

"You know, we can't do this tonight." She hated herself for saying those words, but it was the truth.

India let out a despairing sigh. "I know. I *really* hate it, but I know. I was just battling with myself, thinking the same thing." She kissed her again.

Gina's thought process dissolved into a puddle of goop. Damn it, she had to keep her thoughts straight. Or at least, as straight as they possibly could be.

"I don't want you to go, though." Gina paused, running a hand inside India's top and up her bare back.

India closed her eyes and shivered.

"You think if we slept in the same bed, we'd get any sleeping done?"

India's mouth curled into a smile as she opened her eyes. "The honest answer? No."

Gina covered her face with her hand. "You're right, I know." She removed her hand. "Can we put a pause on this?

Until after tomorrow? But just so we're clear, this is *very much* to be continued."

"Very much so. It's dot dot dot, not full stop. Even though I am away next week with work. But still, dot dot dot." India kissed her, hard. If she wanted to show she meant it, she'd done exactly the right thing.

When they parted, Gina took India's hand and they walked through her room and to her door. Gina's body was alive. She really didn't want India to go. She couldn't ever recall feeling what she was feeling in this moment.

Gina turned to India, composing her face. She wasn't going to pout.

"Only one problem," India said as she opened Gina's door to leave. "I don't have a birthday present to give you in the morning. Poor form."

Gina gave her a slow, sure smile. "Just come to the door, knock, then wrap your lips around mine. That will be the perfect gift."

India gave her a smile that made her clit stand to attention. "That," she said, kissing Gina's hand, then her lips, "I can definitely do. Sweet dreams."

"I think you guaranteed they will be."

Chapter Eighteen

India woke up the following morning naked and hot, her duvet kicked off, her body unsettled. It took a moment to figure out why, but then it came to her.

Last night. Kissing Gina. She hadn't dreamt it. It had happened. Then it had stopped. She covered her face as disappointment slid down her all over again. They'd been sensible. Controlled. She hated it. But she knew it had been the right decision. Plus, they'd both said they'd like to continue at a later date. India hoped with all her heart that was true.

For today though, she had to put it on the back burner and concentrate on Eunice and making a good first impression.

India got up and stretched, before putting on some knickers and a T-shirt. As she moved, her muscles sprang to life, remembering where Gina's fingers had touched her. Her back. Her neck. Her lips. They'd lit a fire on her skin and inside her soul, and her body was still smouldering.

India padded over to the Nespresso machine and flicked it on. She stared at the wall. Gina was on the other side. Was she awake yet? Was she lying in bed touching her lips, thinking about where India had kissed her, too? India hoped so. If this was entirely one-sided, she was buggered.

But last night had definitely not been one-sided. The way

Gina had kissed her had been very real. Which only made India smile that little bit more.

She made her coffee, then took the small white porcelain mug out onto the balcony and glanced across the city. It was one she didn't know, and yet also one that held so many memories for Gina. A formative lifetime, for both Gina and Eunice. Today was a deciding day for both of them. It was also Gina's birthday. Whatever happened with her family today, India was going to make sure she had a good memory of it.

She swigged her coffee. The hotel had a shop near the lobby. Perhaps she could get a gift for Gina before they were due to drive to Eunice? She walked back inside and grabbed her phone. 7.30am. She had time. She gulped the last of her coffee, then stripped off, striding into the bathroom. It was time to get this day moving.

* * *

They got into India's Audi, Gina noticeably agitated. India didn't blame her. Today was a big morning.

"You okay?" India asked, then kicked herself. Stupid question.

Gina nodded, not looking her way. "Sure," she replied.

India ground her teeth together, then held out a white paper bag to Gina. "I got you this. It's not much, but happy birthday."

That got Gina's attention. When she turned, her eyes were misty. "You didn't have to."

India pulled back. "Please don't get emotional until you've seen it. I had very limited options."

Gina gave her a tepid grin, but when she saw what was

inside, it got gradually wider. She reached in and pulled out some rainbow head boppers, along with a packet of rainbow chews. She put the head boppers into her hair and wiggled her head. The rainbow balls on springs duly swayed. "What do you think?"

India burst out laughing. The present was having the desired effect. "You've never looked better."

Gina jiggled the balls again. "This is truly the worst and gayest present I've ever been given. And I love it."

India grinned right back. "Not that I think your parents are going to be anything but thrilled to see you on your birthday. But just in case they're not, I thought you might need an injection of gayness afterwards. What better than this?"

Gina held her gaze and took a deep breath. "Nothing better." She reached over and put a hand on top of India's, then squeezed. "Thank you. I mean it."

India nodded. "You might want to take them off before you see your parents, though."

Gina let out a hoot of laughter, then did just that. "I don't know if you remember, but I asked you if you were romantic when I first took you to see your flat." She held up the bag, before putting it in the glove box. "I think this proves you are."

India sucked on her top lip. "Don't spread it around. I'm a tough business exec, remember?" She gave Gina a wink. "Let's get this show on the road, shall we?"

* * *

Eunice lived in a 1930s red-brick semi, situated on a wide suburban street. The front garden had flower beds, a rockery and a black metal arch adorned with greenery, along with a wooden table with two chairs near the front porch to soak up the morning sun. Deep-green ivy trailed up the front wall above a leaded light bay window.

As India cut the engine and took it all in, Gina let out a low whistle. "Here was me half-expecting you'd walk into an old lady with 12 cats stinking of wee. But if the front garden is anything to go by, I don't think Eunice is that."

India glanced at Gina. "I don't either."

Gina went to open her passenger door, but India put a hand on her thigh.

Gina's head whipped around.

"Before you go, I hope today goes okay. Just remember, I can drive around, go for a coffee, whatever. If you need more time with your family, there's no rush."

Gina nodded. "I'll let you know. But more time is probably the last thing I'll need."

"You never know." India hesitated, then leaned forward and kissed Gina's lips with gentle precision. Even though what she really wanted to do was take Gina's mouth and claim it as her own. But now wasn't the time.

India pulled back and gave Gina a slow smile. "You look gorgeous, by the way. Very birthday-like. Certainly more 31 than 41."

When Gina smiled, the sides of her eyes crinkled deliciously. "Now I know you want to sleep with me, feeding me lines like that."

India kissed her again. "Guilty, but what I said still stands." India's heartbeat was loud in her ears as she stared into Gina's eyes.

Gina gave her a smile. "Thank you." She pulled back,

snapping them back into the here and now. "I hope your morning goes well, too."

They got out of the car and locked up, then India watched Gina disappear around the corner. It was a sunny Sunday, and Gina had insisted she'd walk from here, her parents' house being only 20 minutes away. *"It'll do me good, allow me to clear my head."*

But now, standing at the bottom of Eunice's path, India missed Gina more than she'd thought. Her heart thumped as she pushed the gate, walked up the wide-slabbed path and knocked at the pristine black front door. Above and beside it, brightly coloured stained glass welcomed her.

India's stomach rolled. This was no normal business meeting. Plus, for some reason, she was painting her future love life on top of this, seeing what she could learn. Mistakes she could avoid. She'd read the letters from Eunice. They were cryptic, but the emotion jumped off them. India wanted that in her life. She wanted to feel a similar sort of passion.

She flashed back to last night, holding Gina in her arms. There had been fiery passion. Plus, they had time to see where it might go. Which is the one thing Eunice and H didn't have on their side.

When the door opened, a woman who could only be Eunice greeted India with a warm smile. If India had pictured a typical homely granny, Eunice wasn't it. Her hair was a riot of grey and black, cut stylishly short and swept up off her face. She was the same height as India, and her floaty trousers and block-coloured top were immaculate. She wore big clacky beads, just like India. In fact, if India looked like this when she was Eunice's age, she'd be jumping for joy.

Eunice's emerald-green eyes slid up and down India with interest from behind royal-blue frames. Her glasses matched her earrings, which dangled either side of her face.

Perhaps Eunice had more time than India had imagined. All the more reason for her to step outside her comfort zone and find out if there was a chance with her first love.

"You must be India. I've watched you on YouTube, my granddaughter helped me to find you." Eunice's handshake was steady, and India walked into the parquet-floored hallway, lavender scenting the air. Behind Eunice, a young woman stepped into the hallway, her smile broad, her eyes the same arresting green as her grandmother's.

She extended a hand to India as Eunice shut the front door. "I'm Cordy, Eunice's granddaughter. Really lovely to meet you."

"I haven't met another Cordy since I was at school." India had two in her class, then. "Short for Cordelia, I assume?"

Cordy nodded. "Well done. A lot of people don't know that."

India was ushered through to a modern kitchen-diner at the back of the house, with a skylight and bifold doors opening to the back garden. "This is fantastic. Did you have this done recently?"

Eunice nodded, sitting at the large white dining table, which was already laid out with cups and saucers, along with a plate of biscuits. All from Stable Foods. Was that intentional? If it was, India was impressed.

"Cordy's influence. I moved back in with my daughter while the work was being done. Now Cordy lives with me while she's at university."

Cordy came over to the table with a pot of tea. "Is tea

okay? I know Gran prefers it, but I can make coffee if you like?"

India shook her head. "Tea is great, thank you."

Cordy nodded, sweeping a hand through her dyed-red hair. "I'll leave you to it, then. Shout if you need anything."

Eunice poured the tea with a steady hand, then smiled at India.

India's nerves vanished. "So, tell me. Is this how you imagined this year might unfold when you looked at it in January?"

Eunice laughed. "Very much no." She stirred some sugar into her tea, then put the spoon on the saucer. "But you never can tell where life will take you next. Even when you're nearly 80." She paused. "Cordy tells me I shouldn't age myself. I'm not there yet. How old are you?"

"I'm nearly 40 if we're going by your maths."

Eunice smiled. "Half my age. Use your time wisely, won't you?"

India thought back to last night. "I intend to." She sipped her tea.

"You've read the letters, I take it?"

India nodded. "I did, for my research." That suddenly felt intrusive. She wasn't sure how she'd react if someone read her love letters from another lifetime.

Eunice smiled, her wrinkles bunching on her cheeks. "I gave permission for them to be copied, so it's fine. I know they're going to be pored over once the project goes online. Especially if I agree to try to trace H. Which I imagine is why you've driven all the way from London. To try and convince me to do so."

India sat back with a wry shake of her head. Rumbled. "I'm

not going to lie, that's exactly the reason. But not just for you — for everyone. We all need an ending to the story, don't we?"

Eunice stared into the distance, before turning back to India. "But what if the ending isn't a happy one? What if I don't want to risk upsetting her and bringing it all up again?"

"Only you can answer that. And if the answer's no, then we'll respect your wishes." India glanced around the room at the photos in frames, the bookcase on the far wall, the ornaments brought back from treasured holidays. Everywhere she turned, she could see evidence of a life well lived. A rich, full life. "I know it's a risk doing this. Of course it is." She pointed to the photos. "You've got family. Children. Grandchildren. They all see you one way."

"That's not the reason. I've told them and they've all been terrific. Particularly Cordy, who's gay herself. Or queer, as she says."

India put down her tea. Cordy was on their side. That was a good start. "Then tell me what the reason is, and I'll tell you if it's something you should be afraid of."

Eunice bit the inside of her cheek, then shook her head. The chair scraped on the floor as she pushed it back.

Had India overstepped the mark?

Eunice walked over to the large doors and stared out into the morning sunshine. "I don't care what the world thinks of me." Eunice turned, tapping her chest. "I know who I am. Who I've always been. I'm a lesbian. No ifs or buts. But it wasn't the done thing at the time. So I got married. My husband was a kind man, and I had 30 good years with him. But they were *nothing* compared to the 18 months I had with her." She turned back to the window. "Nothing."

India kept quiet, sensing Eunice wasn't finished.

She was right.

Eunice turned, her eyes brimming with tears. She clutched her beads. They clacked together. India did the same when she was stressed.

"The thing is, we could have been something. She wanted me to be with her. She had plans. She was the driving force. But I said no because I didn't see how we could make it work, how we could survive. It wasn't like today." She closed her eyes, then shook her head. "*I said no*." Eunice blew out a long breath. "So now, if I want to dredge up the past and ask her to reconsider, is it really my place? That's the question I keep asking myself. And the answer that keeps coming back to me is, not when I told her no."

India grabbed a couple of tissues from the box on the table, then walked over to stand beside Eunice. She offered her the tissues, and Eunice took them without a word. India waited a few more moments before she spoke.

"The thing is, I'd say it doesn't rely on what happened in the past. The past is just that. The past. If you still have feelings, surely it's worth a shot." India put a hand to her chest, and her own beads clacked together.

Eunice looked her way, a glimmer of recognition in her green eyes.

"If nothing else, you could tell her what you've just told me. That part of you has always wondered what if? To see where you could have gone."

Eunice let out a sigh. "Probably nowhere fast is the answer. She had grand plans, but I…"

India put a hand on Eunice's arm. "I'm not going to push.

As I said, this is for you to decide. But you have to see if you can forgive yourself for what happened. Because you need to in order to move forward." India paused. "What would you say to a friend who'd done this?"

Eunice moved her mouth one way, then the other, before looking at India. "I'd say, you were young, and we all make mistakes. But also, that it wasn't wholly a mistake, otherwise I'd never have my wonderful family."

India exhaled. "Exactly. You've lived your life and lived a good one. I hope H has, too. But if you can forgive yourself, then maybe H can forgive you, too. Or maybe she already has. If you both get there, then who knows what might happen next?"

Eunice stared into India's eyes. "If it turns out she's no longer with us or with someone else, I wouldn't want to drag her into it."

India shook her head. "We won't. This only goes big if you're both on the same page. You have my word on that."

"In that case, give me some time to think. I'll let you know this week."

"That's all I can ask."

Chapter Nineteen

Gina approached her parents' wooden front door and prepared to go to war. Okay, maybe she was exaggerating a little. They all had to move forward, she knew that, but the future for her and her family was still so shrouded in fog, she couldn't see a clear path.

She fidgeted with her jacket. Was she wearing the right clothes? Did black jeans, olive-green shirt and a black jacket look too gay? She shook her head. It didn't matter what she wore. Her parents didn't see that. She might as well have come wrapped in a rainbow flag, because since she came out that's all they saw. Gina was no longer a successful business woman. She was simply gay. It was the only label that counted.

However, the only way to combat that was to talk to them. Communicate. Make them see she was still the same person she always was. Easier said than done.

Gina knocked on the door of their detached house with garage. Both her parents' Renault and her uncle's flash Mini were there, which meant her journey hadn't been for nothing. That was good at least, because she hadn't told them she was coming. It didn't stop Gina's heart clattering in her chest as she heard footsteps behind the door. When it opened, she braced herself for her mother's disapproval.

Instead, she got her uncle. His dark hair needed a cut, but he immediately broke into a grin.

"Gina! What the hell are you doing here? We were just talking about you! Happy birthday!" He stood back, beckoning her in.

She stepped over the threshold. The scents of garlic and onions frying in the kitchen wafted into her nostrils, along with cumin, coriander, cardamon and turmeric. It was such a familiar smell from her childhood. Gina missed her mum's cooking.

Then Deepak hugged her so hard, he lifted her off the floor. There were only nine years between them, hence he'd never quite been a full uncle to her. More like an older cousin. A friend. Someone else who understood how powerful the disapproving gaze of her mother could be. Deepak had put up with it all his life, too.

He put her down, his smile so genuine, it made Gina smile, too. Her eyes swept the familiar hallway. Photos of her parents' Punjab village on the wall, along with a larger one of the whole family in front of the Taj Mahal. She and her siblings had all been teenagers, as their miserable faces showed. By contrast, her parents were smiling like they'd won the lottery. The shoe racks were still on the left, with indoor slippers for family and guests.

"I can't believe you're here. I miss you coming home. It's fabulous to see you." He leaned in. "Plus, you look at least 20 per cent gayer than when I last saw you." He gave her a wink.

Gina's heart swelled. She couldn't help but laugh. "Can you not say that when Mum's around?"

"Purely between you and me," Deepak replied.

Gina squeezed one of his pert biceps, the arm of his blue T-shirt wrapped tightly around it. "Mum told me you'd built a gym. Looks like it's paying off."

Deepak flexed both arms in a superhero pose.

Gina rolled her eyes, then shed her yellow Converse and swapped them for some white sliders.

"Who is it, Deepak? If it's Nihal, tell him we're still waiting for the quote before he can start on the windows. It's how these things work. Quote first, work and payment second."

Hearing her mother's voice made Gina still. Her power to make Gina quake was undiminished. But Gina wanted to take control of this situation. Not be outmanoeuvred by a five-foot matriarch with a steely stare.

"It's not Nihal, Mum. It's me." Gina walked through to the kitchen.

When her mum turned, her eyes went wide with a mixture of surprise and panic. She was dressed in a pastel-green and white embroidered Punjabi suit, with a lemon cardigan over the top. She shook her head, her short hair not moving. "Nagina? You're here? My little girl on her birthday?" She stayed right where she was, lunch prepping on the hob, a wooden spoon in her hand. "Why didn't you let us know you were coming? There are no phones in London anymore?" She put her spoon down. "I haven't even got you a present!"

It wasn't the first time Gina had heard that this weekend.

Her mum shook her head and turned her attention back to the hob.

Deepak walked in behind Gina, throwing a casual arm around her shoulders. It only went to accentuate the fact her mum hadn't hugged her.

Gina swallowed down the emotion that was threatening to overtake her. She was not going to cry. Not on her birthday.

"Isn't it amazing, Gina's here!" Deepak walked over to the garage door that led off the kitchen and called through it. "Vijay, your daughter's here!"

Her dad peered around the door in seconds, confusion on his face. When his eyes landed on Gina, his face lit up. He held up his hands, covered in dust from his latest DIY project. "Nagina! My goodness! Let me wash my hands." He disappeared back into the garage and they heard the water running in the garage sink. Moments later, her dad walked back in and came straight for Gina, giving her a big hug.

Gina breathed him in. He smelt of wood, and home.

"Why didn't you tell us you were coming? We'd have invited everyone over." He spun around, his grey hair short and newly cut. "Seema, have you called Kishan to come?"

Gina shook her head. "Dad, this is what I wanted to avoid. I don't want a big thing. I've got a friend picking me up in a couple of hours. We're here for a…" she couldn't say the word Pride, could she? "…a work thing." She hated herself for censoring. "I don't have long. But I wanted to stop in and say hi."

Her mum turned. "You only have a limited time for your family? This isn't how we brought you up." Her lips tightened. "And who is this friend? Is she your permanent friend or someone you just met?"

Deciphering the code was exhausting, and she'd only been in the door five minutes.

"She's a friend. As in a friend, not a girlfriend." Or at least, she was right now. After last night, Gina and India were standing on shifting sands. Now wasn't the time to go into what they were and what they weren't when Gina herself wasn't even sure.

Her mum's face hardened. She tried a smile, but it didn't reach her eyes.

Maybe this wasn't a good idea. But if Gina was in her home city, she should be able to call in on her family.

"She doesn't want a present, she just wants a cup of chai. Right, Gina?" Deepak put a pan on the hob before she could answer, and grabbed the masala chai from the cannister on the counter.

Dad guided Gina to the wooden table she'd grown up with, shaking his head as he smiled at her. They'd knocked down the wall to the dining room since she left home, so the kitchen-diner was now open-plan, with patio doors leading out to the garden. "My little baby, all grown up. Forty-one today. What work are you doing up here? I would have thought your Hot London Properties were fairly London-based."

He had a point. "It's a charity project I'm doing on the side."

"What charity?" He'd always been interested in what she was doing. It killed Gina to lie to him.

"You wouldn't know it." She paused. "But when we've had a drink, I do have a bit of a work thing I'd like to run by you. A business proposition."

Her dad beamed. He ran a successful cash-and-carry firm in the city, working with her brother, Kishan, and her other uncle. Dad was a savvy business operator. He liked being looked on as such.

"But no business chat right now," Deepak shouted, stirring

the chai. "Seema, got any samosas? Or that loaf-cake with cherries you were making the other day? I know you have it somewhere!"

Her mum gave Deepak a look, but got the cherry loaf-cake out of the tin and put it in the middle of the dining table, along with some shortbread biscuits. Then she reheated some samosas in the microwave, while Deepak strained the chai into mugs and brought it over. At the table, unease settled on them like an ill-fitting sheet.

Gina glanced around the room at the familiar photos: her graduation, Neeta and Neil's wedding, Kishan's wedding and shots of his sons. On the sideboard, photos of her late grandparents were wreathed in dried flower garlands. From his shrine on the dining room wall opposite, Hindu god Lord Shiva eyeballed her.

Gina ate a lamb samosa amid the weighty silence. It was delicious. Then she cut some cake for something to do. If she had to eat her way through this visit, she was up to the challenge.

Deepak fiddled with his phone until her mum told him off for having it at the table. He rolled his eyes at Gina.

It was like old times. She could have hugged Deepak for being there. Left with just her parents, this would have been even more awkward. If that was possible.

"What business thing do you want to ask us?" Mum cut straight to the chase.

"After cake, Mum," Gina said. "How's Kishan and his tribe?"

"They're all growing up just lovely. Three gorgeous boys." Mum gave her a pointed stare. "Children make your life better, Nagina. They give it purpose."

"If you want them," Deepak cut in.

Gina threw him a grateful look. "Plus, my life has purpose. I work, I have friends, I do charity stuff. Purposeful." She sent her mum's look right back.

"This business proposition — you need money?"

Gina sighed. She wasn't going to let it lie, was she? Gina may as well spit it out. "I do. I can go to the bank and ask for it there, but I wondered, since you invested in Kishan's sideline, if you'd invest in mine. My business partner wants out, so I need to come up with the collateral. It's a solid business and a good bet." Unlike Kishan's start-up, which was still faltering.

Mum pursed her lips again, then glanced at Dad. "It's a tricky climate right now for investing."

Gina wanted to scream "bullshit!", but she didn't. She was 41. She was beyond that. Even though she wanted to shake her mum.

"Dad?" She'd usually been able to appeal to his better nature.

He avoided her stare before he spoke. "We might be able to give you a bit, but I suspect you might need more than that."

Gina closed her eyes. She shouldn't have come, should she? She braced every muscle in her body for rejection. She'd steeled herself that this might happen, but now it was, she wasn't prepared. She might think she was tough, but there were limits.

"Hold up." Deepak put up a hand. "You were just telling me before she arrived how proud of Gina you are."

"Deepak, you don't have to do this, I'm a big girl." Gina stared at her mug.

Deep breaths.

"It's true!" Deepak replied. "They were saying that. Weren't you?"

When Gina glanced up, her parents nodded.

"We are proud of her, of course. We're proud of all our children," Mum said.

"Especially Kishan, who didn't move away and had children; Neeta and I both know." Gina gripped her teaspoon tight. When she looked at her hand, it was shaking. "But you know what? It takes more effort to move away and *not* have children. To build your own life. To be your true self. It takes bravery to come out to your family and risk losing them."

Her lip wobbled, and she breathed deep.

"It also takes time to come to terms with the fact that what you wanted for your daughter isn't going to happen." Her mum's voice was low, but firm.

Her comment sat on the table in front of them, pulsing.

Gina glanced her way. "But this isn't your life, Mum. It's my life. And doing what makes *you* happy would make me miserable, don't you see that?" She paused, then stood up. "You know what, this was a mistake. I'm going to call my friend and go." Gina checked her watch. Had she really only been there for 20 minutes? It felt like a year. This was the stress she'd been trying to avoid in her life by not coming home. She'd been right all along.

Gina hoped India's chat with Eunice had gone better.

Deepak stood up and took Gina's arm. "Sit." He paused. "Please." He wasn't letting go.

Gina stared at her parents, then at Deepak. Then she sat.

Deepak looked from her parents to her, then he sat, too.

"Okay. This isn't pretty." He turned to her parents. "You should be more supportive of your daughter."

"This is not your business—"

"It damn well is!" Deepak told her mum. "I'm not going to sit here and watch you crush Gina. She doesn't deserve that. I agree with her. It took guts to tell you she's gay. But so what? She's still Gina. Life doesn't revolve around you, Seema. If you want Gina to come home more, as you constantly tell me you do, you need to ease up. On Neeta, too. She doesn't have kids yet. So what?" He sighed. "I know it's not going to happen today, but think about it."

Deepak turned to Gina. "And if you need money, you come to me. I *want* to help."

Gina raised both eyebrows. She hadn't even considered asking Deepak. "Are you serious?"

"Deadly."

* * *

Gina lasted another hour before she messaged India to come and get her. Dad had tried to gloss over the altercation they'd had, while Mum had stayed silent. Gina thought her mum would get up and start cooking, like she always did. Instead, Mum got up, turned off the hob, then came and sat back down.

Gina didn't know what to make of it. But they'd sat, eaten samosas and cake, drunk chai, and made small talk. Her uncle on her dad's side in India had cancer. Her cousin in Yorkshire was pregnant (of course she was). Her granny had won a sewing competition. Kishan's son was learning to swim. Nothing about Gina's life, which was off limits as usual.

Then India knocked on the door.

Gina almost fell off her chair in her bid to get there first. When she opened it, she wanted to push India away, slot her into the car and drive off like none of the previous hour had ever happened. But she couldn't do that. She knew it to be doubly true when she caught India staring over her shoulder. Gina turned to find her mum, dad and uncle all standing behind her, waiting to be introduced. So now, even if she wanted to smuggle India out of Birmingham, all routes were blocked.

Especially when she heard a whistle down the street. Gina peered around India to see Kishan heading towards the house, with all of his kids in tow, the youngest, Kiyan, in his arms.

India turned to look, too, then was almost bowled over by Gina's oldest nephew, Aiden, pushing her aside and launching himself onto Deepak. Good to see her uncle hadn't lost his touch.

"Hey, buddy!" Deepak juggled the wriggling seven-year-old in his arms. Seconds later, Aiden slapped his head, then broke free to hug his grandma. Deepak paid no attention. Instead, his eyes, like those of everyone else, were on India. "Aren't you going to introduce us to your… guest?"

If Gina's anxiety levels hadn't been bursting out of her body, she might have laughed at Deepak's struggle to pin a label on India. But now wasn't the time for laughter. Not when she stood in her parents' home, with her potential new girlfriend on their doorstep, and almost her entire immediate family focused on them both. If Gina had ever had a nightmare about her two worlds colliding, she wasn't sure it could have matched up to this level of intensity.

"Everyone, this is India." Gina gave India a look, but she wasn't sure what she was trying to convey. It probably just came off as sheer terror. But India appeared to give her one back saying she understood. At least, that's what Gina hoped it said.

"India, this is my family." Gina waved a hand around the hallway. She knew it was sweeping, and not really to the point. But the thought of introducing India one by one and having her shake hands was a little too much.

"Dadi, have you got biscuits?" said her middle nephew, Devin, walking in the door. He was using the Punjabi term for 'grandma'. He'd been trained well.

Gina had to smile. Perhaps having the kids here would take the pressure off just enough to make this bearable.

"In a minute, Devin," her mum said. She hadn't taken her eyes off India. "Your name is India?" Her clipped accent sounded even stronger when she said the land of her birth.

India nodded. "It is." She stepped into the house, her height and perfume smothering the space. India's beads clacked as she leaned forward and extended a hand. "Lovely to meet you, Mrs Gupta."

Mum stared at India's hand.

Gina held her breath.

Then her mum shook it.

India turned her radiant smile on Gina's dad. "Mr Gupta."

Dad shook India's hand with more certainty.

Gina was impressed she was still standing. This was happening. This was not a drill. Her parents were actually meeting and shaking hands with India Contelli. Even if her mum still looked confused.

"Your actual first name is India? Like the country? Where we're from?"

Gina closed her eyes. Why wouldn't her mum just accept facts? It was a downfall of hers.

"Mum, I'm gay."

"Nonsense, you're just choosy when it comes to men."

"Mum, this is India."

"Like the country? Are you sure?"

But India dealt with it like a pro. "You're not the first person to ask that, Mrs Gupta. But yes, I can assure you, it's my real name. My parents are big fans of your homeland, so they named me after it." India gave Mum a little shrug.

Mum conceded she was telling the truth by giving India a trace of a smile.

If Gina hadn't seen it with her own eyes, she'd never have believed it.

It didn't stop Gina feeling like this was the weirdest Sunday ever, though. Her body felt like somebody else's, her mind completely shredded. She took a deep breath and gathered herself together in a bid to take back control. It hadn't worked when it came to Brexit, but maybe it could work here.

"This is my Uncle Deepak," Gina added to India.

Deepak wasted no time, pulling India into a stiff hug. India was not a hugger, whereas Deepak was the polar opposite.

When he let her go, India's smile was more forced.

Gina would have to apologise later. "And on the doorstep is my brother Kishan and his many sons."

Kishan stepped inside and shook India's hand. "Pleasure. We don't normally meet Gina's friends. Having said that, we don't normally see Gina." He leaned down to kiss her. "Hello, big sis. Happy birthday."

Gina gave him a knowing smile. "Thanks, little brother."

"Now you're here, you'll stay for a cup of tea? We have English Breakfast tea, as well as chai. Plus delicious cake." Deepak looked to India, then to Gina.

Gina shook her head. "Oh no, India has to get back, don't you?" Gina hoped she'd take the hint.

But India was far too polite. She checked her watch. "Half an hour won't hurt," she said, fixing on her TV smile. "While I'm here, can I use your loo?"

Gina closed her eyes. She'd just entered truly uncharted territory.

Chapter Twenty

Gina waved out the car window as India pulled away. As they picked up speed and made their way out of the smaller Birmingham streets, onto the ring road and then eventually the motorway, Gina finally relaxed. All morning, every muscle in her body had been wound into a tight coil. Now, they were all slowly releasing, the tension seeping out of her body. She pressed back into the headrest and let out a long sigh.

In front, the motorway opened up into four lanes of traffic, and India put her foot down.

"I seriously cannot believe that just happened." Gina pointed a finger at her chest. "I was just in my parents' house, with you, the woman I kissed last night. My *parents*, who do not accept I'm gay and can't even bring themselves to discuss anything about my life in any way just in case they catch it, too."

Beside her, India smiled. "Do you need to eat some rainbow chews to recharge your gayness, or wasn't it that bad?"

Gina blew out a breath and shook her head. She was still processing. "It was… I don't know what it was. My mother stopped cooking her meal, which is a first. It was a morning I'd rather not repeat." She opened the glove box and took out the rainbow chews. "But let's have a chew anyway." She unwrapped two and gave one to India.

"These are good." Tropical fruit flavours coated Gina's mouth. "Fruity."

India snorted. "They taste pretty gay to me," she replied through a mouthful. She took a few moments to eat the rest before continuing. "If it helps any, you did really well. And maybe, just maybe, meeting me and seeing I'm not an ogre will make them think about their behaviour."

Gina waited a few moments before she turned her head. "Let's not get too far ahead of ourselves."

"Just trying to be upbeat about this morning." India glanced over at Gina. "I'm very positive about last night, in case you were wondering. Particularly the bit where we kissed. That was a good part, right?"

Gina's muscles tightened again, but this time for positive reasons. "Kinda great, I'd say." Then she put her hand to her head. "But the whole time we were sitting there eating cake, all I could think was, 'We're gay! This is what gays look like. Like anyone else!' But I think that might still be a little early for my parents to absorb."

"One step at a time."

"Says the woman whose parents are super-accepting."

"They took a while to come round, too. Like you said, it's harder for you with the distance."

"And the expectations. It's just… frustrating. I'm 41. I'm an adult."

India glanced her way. "You're always a child to them."

"I'm just sorry you got caught up in the middle of it."

India shook her head. "It wasn't too bad. And if you

think your parents are stuck in their ways, you should meet my grandmother. She hasn't spoken to me since I came out on national TV. Her loss. So yes, today was awkward, but it was a start. Plus, if meeting me moves them forwards, it's a win, right?"

"I suppose. Although I wanted the ground to swallow me whole when they invited you in."

"They're curious about your life. That's a good thing. Plus, it was nice to meet your family, including your brother. You should meet mine. He's having a child with his husband. Maybe your brother could give him some tips."

Gina coughed. "He could, actually. He may be many things, including annoying, but he is a very hands-on dad."

India was right about her family. However, Gina felt exposed after subjecting India to them. She bet hers didn't sit around a table eating cake and grilling their visitors. They probably had a mansion that was laid to lawn, and were the ultimate cool and calm family. Hers had never been that.

Gina grabbed her phone from her bag, after hearing a couple of messages come through. One was from Deepak, telling her he'd call her about the investment. He'd also added a ton of emojis that Gina couldn't translate to mean anything other than he liked horses, sunshine, parties and Spanish dancing? Whatever, he made her smile.

The second text was from her mum.

That made Gina sit up, the tension hastily rebuilding in her limbs. If this was a 'never grace our door again' text, she'd better be ready. Gina clicked, then held her breath.

'Next time, let us know you're coming so we can buy you a gift, please. Nice to meet India. She seemed nice.'

Gina let go of a breath she didn't even know she'd been holding, then closed her eyes.

A hand on her thigh made her open them with a start.

Desire shot through her.

Right now, there were far too many emotions cruising around her body.

"Everything okay? Was that from your family?"

Gina nodded. "Yep. Mum thinks you're a nice girl, and my uncle wants to learn Spanish dancing." She shook her head. "Don't ask me to explain."

India squeezed her thigh. "Okay, I won't." She removed her hand.

Gina stared at the space where it had been. Her breath caught in her throat.

She wasn't going to forget this Sunday in a hurry, was she? Bridges were being repaired, and new horizons hastily assembled.

***

They pulled up outside Gina's apartment block, a far cry from India's historic street in town. Canary Wharf was the financial centre of London, a modern district of tall, metal structures, gleaming glass and sleek lines. Gina's block was stylish and near the water, so India saw the attraction, even if it was a little sterile. Gina was the opposite of that.

Plus, this weekend had given her a view of Gina in her entirety. The real Gina. Meeting someone's family always stripped away the layers in an instant. Gina might think her family were complex, but the truth was, all families fitted that description. It was just what you were used to. India cut the engine and turned to Gina. Her dark hair shone in the evening light, and the shadow on her face showed off her striking cheekbones. India wanted to reach out and run a finger down them, but she held back. They weren't there yet.

"I had a great time this weekend."

Gina stared, not turning from her gaze. "Weirdly, so did I. Even today."

Something flickered behind Gina's eyes as she spoke. India was still trying to work her out.

"You never told me what happened with Eunice. You just gave me the headlines, not the inside track."

India shook her head. Outside the car, a man dressed head to toe in Armani walked by, his Cuban heels clicking on the polished pavements outside Gina's block.

"There's not much else to tell. She was like her garden — immaculate. I want to be her when I grow up, minus the losing-my-first-love bit." *Could hers be Gina?* India's heart warmed at the thought. "She's going to make such a great poster for the Pride campaign if she says yes. She was a fashion designer back in the day, and you can tell."

"But is she going to search for H? Her long-lost love? I might if she doesn't. I need to know the end of the story."

India smiled. She'd thought exactly the same thing. "I think she will, she just needs a little help. Luckily, her granddaughter is queer, so she wants her to do it. I think with some gentle persuasion from her, Eunice might agree. I'd love it if she did, but also, I don't want to be the cause of heartache for her. She just has to work up the courage."

India held Gina's gaze. "Talking of courage. I don't regret what happened last night." She reached out and took Gina's fingers in hers. They were so soft, and she still recalled the effect they had on her last night. She gulped as she continued. "I hope you don't, either."

Gina shook her head, sucking in her bottom lip before letting it go.

India dragged her gaze from dwelling on it. Heat crept up her spine, her neck, reaching her ears.

"No regrets here," Gina replied. "My only regret is that you have to go now."

India shook her head. "I know. But family calls. They've already delayed the monthly Sunday dinner for me. I can't be a no-show." She paused. "Unless you want to come with me?"

The sexual tension in the car dipped, as Gina shook her head decisively. "I'm sure your family are lovely, but I've had my fill of family for today. But I'd love to catch up again soon?"

"It's going to be the thing at the forefront of my mind this whole week while I'm away with work. But we'll make some time soon." India took Gina's hand in hers, then turned her palm upwards. She traced her heart line.

At India's touch, Gina drew in a sharp breath.

India ignored the thud of her heart as she traced Gina's skin, which was eminently kissable. India wanted to see if Gina's skin was soft all over her body. But that was going to have to wait for another day. "Someone I once knew used to read palms. Or at least, she pretended to. Told me stuff about my heart line and what was coming in my future."

Gina dropped her gaze to her palm, then back up to India. "Were her predictions right?"

India licked her lips. "She told me I'd meet someone who

looked suspiciously like her and fall in love, but it never happened." India swept her thumb across Gina's palm again.

The tremble that passed through Gina was almost imperceptible, but it was there.

"Do you want me to try to dredge up my knowledge and read your palm?"

Gina's mouth curled into a sultry smile. "Do your best."

India traced the curve nearest to Gina's thumb, the rattle of their connection vibrating to her core. "This is your life line. I see vitality, and long life in your future." She took a breath, then glanced up at Gina. India's stomach rolled. She'd thought Gina was pretty before this weekend, but now, she was beyond that. Something had changed. One dynamite kiss they couldn't back away from.

India focused back on Gina's palm, tracing the curve at the top. "This is your heart line."

"I'm interested in this one." Gina leaned forward, her breath tickling India's face.

India kept her hand steady. "You didn't want to know if you were going to live a long life?"

Gina's tongue traced her bottom lip. "Only if there's love in my future. What do you think, in your professional opinion?" Her words were laced with honey. Her eyes dropped to India's lips.

India's breath quickened. "You've got a strong heart line," she replied, her voice low. "In fact, I see lust in your future." She lifted her gaze to Gina's face. "Steaming sexual desire. All with a tall, dark, mysterious woman who's set to sweep you off your feet."

Gina leaned in some more, her lips glistening where she'd

just licked them. "Is that so? Does this woman have a name?"

"A weird one, according to your mother." India leaned in, too.

"Does this woman want to kiss me now?"

"Like you wouldn't believe," India replied, the heat that had crept up her body now bursting out of her skin.

Their mouths were drawn together in seconds and it was all that India could do not to climb across the gear stick and mount Gina.

India's body shook as their lips and tongues collided, desire smashing into her like a tidal wave.

What did Gina do to her? The normally calm and collected India Contelli was fluid in Gina's hands. Their chemistry was off the charts, as evidenced by this kiss. India twisted her body to deepen their connection. Was Gina what she'd been searching for all this time?

A horn blasting nearby interrupted them.

India jumped, smacking her head on the roof. She let out a howl of pain, clutching it as she pulled away.

"Are you okay?" Gina's voice was studded with concern.

India grimaced then nodded. "I'll live." They'd been caught in the act. Like furtive teenagers.

She needed a fan to cool herself down. Or a bucket of ice.

"Next time we do this, can we make sure we're not in a car, with no upcoming family or work commitments, so that perhaps we can progress to the stage of being naked?"

India closed her eyes. "Getting naked with you is now my ultimate life aim."

The car horn blasted again. India turned around and gave the car behind a wave.

Gina looked at her, then kissed her one more time. "I'll text you. Don't forget about me this week."

India stared into Gina's eyes. "You just made that an impossibility."

Chapter Twenty-One

The weekend in Birmingham had given Gina more grit. More determination to order her life as she wanted it. If she could make headway with her family, she could definitely do the same with work.

Over the last year, she'd started to see cracks in Bernie's input and enthusiasm, but she'd overlooked them. Bernie had swept into her life with cash and a book of contacts. At first, she'd been gold, and that still counted for something. However, now she'd stepped over multiple lines — work and personal — Gina couldn't look the other way anymore. Sara was the tip of the iceberg. Gina was doing more of the work for less of the profit.

If Bernie was a pain point in her life, India was balancing things out by being the polar opposite. If Gina looked beyond her kissing ability — and she didn't do that lightly — India was also proving a saviour when it came to sorting out the business. She'd hooked Gina up with her legal adviser the night before, and Gina had received some great advice on how she should move forward.

Plus, even though India had been away on business this week, they now had a semi-routine of sending texts at the start or end of each day. This morning, India had wished her luck for her meeting. It was still making Gina smile.

Gina breathed in the fresh spring air as she walked across Tower Bridge, trying to ignore it was laced with petrol fumes, too. This was London, after all. To her right, the traffic crawled and honked, the bridge vibrating to its beat. Up ahead, the biscuit-coloured buildings of Shad Thames and beyond stood tall, glinting in the morning sun. To her left, the Thames flowed wide and deep, its surface a soup of blues and greys.

Gina often did this loop walk when she needed time to think, or to gee herself up. Walking across Tower Bridge and back, breathing in the crackle of history when she passed the Tower of London always made her see things more clearly. Yes, her issues were important, but she wasn't about to go to the Tower to get her head cut off. Things could be worse. She could have been married to Henry the Eighth. That thought almost made her forget she was meeting Bernie in a matter of minutes.

In fact, Bernie was ahead of Gina, her silver Range Rover already parked in her designated parking space outside their offices. Gina pulled her shoulders back when she clocked it, ready for battle. A little like meeting up with her parents, she had to try to keep the emotion out of this meeting. This was about cold, hard business facts, and that was what Gina planned to present to Bernie. She didn't plan to bring up Sara. However, if Bernie played hardball, it was a tactic Gina wouldn't hesitate to use.

As soon as she walked in, Bernie hopped up like a popcorn kernel in a hot pan. She had her closing suit on. The one she wore when she was on the verge of a deal and needed confidence. Gina couldn't quite decide if that was a good thing or not. On her desk, Bernie's sunglasses sat abandoned, along with her bunch of keys.

"Coffee?" Bernie was already at the machine, snapping into action.

Gina frowned. "Sure, thanks."

With drinks in front of them, Gina leaned back in her chair.

Bernie stayed still. That was weird.

The air in the office grew thicker.

"So are we—"

"I just want to say—"

They both stopped.

Gina swung left, then right.

Still Bernie didn't move.

"You first," Gina said.

Bernie stood up, walked to the edge of her desk and leaned. "I just want to start by saying sorry. For everything. But especially for the money going missing. For giving Sara access to our business card. After everything she put you through, it was unforgiveable."

Gina narrowed her eyes. If this was a calculated ploy, she had to hand it to Bernie. She was convincing. But Gina had seen Bernie in action too many times. She wasn't falling for it just yet.

"You're not wrong."

Bernie frowned. "You think I'm bullshitting? That I'm just saying this to butter you up?"

"We've worked together too long, Bernie."

Bernie shook her head, folding her arms across the buttons

of her waistcoat. "I've had one foot outside Hot London Properties for a while now. We both know that. You've been running the show more for the past year at least."

Gina nodded.

"I enjoyed the first two years, they were great. But it's time for me to move on, and I don't want to stand in your way. You offered to buy me out. You gave me a figure. I'm happy to accept it."

It couldn't be this easy. Gina had come with arguments all prepared. "What's the catch, Bernie?"

She shook her head. "No catch. This is legit. I don't want to blow up our friendship for the sake of a business I'm happy to exit." Bernie held up a hand. "And I know that while I'm still seeing Sara that might be tricky, but maybe in time things might change. You matter to me, Gina. You're not just someone I did business with. We *know* each other."

"I thought we did," Gina replied. "Until you started fucking Sara. Then I questioned if you'd actually witnessed what happened when *I* did that." Gina got up and leaned on the edge of her own desk. Standing opposite each other like this was such a practised move for the pair of them, and yet, this felt final. The end of an era. Mainly because it was, whether Bernie was telling the truth or not.

It almost made Gina get sentimental.

Almost.

Then she remembered what India's business manager had said to her. The instructions she'd given. Don't let Bernie get on your good side. Not today.

"We're going to have to disagree on this." Bernie chewed on the inside of her cheek. "Just get the paperwork drawn up and I'll sign it. Then I can be out of here and on to my next project."

"Unless Sara bleeds you dry first."

Bernie gave her a sharp look, then covered it up with a half-smile. She picked up her bag, slung it over her broad shoulder, then put on her sunglasses. "I'll be expecting your call."

* * *

Gina paced the office like a caged animal after Bernie left. Her emotions were on a see-saw. Could she trust Bernie? Was she serious about just walking away? If she was, this was the absolute best outcome she could imagine.

Gina texted Deepak to let him know it was all systems go. She received an immediate thumbs-up emoji in reply, along with more horses, sunshine and some heart eyes. Was this the way Deepak did business with everyone? Perhaps it was the new way to go. Lull them into a false sense of security as if you had no idea what you were doing, then land a cracking deal.

Gina twirled in her seat. Bernie hadn't twirled once. If she was happy with Sara, she'd kept it well hidden. However, that wasn't Gina's problem anymore. Both Sara and Bernie were almost off her plate, and now she could concentrate on making Hot London Properties the best it could possibly be. She had some ideas. She needed to get somebody on board quickly once Bernie was out of the picture. Gina made a note to ask India about the woman she'd mentioned. A friend of her PR consultant, Eden?

She couldn't have done any of this without India's help. Her business adviser had been invaluable, as had her prompting and encouraging messages all week. Gina wanted to do something for India in return. But perhaps getting India's flat over the line would be payback enough.

She was just replying to Deepak when a call came in.

India.

Gina couldn't help the grin that spread across her face.

"I was just thinking about you."

"I've been thinking about you, too. How did this morning go? Are you still in one piece?"

"Surprisingly, yes. Bernie was a pussycat, which makes me nervous. But she's agreed to sell me her part of the business and agreed to the numbers, so I can't complain. I can still be suspicious, but I can't complain." She paused. "Actually, I was just sitting here thinking that I owe you. You've helped with my parents, and my work. It's about time I did something for you."

Gina couldn't see India's smile, but she heard it. "I'm sure we can work something out this weekend." The low timbre of her voice made Gina's insides quiver. Memories of their weekend in Birmingham came flooding back. It was less than a week ago, but it seemed far longer.

She needed to see India again.

She *wanted* to see India again.

India cleared her throat. "But beyond that, I have another idea how you might be able to make up for all the help I've been giving you."

Gina sat up. "Shoot."

"Remember Eunice?"

"How could I forget?"

"She called me last night. She's coming to London this weekend with her granddaughter, and she wants to meet up. She says she's ready to talk about H, reveal her identity and allow us to start the search and see if she's interested in reconnecting."

Gina spun in her chair again. It was a spinny kind of morning. "Wow, that's huge. Well done."

"I did nothing."

"I think you underestimate your powers of persuasion."

"I'll let you know after the weekend if they're still working where I need them most."

Gina's stomach did another loop. "You are being bold this morning."

"It's the Eunice affect. She's being bold. I figure if she can take the leap, I can too. Her situation is far more precarious. She's got so much more to lose. Whereas I hope I've got a foothold already. I'm not wrong, am I?"

"Not one bit." Gina's mind was now a classic summer portrait, all blue sky and sunshine. She snapped back to Eunice. "But she's coming *this* weekend? When we were hoping to spend some time together?" She couldn't help the twinge of disappointment at yet more crashing of their plans. Because Gina's plans had been big. And mostly naked.

"She is, but we'll still have plenty of time together. I want to wow Eunice, but also put her at ease. Put her in a situation where she's got distractions to take her mind off what she's revealing."

"Makes sense. I'm still not sure where I come in."

"I was thinking what distracts me? Makes me feel relaxed?" India paused. "The answer was rooftops. But I don't have my rooftop yet. I wondered if you could supply one? Any chance we can get the keys to my flat for the weekend?"

Gina winced. "I don't think so. It's a little too close to the exchange date being agreed. I wouldn't want to rock the boat."

"I thought you might say that. So, option two. Could we possibly get the keys to that London Bridge flat you took me to the first day after you showed me my future home? We could set up there, and make Eunice feel like a queen. Ask if we could have the flat for the weekend? Play the Pride angle?"

Gina flashed forward. She had a good relationship with the management of that flat. They could only say no. "I'll ask them and let you know."

"Great. I knew I could count on you."

"It's not a done deal yet."

"I have a good feeling, though. About the flat and about you."

"The feeling's mutual." Her heartbeat pulsed in her ears. "I've missed seeing you this week, but I'm loving these calls and texts." Gina had no control over her mouth when she was talking to India. Thoughts just slipped out.

"Ditto. I gotta run. I'll call you later with details about Saturday. Let me know on the flat. See you then, whatever?"

Gina nodded. If nothing else, she was determined to do that. "It's a definite date."

Chapter Twenty-Two

India leant on her car bonnet, head turned towards the May sunshine. She couldn't have written the weather better today. It was as if, finally, this year was taking shape. She could feel it under her fingers, like putty in her hands.

First, she'd kissed Gina. Then, Eunice had said she was open to looking for the mysterious H. With that *and* the Pride biscuits ad campaign signed off, she was on top of the world. Even Andi had stopped messaging her. Maybe she'd finally taken the hint. This week had been a good week. If it carried on like this, it could even start to be a good year. From starting the year in a black hole in New York, India was now cautiously optimistic.

A car pulled up beside her and she turned. Gina.

India's body flooded with pheromones as she waved.

Gina waved back shyly.

She loved that about Gina. She was this ballsy business owner, yet she was tentative and shy, too, and not afraid to show it. She brought out the vulnerable side in India in return. They'd had a strange start to their… *whatever this was*, but now, Gina was a welcome blast of fresh air.

Gina dug in her bag as she approached India, then stopped a few feet away.

They hadn't seen each other since Sunday. Six days since

that scorching kiss in India's car. How were they supposed to greet each other now? It wasn't quite a work thing, but it kinda felt like it. Plus, Eunice and Cordy were due in half an hour. It wouldn't do for them to turn up to find India and Gina snogging on the street. She could see the indecision in Gina's eyes, too. India wanted to kiss her into next week. But she had to have patience.

"Hey." India settled for a hand on Gina's arm.

They both stared at it for far too long.

"You look lovely today, by the way. That shirt dress is gorgeous on you." Gina's eyes were glued to it. "A change from your usual work suits."

India smiled. "It's my weekend look." She'd got compliments the last time she wore this denim shirt dress with a pair of box-fresh white trainers. She was glad Gina liked it, too.

"I approve." Gina produced the flat keys and they took the lift up to the penthouse. The flat was just the same as it had been the first time India had been here.

Or was it? On the side was a tray with fresh tea and coffee, a teapot and a cafetiere, plus biscuits. India's biscuits.

She turned to Gina, pointing. "You bought our biscuits? You could have just asked me."

"I got my assistant to sort this out, and I just had to turn up last night to let the delivery in. I wanted today to go off without a hitch. There's even milk in the fridge."

India wasn't going to wait any longer. She walked over to Gina and pulled her close. "I could seriously fall for your organisational skills, you know that?"

"I was hoping you might say my dazzling good looks, but we'll get to that later."

India nodded. "We will." She stared at Gina's lips. So full and inviting. She was done waiting for a formal invitation. She pressed her lips to Gina's, and the room swayed. She'd meant it just as a brief kiss, a reconnection after the weekend. But it soon ramped up of its own accord, Gina's hand sliding round to India's arse, their bodies pressing into each other. When Gina opened her mouth, and India's tongue slid in, they both groaned.

India was ready to push Gina onto the kitchen counter and have a quickie there and then.

However, the insistent buzz of the doorbell pulled them both back to reality.

India's eyes went wide. "They're early."

Gina nodded, her breath heavy. "They are."

* * *

Eunice looked nervous when she walked in the door, and India didn't blame her. India would be, too. However, India was thrilled that the trip to Birmingham hadn't been a waste of time. Eunice trusted her, and without it, she wouldn't have agreed to a second meeting, or to revealing the identity of her secret lover. India hoped she was ready to tell the full story. She couldn't wait to hear it. Between India's own unfolding romance and this one, work had been relegated to a distant third place. Even her new flat wasn't getting a look-in. If you'd told her that in January, India would have laughed in your face.

Gina busied herself making tea for everyone, while India led Eunice and Cordy out onto the terrace. They made all the right noises.

"Wow," Cordy said, as she and Eunice walked to the

edge. "This view is spectacular." She turned to India. "Is this your flat?"

India shook her head. "I wish. We've got Gina to thank for it. She's the letting agent, and the owners graciously let us use it while it's empty. I thought it'd be a nice treat to see London from a view only a few get. London Bridge, the River Thames and beyond."

Eunice stared across the river. "It certainly is. I used to walk over London Bridge with her every day on the way to work." She clutched the railing at the end of the terrace, her knuckles turning white. "We used to say it was our favourite bridge in London. It was *our* bridge."

Cordy caught India's gaze, then guided her gran to the table.

Eunice bristled. "You don't have to escort me. I might be 79, but I'm still perfectly capable." She shook her head. "I know I got emotional on the way here, but it's all still so new. All this remembering." She breathed the air. "Even the smell is familiar. A *London* smell. It's got grit, oil, promise. It smells of freedom. That's what I associate London with. Freedom. It was where Joan and I met. It was where my life was happiest until I got married and moved away to the midlands. Then it took a different turn, and I had to bury whatever had happened in London. It was a different time. Things didn't happen like they do now."

Eunice reached out and grasped Cordy's hand. "Even if I'd said yes to her, it would have been so hard for us to live our lives together. But I'm so glad things are different for Cordy." She shook her spare fist. "You can live your life. Fall in love and be happy with who you want. That's why I agreed to this when the letters were found. To show you should never hide your feelings down the back of anywhere. A cabinet, a sofa or down the back of your life. Be who you are. Love who you want to love."

Eunice was quiet for a few moments. The only sound was a plane overhead, on the flight path to Heathrow.

Gina came in with the tea and biscuits, then left again.

India flicked her eyes from Cordy to Eunice, then back again. "Let me get this right. H's name is Joan?"

"That's right." Cordy gave Eunice a warm smile. "Gran was telling me on the train down yesterday. She and Joan were best friends. Then secret lovers. Right up until Gran's parents introduced her to a friend's son, and he was very keen on her. They had a couple of dates, and after a few months he asked her to marry him."

Cordy put a hand on her gran's arm. "Back in those days, getting married was still the done thing, and I can't imagine the pressure Gran was under. I still can't quite believe what a story it is. Gran's girlfriend was called Joan Hart. She'd be 80 now. The last time Gran had any contact with her was when she told Joan she was getting married."

Eunice's hand trembled as she brought her tissue up to dab her eye. "Like I told you in Birmingham, if she doesn't want to see me, that's fine. I understand. But I thought about what you said. I only have one life. I've already made one wrong decision because I was afraid to try. I don't regret my life or my lovely family one bit, of course. But when it comes to Joan, I'm not making the same mistake again. I can only try. Cordy persuaded me of that, too. I want her to be proud of me, so I decided to take a chance." She gave India a wobbly smile. "Even if the next couple of weeks might be the most nervous of my life."

Cordy reached over and kissed Eunice's cheek. "I've always been proud of you, Gran. Who you love doesn't change that. Just like you told me when I came out to you." Cordy glanced up at India. "It's like what Pride says. 'It's Never Too Late'. We're testing that theory with Joan. Let's see if she agrees."

India reached over and put her hand on top of Eunice's. "We're going to treat this with the utmost respect and importance. You'll still come to tell your story on video next month, as planned. But if we can get Joan there too, we will. Leave it with us. And thank you for trusting us."

Eunice nodded, then squeezed India's hand with her own. "I wouldn't have trusted anyone else."

* * *

India stood on the terrace for a while after Eunice and Cordy had gone. Gina had seen them out, and slipped to her office to retrieve a folder she needed. India was glad to have a little while to gather her thoughts.

She was so moved by Eunice's story, and the responsibility of finding Joan was heavy on her shoulders. But she was also excited. India wanted to give Eunice a happy ending, but she was well aware it was out of her control. If Joan was still alive, that would be great. If she wanted to see Eunice, that would be the icing on the cake. She made a note to contact Eden about what was going to be needed if they found Joan and she said yes. Two major hurdles to overcome first.

India raised her gaze to the London laid out before her. She scanned the tiny bodies on the street scampering about below.

Was one of those people related to Joan? Was Joan sitting somewhere in London right now, wondering where Eunice was? Had Joan carried a torch for years, too? The lost time was almost too much to contemplate.

India walked over and sat at the terrace's table, Eunice's face still bright in her mind. Eunice had been vulnerable. Just like Gina had taught India to be. Putting yourself on the line was scary. India had done that with Andi, and she'd been burned. But it was only when you put yourself out of your comfort zone that you were truly able to move to the next level of your journey. Eunice and Gina had showed her that this week. They'd both been brave and confronted major issues in their lives. India was ready to learn a lesson.

Her phone buzzed, and she grabbed it. Frankie. India clicked on the message.

'Don't know if you've seen the news today, but Andi has announced she's split up with her heiress. Apparently they had differences they couldn't quite get over. I bet they did. Just thought I should let you know. Hope you're having a good Saturday x.'

India let out a long sigh, then bit her lip. She wasn't surprised. Was that what Andi had been trying to contact her for? Was she having regrets about them? India wouldn't put it past her. A shiver ran down her body. Andi was lost, and India hoped she wasn't looking to her for advice on being found.

India didn't want to think about Andi. She wanted to focus on Gina now.

As if sensing her thoughts, the door to the flat slammed. Gina was back.

When she walked onto the terrace, Gina squinted into the

midday sunshine, putting a hand up to shield her eyes. She dropped the folder she was carrying onto the wooden table, then stood beside India.

India was transfixed. Gina's smooth skin, high cheekbones and delicate nose were perfect. Everything about her was perfect.

In seconds, India snaked an arm around Gina, butterflies fluttering inside. She leaned closer, then pressed her mouth against Gina's. Her whole body stirred on contact. Gina's lips were warm, just like the sun.

When India let go, Gina blinked. "That was a nice welcome back."

India shook her head, staring out at London Bridge. "After hearing what Eunice said about her lost love. How they used to walk to work together every morning across London Bridge — *their bridge*. I don't want to waste any more time. Plus, I was right about bringing her to this rooftop. Rooftops have magical powers over people. Eunice was nearly brought to tears. Cordy couldn't tear her eyes away." India snagged Gina's gaze. "Plus, it's where we first started talking. Where I first knew you could be someone important in my life. Someone who stuck."

Gina reached up a hand and brushed a finger down India's cheek. "You *are* stuck with me." She glanced out to the view, then back to India. "And right now, I want to seize this moment before anything else interrupts us. What do you say?"

India almost swallowed Gina's final words as she crushed her mouth to hers. She couldn't wait any longer. She'd planned a long, leisurely lunch, a stroll on the river, then to take Gina back to her place. But time was of the essence. Eunice had taught her that. Don't put off what you can do today. She was going to do just that.

She trailed her teeth along Gina's top lip, before dropping lower, kissing and nipping at her neck. India breathed her in, the scent of Gina filling her lungs and her heart. She wanted to gather her up and never let her go. She was doing this for Eunice, and for all the lovers out there — both lost and found.

Gina responded with urgent kisses. Then, when India's head was spinning, she pulled back and guided India to one of the loungers, then lowered her onto it.

To say India was surprised would be an understatement. She'd gone from being in control to the tables turning. But she was more than okay with that. Every muscle in her body, currently pulsing, was telling her so.

She wasn't prepared for Gina to straddle her though, and then for Gina's hands to travel over the top of India's shirt dress.

India was transfixed. Her heart rippled in her chest.

Gina slowly and deliberately popped open India's top three buttons, then pushed back the material to reveal her black lacy bra. She left wet kisses on India's neck and collarbone.

India almost stopped breathing.

Seconds later, Gina's alluring lips were back on top of India's.

India went with it, arching her back. Her heartbeat accelerated as Gina's hands clung to her. India's mind flicked through the showreel of their times together. The weekend in Birmingham had top billing. That balcony kiss had been fire-stamped in India's mind ever since. But this rooftop kiss blew it out of the water. Every part of India's body told her so.

Their mouths broke apart briefly, India's hand stroking Gina's side. She stared into Gina's conker-brown eyes, seeing new tones of amber and gold. Her lips glinted in the sunlight, pink and inviting.

A flush of desire travelled down India's body, ending in her groin. "I can't believe we've finally got five minutes together, no interruptions."

Gina put a finger to India's bottom lip and skated along it, quickly followed by a kiss. "You certain about that?"

India nodded. "My diary has only one entry. You."

"I like that very much." Gina's tone was breathy, waiting to pounce. She kissed India hard, before pulling back. "I was thinking we should leave and take this elsewhere. But it's kind of perfect, isn't it, given our history with rooftops?"

"You could say that." India's words were between breaths, as Gina moved a hand between her legs.

Fuck, this was happening. As India inched her legs apart, a steamy breeze swept through. The temperature was only going to rise from here on in.

Gina brought her face closer to India. "Have you ever had sex on a rooftop?" Gina pressed her fingers through the fabric of India's knickers, to her core.

India couldn't speak. She just shook her head, never taking her eyes from Gina. When did she get so masterful?

"Let's see if we can change that, shall we? Plus, your shirt dress is the perfect clothing for it."

With its buttons all the way up the front, Gina had a point.

Before India knew what was happening, Gina had flicked open the buttons on the lower half of her denim shirt dress, and began stroking her inner thigh.

India's mind went blank. All she could see was Gina

above her, her eyes dark pools of want as they zeroed in on India's body.

She unhooked India's bra and pushed it above her breasts.

India was no prude, but being semi-naked on a rooftop, she suddenly felt exposed. A shiver ran down her body as her eyes scanned the surrounding area. It was automatic. However, they weren't overlooked here. Nobody could see them. No paparazzi could get a shot of India's breasts.

"You sure about this?" Gina asked, reading her mind. "We can take this inside if you want to. There's a bed and a sofa to choose from." Gina's low tone was smoky.

India felt it *everywhere*.

As Gina lowered her mouth onto India's nipple, tweaking it with her teeth, India shook her head. "I just want you to fuck me," she said, spreading her legs a little further apart to back up her point.

Because sex on a rooftop was perfect. *Too* perfect. It was *them*.

Gina let go of India's nipple and looked up at her. She gave her a grin. "Just know, this is a rooftop fuck. This isn't fully what I want to do to you. But I'll save that for when we're alone with walls around us."

India's clit stood to attention at Gina's words. "Your dirty talk is effective, you know that?"

Gina stopped talking. She flicked open all the buttons on India's dress, moving the material to the side, then peppered India's breasts and stomach with kisses. Gina's short, dark hair was soft on India's stomach, and she couldn't help but flash forward to what it might feel like on the inside of her thighs, with Gina's tongue taking centre stage. They'd have to go inside for that. Although watching the London skyline with Gina's tongue on her centre would be beyond glorious.

India closed her eyes at the thought. She could feel how wet she was already. As Gina worked her way back up India's body, she was only going to push her to still newer heights.

Gina's mouth nipped at India's neck before she brought their faces level. She cupped India's cheek as her tongue licked along her bottom lip. Then, Gina's deft fingers skated across her thighs, before sliding into her underwear.

India's breath hitched. She reached up and grasped Gina's face between her hands and kissed her roughly.

In response, Gina dipped a finger slowly into her, and then out.

India threw her head back, her mind scrambling, her brain fogged.

Gina did it again, never taking her eyes from her.

India was rapt. She went to say something, but nothing came out of her mouth. She had no idea what she was going to say. Words fled her brain. The only thing she could focus on was Gina's finger inside her. Also, that she wanted more.

Again, as if reading her mind, Gina discarded India's underwear, then slipped a second finger into her.

The sky swayed and the sun pulsed.

Gina's lips found India's again, sliding over them, her tongue moving in time with her fingers.

With every thrust, India's body rose to meet it.

When Gina moved her thumb to brush across India's clit, a whole new level of bliss was reached.

India heard someone's moan cut through the air. She was surprised to realise it was her own.

She sat up a little, her face contorting at the delicious angle that made. Rooftop sex was the absolute best. Why had she never done this before? But India knew why.

First, she'd never had a rooftop. Second, she'd never had anyone she trusted enough to do this with. But now, here she was, half-naked, with Gina deep inside her. But it wasn't just Gina's fingers that had taken root. It was something else. Something more. Something that tugged at her heart. Which only made the low rumblings of India's orgasm flood through her body with more force than normal. Her shoulders tensed. Her calves heated up. Her back arched. Her mind fizzed.

Gina kissed her again, making India's brain spin around and around. When Gina's rhythm brought India all the way to breaking point, India's eyelids flickered open. Her body bucked.

Gina caught her gaze. "Like that?"

She could *so* get used to this. India gave her a slow nod. "Just like that," she replied.

Exactly like that.

Moments later, India sat forward and clutched Gina's shoulders as she came hard, her body rocking as Gina brought her to a safe landing.

They sat, clutching each other, their breathing laboured, before India leaned back and Gina eased her fingers out of her.

When their gazes locked again, India could only shake her head. Her feelings for Gina were the real deal. That realisation made her body shake a little more, but it didn't scare her one bit. "Wow. I think I said that the first time I stepped onto this rooftop. But this time, the wow is even bigger."

Gina grinned, then kissed her lips. "You can thank your

shirt dress. As soon as I saw you in it, I thought, 'that's got easy access'."

India smiled and kissed Gina's lips again. Then she leaned back on the sun lounger, doing up her top buttons. Gina did up the bottom. When they met in the middle, they kissed.

Bliss swept through India once more. "I was just thinking that I rarely wear shirt dresses, but maybe I might start to wear more."

"It's a plan I could really get behind." Gina did up her last button, then straightened India up. "There you go, you're respectable again."

India gave her a louche grin. "I hate being respectable, that's one thing you should know about me." She kissed Gina's lips, lingering when their mouths pulled apart, keeping their noses touching. "I'd also love to feel you, too. But would you like to go somewhere a little more private?"

Gina nodded. "I'd love that."

India blew out a long breath. "Let's go. Too much talking after an orgasm makes me feel exhausted. Plus, I'm starving. Shall we get lunch, then I can take you back to my flat to pick up where we left off?"

Gina stood up and held out her hand. "I thought you'd never ask."

Chapter Twenty-Three

Gina had a spring in her step when she took the stairs up to her office on Monday morning. India had seen to that over the weekend. However, her smile was short-lived when she saw Bernie on the sofa with Sara.

"What the hell are you doing here?" Clouds descended on Gina's brain. "What part of you giving this up and going quietly is this?" Gina stared at Sara. "And why have you brought her?" The sight of her ex still made Gina mad. Mainly at herself.

Bernie stood up, her dark hair so short on the sides, Gina could see her skull.

"I knew you might react like this." Bernie held up a hand. "Sara and I have been talking."

Gina closed her eyes. Seriously? She tried to think happy thoughts, but her world was closing in by the second.

"The thing is, Sara convinced me that walking away isn't the answer. This is a good business. So maybe we could have a rethink about splitting up? Just because Sara's in my life now shouldn't affect that. We can keep our work and personal lives separate, can't we?"

Gina couldn't quite believe her ears. "Like you're doing now, you mean? With Sara sitting on the couch in my office."

"Bernie's office, too," Sara intervened.

There went Gina's good mood. She shook her head with some force. "Just shut up, Sara. This has got nothing to do with you."

Bernie's face fell. "It kinda does if we're together."

"And that's the fucking point, Bernie! Let me spell it out for you. Sara is my ex. She's a pain in the arse who stole my money."

"I never stole anything." Sara stood up, hands on hips, spoiling for a fight.

She'd chosen the wrong woman.

"You took the final £500 from our joint account!"

"I'm going to pay you back once my paintings start selling."

Gina shook her head. How many times had Sara told her that before? "Really? Have you done your website? Got them up for sale?"

Sara dipped her head.

"I didn't think so." Gina turned her attention back to Bernie. "There's a reason I split up with Sara. I didn't want her in my life anymore. I still don't. Plus, you already told me your heart's not in this anymore. Just do what you promised and let me buy you out, Bernie. It's the least you can do after this mess."

But Bernie shook her head. "Sara and I have discussed this, and we don't want to do that. Isn't there a way we could work this out?"

"You're not listening, so I'm going to make this *really* clear. I don't want to work with you anymore. I don't *trust* you. Plus, I don't want Sara anywhere near the business. So no, we can't work this out. Stop pandering to Sara just because she gave you a couple of good orgasms."

Gina put her hands to her head. A headache was beginning to form behind her eyes. It was the same headache she'd had for the past year, and it was always to do with Sara. *Always.*

But suddenly, she saw the reason why. Money. Sara had got to Bernie. "Is this about money? You want more for your share, is that it? Or rather, *she* does." Gina pointed at Sara.

Bernie shook her head. "Not necessarily." She paused, splaying her hands. "Although, when I took another look, what you're offering me is a little on the low side. Add another 20k and maybe we could work something out."

Crimson coloured Gina's vision. "Get out, both of you. I almost believed you before, Bernie, with your contrite words. I should have known, shouldn't I?"

Things were never that easy.

***

Gina jumped in her car and gunned the engine. She wasn't sure where she was going, but she had to get away from the office. Plus, driving and walking always allowed her time to think. Bernie was being a pushover, but Sara could be persuasive when she wanted to be. Gina knew that all too well.

Gina was at a traffic light when her phone pinged. The text message came up on her screen — it was from the legal team dealing with India's flat. They had a proposed exchange date. June 1st. Gina's mind flashed back to the weekend they'd spent in each other's company, laughing, loving, getting to know each other more intimately. When she'd had to leave on Sunday night to go home, it had felt wrong. Like this wasn't the life she was meant to be leading anymore.

Gina loved that feeling. She wanted it back. But then India

had been whisked away to some last-minute TV meetings. India's life was impossibly fast-paced and ever-changing. She was a celebrity of sorts. A high-flying business exec. Could that match with Gina's life?

Gina hoped so, with everything she had. This weekend was the first time she'd felt a seismic connection with a woman. That the world might be about to open up. Gina loved the way India made her feel. How her whole body lit up when India touched her.

She wanted to speak to her right now. She pressed her number.

"India Contelli." Even the way she said her name was sexy.

"Say it again."

There was a pause on the line, then she repeated, "India Contelli."

Gina smiled. "Yep, it was even sexier the second time."

"Glad to be of service."

"How's the world of TV?"

"Not nearly as glamorous as you think. We're in central Manchester and last night there was a major power cut. My producer got stuck in the lift for an hour. I had to finish my shower in pitch black as it was an internal bathroom, and nearly face-planted into the sink."

"But if I was there, we could have been in the dark together."

"That would have made it a whole lot better. I have a big bed that would look perfect with you in it. Like it was made for you."

Suddenly, Bernie and Sara fled Gina's mind. "I can just picture it."

The traffic lights changed.

Gina blinked.

She put her foot on the accelerator like it was the first time she'd ever done so, all the while her mind picturing India's long, tanned body. She still couldn't quite get her head around the fact she was sleeping with her.

"Anyway, sorry to rush you, but I have a meeting in five. Did you need anything from me?"

Gina swallowed. Of course. India was busy. "I have flat news for you. Also, this morning has not gone quite as expected."

"Oh?"

Gina gave India the short, sharp version of the Bernie-Sara saga.

India gave a low sigh. "What the hell is going on with exes these days? First Andi, now Sara. You think she's in it just to piss you off, or does she like Bernie?"

"Who knows. Sara likes anyone with a bit of cash. I fell for it. Bernie is only at the start of the ride. She's still got that 'just fucked' look in her eyes."

India coughed. "I can totally understand that. My mind might have wandered off in a couple of my meetings this morning."

Gina smiled. "I was hoping I might have time for a few illicit daydreams, but no, Bernie poured a bucket of cold water on that idea. I was even whistling this morning. *Whistling*. I don't whistle. Whistling is not me."

"I wanted to shout from the rooftops about the amazing weekend I had, but I figured the rooftops had already served me well, so I shouldn't push my luck."

Gina moved the car forward in the morning traffic, driving

past where India had found her sobbing weeks ago. How times had changed with them, although not with Bernie and Sara.

Gina shook her head. She wasn't going to think about them now.

Instead, she grinned as she thought back on their rooftop sex. Where the courage had come from to straddle India and fuck her, she had no idea.

"I can't wait until you get your own rooftop, let's just say that," Gina replied. "But Bernie is still a massive pain. I thought it was sorted. Would your consultant have any other ideas for me to try?"

India was silent for a moment. "I'm not sure going that route is the way to go now. Leave it with me. Frankie knows her from old. Just like there's an old boys' network, there's a moral code in the gay women's world, too. Maybe she can have a word. It might help."

Gina raised her eyebrows as she pulled into a side street and parked. "There's a gay women's club, too? How come I never got an invite?"

"You have to fuck at least five of them, so I thought I'd spare you."

Gina stopped breathing. "Seriously?"

"No, I'm joking."

"Right." Gina let out a strangled laugh. "Sorry, it's been a long morning. But seriously, if Frankie could say something, it would really take a load off my mind. I'm speaking to Deepak in a minute, and I'd love something concrete to tell him."

"Leave it with me," India replied.

"Before you go, I have news. Your solicitors just contacted me to say there's a proposed exchange date. Keep an eye on your email. You should definitely be in before Pride. It's June 1st."

"Brilliant news. Plus, like you say, then I'll have my very own rooftop. And by then, I might even stick around long enough to use it. Maybe I can return the favour you did for me on Saturday."

Gina's clit pulsed. "I'm driving to the shop to buy a shirt dress right now."

Chapter Twenty-Four

India got back to her flat and flung her keys on the coffee table. She flicked on the TV and slumped on the sofa. It had been a long few days of meetings in Manchester, but she felt like they were getting somewhere even though she'd been promised a break. She'd taken work with her, though, because she'd needed to. She and her dad had worked together side by side since she'd got back, and he'd told her on the way home that the company was her baby now. He was stepping down at the end of the year, and India should consider the next six months her formal transition period.

India had gulped, but also, she'd been flushed with pride. Her dad trusted her with the company's future. She'd worked hard for it and she deserved it. However, it was also a turning point. If she wanted to be the best at being the company CEO for real, she might have to take a step back from her TV work. They both understood that, and it was something India was prepared to do. Less TV work hopefully also meant more time at home. More time when she wouldn't be working super-long hours trying to do two jobs.

With luck, more time for her and Gina to explore where their relationship might go.

Should she be factoring Gina into her future? India had no

idea. She was just going with her gut. It told her she wanted Gina in her life, so she was going for it. If the constant stream of texts this week were anything to go by, Gina wanted India in her life, too.

She reached over and picked up the pink velvet cushion, the same one Gina had hugged in her flat a few weeks earlier. Bernie was still giving her grief. India had spoken to Frankie, and hopefully she could sort it out. India didn't want to wade in and fight Gina's battles for her, but she would if she had to.

She took a quick shower, then dressed in some casual trousers and a white shirt. She picked up some big clacky beads, then put them down. That was more part of her work uniform. Her carefully cultured public persona. Yes, it was her, but she wasn't feeling that today. Instead, India went to her jewellery box and fished out a plain silver necklace with a compass on the end that her mum had given her on her 30th birthday. It was before big clacky beads took over her life. Plus, hadn't Gina said she liked her weekend look? Now, India wanted Gina's approval.

She put it on and nodded at her reflection. Maybe she needed to mix up her jewellery. Maybe she needed a compass. Although, she seemed to be taking better roads these days. Roads that led somewhere, rather than dead ends. Roads with Gina waiting in the wings.

Her phone flashed and India grabbed it. It was a message from Frankie, telling her she'd spoken to Bernie. 'I think it should be sorted.'

India sent her a thank you text. She hoped that was the end of it. Gina was too lovely to need any more aggravation in her life. India was determined to bring nothing but chill to her. Starting tonight.

Her phone buzzed again and she glanced down.

'Still on for later?'

India grinned. She couldn't help it. She was due at Gina's for dinner at 7pm.

'Leaving in five,' she replied. Then hastily added three kisses.

She wasn't leaving anything to fate this time. She'd believed in fate with Andi, and look where that had got her. This time around, she wanted her intentions to be crystal clear.

* * *

Gina was waiting for her outside her building when she arrived. Was she thinking about the scorching-hot kiss they'd shared outside her flat last time India was there? India was, and she had no shame.

Gina beamed, then reached up for a kiss. It was light, but it reconnected them. As soon as their lips touched, calm washed through India. She could *so* get used to it.

"What's in the bag?" Gina pointed at the white holdall on India's shoulder, packed tight and bursting at the seams.

"Chocolate Rockets, Rainbow Rings, plus a few others. You said we had to make a pit stop to meet your sister, and she loves biscuits. I keep a stash in my flat for just such an occasion."

"To impress potential suitors' sisters?"

India gave her a grin. "Exactly that. Lead the way."

Gina walked India to the lift, stabbing floor 14 and waiting for the door to close. As soon as it did, their eyes locked.

It'd been a long week apart after the weekend they'd

shared. Gina seemed to have the same thought at the exact same time, as she stepped towards India.

The lift juddered to life.

India dropped her bag on the floor.

Gina's hand stretched up behind India's head to pull her closer, and their lips connected again, this time with more purpose. India's insides lit up as they touched.

This was what had kept her going through this week of negotiations. The thought that when she got back, Gina would be waiting. India slid her tongue into Gina's mouth.

Gina clutched her harder.

Desire drenched India. They could have carried on kissing if the lift hadn't stopped.

"Floor 14!" said the voice.

India pulled her lips from Gina's. They both checked themselves in the mirror, Gina's hand on the button keeping the lift in place.

"Do we look presentable and not like we've just been snogging each other's faces off?"

India nodded. "I think we do. No stubble rash here." She gave Gina a wink.

"I hope not," Gina said, squeezing her arse.

Gina's sister was waiting at the door when they turned the corner, nervous energy radiating from her. She gave them both a wide smile, before her arms encircled Gina, then she held out a hand to India.

"Lovely to meet you. My sister has been troublingly short on detail about you."

India turned to Gina. "You need to do better. Family gossip is the lifeblood of any relationship."

Neeta nodded towards India. "I like her, she speaks the truth."

"You're going to like her even more when you see what she's brought you."

Neeta took the offered bag, peering inside and giving India a thumbs-up. "Biscuits galore, including Chocolate Rockets!" She pointed at Gina. "Did I mention I like her?"

India immediately warmed to Neeta. She had spunk, just like her sister.

They walked through to the living room, with its open-plan kitchen at one end, and its large windows looking over one of the many waterways of Canary Wharf. India admired the view. "Do you have the same view from your flat?"

Gina nodded. "Yep, just three floors higher."

"We bought them off plan, and Gina was sad we couldn't be neighbours. I like the three floors' separation. You know what they say about family." Neeta gave Gina a grin.

"Lies!" Gina laughed. "I was going to buy in the next block, but Neeta almost cried."

Neeta boiled the kettle, her words drowned in steam. "That is actually true. Mainly so I could come and get food from Gina when I needed it. She's a much better cook than me."

India raised a single eyebrow. "Is that so? I haven't had the pleasure of eating any of her food."

"You haven't been back to my flat, so the chances have been slim." Gina paused. "But we're going to rectify that later." Her gaze was loaded as she spoke.

Gina patted the seat beside her and inclined her head.

India did as instructed.

Gina put a hand on her thigh.

Every single action Gina did put India on high alert. Their kiss was still swirling around her brain. She wanted to do it again. How quickly could they drink their tea?

In the kitchen, Neeta was oblivious. "Also, you're actually just as tall in real life as you are on the TV." She brought the mugs over to the coffee table, followed by a plate of Rainbow Rings, then sat on the armchair facing Gina.

India picked up a biscuit, holding it in front of Gina. "You didn't eat one at my flat. You can't say no a second time, I'll be offended. This is my life's work."

"Will they make me gayer than I already am?" Gina took it, along with a small plate.

"You won't know until you try."

Neeta took one when she was offered. "I always thought I'd make a really good gay, so I'm excited for the possibility of change."

Gina chuckled through a mouthful of biscuit. "What about Neil? What would he say?"

Neeta waved a hand. "He'd be fine with it. So long as I only do it when he's working, how will he ever know, anyway?"

India laughed, too. "Maybe that should have been part of the marketing campaign? 'This biscuit will turn you gay.' It would have been an interesting concept."

"It would certainly have caught people's attention," Gina said. She paused, pointing to the counter-top. "Why have you got a gold-embossed statue of Lord Ganesh? Have you been born again?"

Neeta rolled her eyes. "Mum sent it to me because Lord Ganesh removes obstacles in your life. I'll leave it to you to work out which obstacle she wants removed."

"Not getting pregnant?"

"Bingo. Neil thinks we should create a shrine and not tempt fate. I think we should hide it in the wardrobe." Neeta turned to India, hardly pausing for breath. "Gina tells me you've got a Pride bus and you'll be giving these away. You're going to be very popular."

"That's the idea." India paused. "You should come if you're free." She glanced at Gina, then back to Neeta. "If that's okay with Gina and something you'd like to do."

"If I'm not working, I'm there. I get my new rota next week, but if I can, I'd love to!"

India fished out her phone and gave it to Neeta. "Put your number in my contacts. I'll add you to the Pride Bus message group."

Neeta looked as if she'd just won the lottery. "I *really* like her," she said, pointing.

Neeta gave India her phone back just as another message came in. India glanced at the screen. It was from her PR guru, Eden.

'Just to let you know we've found Joan, and she wants to meet Eunice! To say I'm excited is an understatement. I'm arranging a suite at The Savoy so they can come to London before Pride. I'll sort everything out. Call me when you get the chance.'

India couldn't help the grin that spread across her face. Joan wanted to meet up with Eunice. Their love story might have a happy ending. But she shouldn't get ahead of herself. Instead, she pumped her fist before stashing her phone back in her bag.

"That was Eden. Eunice's long-lost love is still alive and

wants to meet up with her." She stared at Gina. She wasn't sure why this was so important for them too, but it was. Like their relationship was intrinsically linked to the success of Eunice and Joan.

"She said yes?" Gina grabbed India's knee as she spoke.

India nodded. "Eden is going to sort out dates, but she's coming."

Gina put a hand over her heart. "It's too much. I can't wait to meet Joan. It's like an old-school Hollywood romance come to life."

"Only better, because it's full of lesbians," India added.

"India's going to ask them to be in a biscuit ad, too," Gina told her sister. "We've already got a gorgeous couple doing it, but think of the squidge factor with two women reuniting after 60 years."

"They might not agree, so let's not get ahead of ourselves." India stroked Gina's arm, giving her a loving look.

"If they don't do it, you two should. The looks you're giving each other right now are enough to scorch my sofa."

India pulled back reflexively, giving Neeta a sheepish look.

"Don't stop on my account. I'm just going to ask if you could not shag on the sofa. I only just washed the covers."

Neeta grabbed another biscuit and gave her sister a smug, triumphant look.

Chapter Twenty-Five

They barely made it out of the lift before India's mouth was on Gina's.

Gina didn't complain. She managed to guide them down the corridor while not removing her lips for long, unlocking her door and guiding India inside.

India walked ahead through to the main room, her tall, lithe body tantalising Gina every step of the way. The air was already stamped with her. India's smell was intoxicating.

India ran a hand along the breakfast bar, and Gina immediately wanted to be the breakfast bar. Then India walked up to take in the view, just as she had in Neeta's flat. When she turned and parted her lips, Gina was mesmerised.

They stared at each other for a good few moments before Gina spoke.

"I know it's not as fancy as your flat. Your old one or your new one. But it's home." Gina shrugged like it meant nothing. But that wasn't true. It meant a great deal. She wanted India to like where she lived, because Gina was proud of her flat. Getting the keys had been one of the best moments of her life. To finally have something that she could call her own. She interlocked her fingers and squeezed hard.

India turned up her smile. "I was just thinking it's very you. Warm. Stylish." She patted Gina's golden wing-backed armchair. "I love this piece, it's gorgeous." She glanced up, shaking her head. "This space is the same as your sister's flat, but I prefer this one. Mainly because it's about you." She walked towards Gina.

Gina's stomach flipped.

"It's beautiful, considered, and somewhere I would willingly come back to time and time again." India stopped just before she got to Gina, her stare intense.

Gina tilted her head. "You'll come back, even though there's no rooftop view?"

India mirrored her head tilt. "I like a bit of variety in my life."

"Good to know." Gina paused, lust sweeping through her as she focused on India's lips. "Plus, if you like the living room, wait until you see the bedroom." She was being bold. Although, then she took a step back. "Unless you want a drink first?"

India shook her head, her eyes dark and brooding. "I just want you."

Once inside the bedroom, India stepped up behind Gina and put her hot lips to the back of her neck.

Gina's insides turned liquid on contact.

"I've wanted you since I saw you downstairs." India pulled at Gina's black-and-white top and tugged it off. "Even the way you were drinking your tea downstairs was sexy."

India's words drifted across Gina's brain, but it was her touch that was at the forefront of Gina's senses, lighting her up.

India unclipped Gina's bra, letting it fall to the floor before cupping her breasts from behind, claiming Gina as her own.

Gina had never been happier to be claimed in her life.

India rolled Gina's left nipple between her thumb and index finger. "Did you know left nipples are more sensitive than right?"

As if on cue, Gina's nipple sprang to attention. "I didn't," she rasped, looking down. "But mine seems to be proving your point."

"Seems so," India replied, nibbling the side of her neck.

Gina concentrated on staying upright, even though her whole body wanted to collapse.

India cupped both breasts from behind, then pressed herself into Gina.

Gina's heart drummed a whole new beat.

"And these jeans need to come off, too," India whispered in her ear.

Gina wilted, her growing desire for India etched into every breath she took. She wobbled as she stepped out of her jeans, then her underwear. Goosebumps broke out across her legs.

India pressed herself into Gina's naked back, her hand reaching down and cupping Gina's bare arse cheek before moving between Gina's legs. When India connected with her core, she groaned into Gina's ear, kissing her lobe, before sucking on it.

A blaze of desire burned through Gina as India bent her over her bed, then slid skilled hands across her behind.

There was a hitch in India's breathing as she moved her fingers through Gina's silky heat.

Gina shuddered, biting her lip as India slipped one finger slowly inside her, closely followed by another.

"Oh fuck," Gina said, as India placed her other hand on Gina's bottom, then slowly began to fuck her from behind.

"The thought of doing this to you again has been tormenting me all week," India said, leaning forward and whispering into Gina's ear.

Gina closed her eyes as wetness pooled between her legs. India's words sent shockwaves to her very core. Gina couldn't get enough of her; she spread her legs some more, letting India have the easiest access possible.

As India sank into her, her hips pressing into Gina's bum, Gina surrendered herself to them, to whatever this was, this fledging relationship with their off-the-scale connection. She relinquished any control over her feelings in this second, trusting India to keep her safe. As she rewrote her life script, Gina gave in to her lust, knowing it was the kernel of something that might turn into something far deeper. It already had the power to do so very quickly. Gina knew it, and the way India had stared at her in the lounge, Gina was pretty sure she knew it, too.

She was so close, but Gina wanted to see India's face. She turned her head, hoping she could convey that without words. She couldn't manage them right now. Her brain was too scrambled. India seemed to understand.

Gina twisted her body slowly, every movement intense as India twisted her hand along with her, never leaving her. Where had India been all her life?

Gina's breath bunched in her throat as she eased up the bed, India never taking her eyes from her. Moments later, India settled on top of her, her weight pressing down, her fingers curling into Gina deliciously.

Gina arched her back and rolled her hips, then pressed her head into the pillow as India picked up a delicious rhythm, driving Gina higher and higher.

She let out a low moan as her orgasm ignited deep inside. It started out as a low beat, before the volume increased and rattled through her body. Colours cascaded across the back of her closed eyelids, as Gina reached out and gripped India's body, pulling her down as she rose up. She was close, *so close*. She could feel it in her bones, in her veins. She could feel it *everywhere*.

India slipped her other hand under Gina, raising her bum onto India's bent knees. Then she circled Gina's swollen clit, avoiding where Gina needed it most.

Gina cried out again as India's circles began to close in. She bucked her hips, with no idea what to focus on anymore. India was on top of her, above her, all around her.

Gina opened her eyes to connect with India, just as a flash of intense light throbbed in her eyeline, blazing-hot lust bowling through her. She came undone in seconds, making noises she'd never heard before, because India was making love to her in a way she'd never felt before. India didn't let up, either. Not until Gina had come again, and she reached down to still her hand. Then India collapsed on top of her, covering Gina's face and neck with seductive kisses. When Gina finally opened her eyes, her fists clinging to the sheets to hold her in place, India's fingers were still inside her.

She curled them once more, and Gina gasped.

India kissed her lips again, before finally withdrawing. She rolled onto her side, before gathering a quivering Gina into her arms. Then she trailed her index finger — the one that had just been inside Gina — up Gina's neck and over her chin, making her insides quiver. When India pressed that finger to Gina's lips, she wilted again.

"Look at me," India said, her voice soft but firm.

Gina gushed on the spot, doing as she was told.

"Suck my finger." India's stare was intense, which only sent Gina's levels of want higher.

The erotic scent of herself was making her even wetter, and when Gina took India's finger inside her mouth and moved her tongue around it, she had no idea this level of desire even existed: it was beyond anything Gina had experienced before. India added another finger and Gina sucked it, her thirst overflowing.

Judging by the lust pooling in India's eyes, it was working for her, too.

After a few more seconds, India withdrew. Then Gina's eyes widened as India's fingers travelled south before slipping back inside, fucking her hard, making her come again all over her fingers. Gina no longer had any idea who she'd been before this moment. There was only this day, this hour, and nothing else mattered. India had depleted her utterly, gloriously.

Gina waited a few moments to get her breath back, as India kissed her shoulders. She eventually composed her thoughts before sinking back into India's arms. "I think I might demand you go away for another week if this is what happens when you get back." She leaned her head back and kissed India's cheek lightly.

"I like the sentiment, if not the practice," India replied, kissing Gina's lips. "Besides, the whole point of me getting my new flat is so I can spend more time in it. When I first decided to buy it, it was for me. But now it's for you, too. It's for *us*."

Gina gave her a hazy grin. "For us?" They hadn't even spoken about what they were as yet. Were they exclusive? Was India her girlfriend? Gina wasn't going to ask, as it seemed a little juvenile. For now, she was just going with the flow. "I can totally get down with that."

She shook her head, still dazed from the pleasure India had wrapped her in. "When did you become such a goddess?" The words were out before Gina could contain them. Was it too much? She didn't care. Gina sat up, still shimmering with desire. "However, you'd be more of a goddess if we got you out of your clothes."

India gave her a grin before she undid her shirt and slipped it off her shoulders, followed by her bra.

She had Gina's attention now.

India put her fingers to Gina's lips again, and she sucked obediently. Then India took that finger, and rolled her own nipple between it and her thumb.

Gina was transfixed, her pussy wetter by the second.

India stood up and slipped off her trousers, then her knickers. She was so strong and beautiful; it took Gina a few moments to truly drink her in. But when she did, India was almost too much to take. Until she wasn't.

India's toned physique made Gina suddenly more switched on. Everything came into sharper focus. Gina didn't want to just look. She wanted to touch, to feel.

She pulled India onto the bed, kneeling up beside her, running her hands over India's skin that went on for miles.

She breathed her in, India's scent raw and alive. Gina could bury herself in it.

As Gina's mouth travelled down India's neck, she made sure to take in every part of her, especially India's deliciously wide collarbone she'd admired from afar. Now, it was on the tip of her tongue and it was glorious. Gina licked a hungry trail along it, making India squirm. Then she dropped to India's perfect breasts, taking India's right nipple into her mouth and swirling her tongue.

India sucked in a breath.

However, Gina wasn't staying long.

Throughout India pleasuring her, Gina had one thing on her mind — to drink India in. Literally. Now, she lowered India onto her back, kissed a path from her ribs to her navel, then sank lower still, Gina's inky hair caressing India's stomach. Then her mouth and body travelled south, settling over India's core.

"Spread your legs," Gina said, her voice gravelly, speaking right over India's centre, knowing her breath was right where it needed to be.

India groaned again, but complied.

And when she did, Gina swelled with desire, licking her lips: she was *desperate* to taste her, to be inside her. Gina ran her tongue up the inside of India's thighs before pulling India closer to her mouth. She parted her legs wider with both hands, before using them to open India's lips and flick her tongue through her liquid heat, then back down. Slowly, tantalisingly. Just the way Gina knew would drive her mad if India tried the same thing on her.

It had the desired effect as India squirmed beneath her.

It was taking every ounce of willpower Gina had not to bury herself up to her elbows in India, to bring her to a quick climax. But she wanted to take it slow, to give India the best she had.

She swished her tongue around India's clit with syrupy precision. When she eventually pressed her tongue flat and drove it upwards in grand, masterful strokes, as if she were painting a grand opus, India cried out, her body stiffening as Gina got into her groove. Even more so when Gina slipped two fingers inside her lover: India grabbed her hair and held on.

As Gina swept India over the edge with a luxurious flick of her tongue, bright lights danced in Gina's soul. India came hard in a hot rush of passion, studding the air with her cries.

Gina's heart raced. She wanted to stop time in this moment. Finally, she got it. She was experiencing what all those love songs talked about. What everyone else raved about. The club that Gina had assumed had no room for her had finally opened its doors and welcomed her in.

She was the happiest she'd ever been. Light on her feet.

Simply put, Gina was falling in love.

Desire drenched Gina's body as she gave India another crescendo, before crawling back up her long body and bringing their heads level again.

"Kiss me," Gina panted, only vaguely aware of where she was and who she was.

India did as she was told, their kisses soft and cushioned after such a frantic workout, their lips warm and tender.

When Gina pulled back, she let a languid smile stroll onto her face. "I could so get used to you." She stared into India's crystal-blue eyes, her face red, her breathing sketchy. "You're beyond exquisite."

In response, India blew out a long breath. "My brain can't think of an adequate reply. But I'm glad you're mine." She paused, before kissing Gina's lips again. "I hope you're mine."

Gina gulped, then smiled. "If you want me, I'm yours one hundred per cent."

Chapter Twenty-Six

The next morning, India woke up, her mouth dry. She turned in the bed and rolled straight into Gina. She could do nothing but smile. India kissed her smooth shoulder, drawing a mumble of recognition, but nothing more. India rolled onto her back, not wanting to wake Gina too quickly.

Her mind wandered forward to the next weekend, when she was meeting Eunice and Joan at The Savoy. Eden had sent her a text to tell her everything had been arranged. How was that meeting going to go? India wanted to be there when they arrived, to sit down with them, to learn everything about why they hadn't worked out. But it was their story, their lives, not hers. She just had to ask them the surface questions, to get some good sound bites and film their reunion, before leaving them to it. Pride had supplied the pair with a suite at The Savoy for the weekend. Would they spend it in bed, making up for years of lost time? Would Eunice wake up the following morning kissing Joan's shoulder, just like Gina and her today? The thought made India smile.

Life could go off course very easily. If India hadn't met Gina, she might not be moving into her flat in a few weeks, living her rooftop dream. Last night had been incredible, like nothing India had ever experienced before. Where did they go from here? She didn't want to leave anything to chance, but she also didn't want to push too soon. However, one thing she *was* certain of: Gina was going to know how she felt. She wasn't going to leave it to someone else finding some love letters down the back of a drinks cabinet to reach her destiny.

Gina stirred and rolled over. Her face was marked with sleep, red lines running down her cheeks. She was adorable, and India told her so.

"I bet I look a sight."

"A gorgeous sight," India replied, kissing her lips. "How did you sleep?"

Gina blinked a few times, before raising a single eyebrow. "Once someone stopped having sex with me and let me sleep, it was pretty good." Gina wriggled. "But damn, I'm aching this morning."

India grinned. "It was worth it, though, right?"

"Every last second." Gina smiled at her through sleepy eyes.

"I was just thinking about Eunice and Joan. Eden's set up a meeting for next Sunday. Eden's bringing her friend, Lib. Are you still good to come along and meet her? I'll give you the company credit card and stump up for a coffee for you both."

"How can a girl refuse an offer like that?" Gina yawned. "I've interviewed a couple of people for the job, but haven't found anyone suitable yet. It'd be good to meet someone who's already known. She seemed nice when I messaged her."

"Eden vouches for her, and that's good enough for me." India ran a hand down the side of Gina's cheek. "I was wondering if Eunice and Joan were going to end up like us next weekend, after a night of hot sex."

Gina smiled again. "Lucky them if they do."

"Imagine, though. Sixty years since you were naked with the love of your life."

"They might never have been naked. It might have all been stolen kisses and sex against a door."

"Stop it, you're turning me on." India rolled into Gina and kissed her lips, this time with more intention. When she eventually pulled back, her brain was scrambled, her thoughts shredded. She blinked again. "What was I saying?"

"About Eunice and Joan fucking against a door." Gina laughed. "I hope they find what they're looking for." She held India's gaze with her own. "It can happen when you least expect it."

India drew in a fractured breath. "It certainly can." She kissed Gina once more, before pulling back. "You know, I haven't had many nights like last night. You've raised the bar."

Gina shook her head, then rolled onto her back, blowing out a breath.

India backtracked down her conversational cul-de-sac. Cold dread gripped her. "Did I say something wrong?"

Gina turned back, giving her a slow, sure smile. "I don't think telling a woman she's raised the bar could ever be seen as saying the wrong thing." Gina propped herself up on one elbow, her cheek cradled by her palm. "You're doing all that and more for me. You brought me new business via your flat. You've helped me with Bernie — did I tell you she emailed and did a U-turn? Just like that. Frankie has magical powers."

India smiled. "It helps to have friends in powerful places."

"It certainly does." Gina snagged India's gaze with her own. "Plus, you're the first woman my family have met, and they all seem as smitten as me. On top of all that, you gave me multiple orgasms that almost made my body explode." She pressed a finger into India's bare chest. "And you've got great tits."

"You say the sweetest things," India replied.

Gina touched her cheek, a loving look in her eye. "You've emboldened me. Made me a little more fearless. So, thank you. You turn an ordinary day into something special."

India gulped. She was so close to saying those three little words but she was pretty sure it was too soon to reveal her feelings. So she held back. But the rush of emotion filling up every inch of her body could easily be mistaken for love. However, she'd been burned before. She wasn't going to fall so easily again. Gina was so different to Andi, but India still needed to have some sort of armour covering her heart. At least, for a little while longer.

"One thing, though. I still haven't told my family back home about us being more than friends. Until I do that — which I will, soon — can we keep this to ourselves? No social media, that sort of thing."

India nodded. "Of course. But for now, not forever, right? I don't want to keep you under wraps for too long."

Gina kissed her lips. "I know. I just need to work up the courage. Soon, I promise."

Chapter Twenty-Seven

Gina hadn't been for a run in a while, but she wasn't chancing another game of squash with her sister, and Neeta was very insistent.

They began on the waterway beside their building, the stone flags underfoot uneven and hot from today's sunshine. They ran over the chrome bridge that vibrated under the pounding of their feet, past the busker on the other side singing a dodgy version of Oasis's 'Wonderwall.' Was there a non-dodgy version?

Gina breathed in the smells of coffee and chorizo from the street stalls on the north side of the water, then ran under the Docklands Light Railway, which rattled overhead, the sun hot on her skin. They carried on along the water, until they ran past a line of small boats — then the vista opened up. Before them, the Millwall Docks shimmered into view, the weekend dragon boat crews ploughing up and down the aqua carpet, making the water fizz white and frothy.

Once there, Gina and Neeta raced to the bridge on the other side, as was their custom, then doubled over, wheezing and grinning at each other.

It was a few seconds more before Neeta got her breath back. "You never told me what happened with Bernie, by the way."

"That's because I never see you." Gina was still out of breath. She needed to run more often.

"Is she still bringing Sara to the office and making your life hell? I never liked her, I told you that, right?"

"A number of times, yes." She didn't want to tell Neeta she'd been right in her assertion that Bernie was crooked, which her sister had said from the start. Gina was hopeful she'd soon be rid of her, and that her life would be as smooth as India's bum. Which was the smoothest she'd ever felt. The corners of Gina's mouth twitched just thinking about it. Luckily, her sister was oblivious. Some things Gina was more than happy to keep to herself.

"Bernie backed down after some choice words from Frankie, India's friend. Plus, I worked out everything that needed to be done with the help of India's legal team. I made it easy for her to get out. Bernie just had to realise that, which she eventually did."

"So, Bernie gets cash and Sara to spend it for her. She's a glutton for punishment."

"She's going in with her eyes wide open. What can I do but wish her luck? She's going to need it."

A man and a woman walked by with a toddler between them, each holding one hand. They swung the small girl, whose feet left the ground as she was propelled forward, the glee on her face palpable. Both Gina and Neeta grinned.

"Now you're in business with Deepak. Which is better?" Neeta elbowed her sister.

"I know how to handle Deepak. Plus, he's a pussycat around me."

"You always were his favourite."

"He's a shrewd business owner, too. I'm not expecting an easy ride, but at least this will give me the money to do this properly. I'm excited about driving the business forward. It does mean that Deepak might come down to London a bit more. Which means you're going to have to come out with us, too."

"Us? As in you and Deepak, or you and a certain tall, biscuity woman?"

Gina rolled her eyes. "India might be involved, but I'm sure he'd like to see you and Neil, too. Heck, I'd like to see Neil. You are still married, right?"

"Last time I checked."

"Good. I spoke to Deepak last night, and invited him to Pride. He's coming on the bus." Gina was still wondering whether or not that had been a sound move. "Am I totally mad to do that?"

Neeta shook her head. "Not mad. I spoke to Mum this week, and she told me she was pleased Deepak was going into business with you. She might be coming to London a bit more, too. Tagging along with her brother. Your personal lines might start to become blurred. So please tell them you're with India soon. Mum was badgering me the other day, and it took everything I had not to crack."

"I will. I promised India too, so I have to do it now."

"You have to do it before Pride, if Deepak's coming. He won't be able to keep his mouth shut."

"I know." Gina held up her hands, her insides twisting. This wasn't her favourite topic. Dealing with her sexuality and her parents was never easy. But now she had someone who counted, it was time. She just had to work up the courage.

"How are things going with India?" Neeta glanced Gina's

way. "You seem… I don't know what you seem. Like you're more at ease. More sure of yourself. Whatever it is, I like it. It looks good on you."

Neeta had hit the nail on the head. It was still early days with her and India, and there were still many things that hadn't been said. But India had nudged Gina towards change. Her family lines were blurring, Neeta was right. It had to happen, and Gina wasn't sad. Scared, yes, but change happened with small steps. It had started with the weekend in Birmingham, it was shifting with Deepak, and who knows, one day, her mum might ride the Pride bus. Not this year, but one day.

"I like her, and I think she likes me, too. We'll see where it goes, but fingers crossed. It *feels* different." That was the understatement of the year. Gina had *never* felt this way before, and it was a constant surprise. "Plus, she's got a Pride bus, so we're riding in the parade. That's different, right?"

Neeta put an arm around her. "A marked difference to Sara. You deserve happiness, and I'm backing India to bring it to my little Nagina. Otherwise, she'll have me to answer to."

* * *

Gina picked up an orange from the pile in the greengrocers and squeezed. Not too soft, not too hard, just right. She dropped it in her basket and grabbed a bunch of bananas from the shelf above. She needed more fruit in her diet, and the only way she was going to get it was to buy it.

Her gaze shifted, and she was just deciding between blueberries and raspberries when her phone rang. She checked the screen. Mum.

Gina wrinkled her forehead. She'd already decided to ring

later and tell her about India. However, Gina wasn't ready to have the conversation just yet. Not in the greengrocers. Then again, she was probably never going to be ready.

Gina stared at her phone. It was still ringing. She should ignore it.

Her finger pressed the green call button.

Damn it.

"Hi, Mum." Gina selected a punnet of blueberries and put them in her basket. Whatever her parents' reaction, Gina was going to stay healthy.

"I've been waiting for you to call, but I could be waiting forever for that to happen."

Hello to you, too. What was it with mothers and daughters? Gina was sure her brother never got calls like this.

"I was going to call later."

Her mum made a noise like she didn't believe that for a second. "How is your business going? Deepak said things are progressing well."

Gina nodded, picking up a cauliflower. She'd heard you could roast them to great effect, make a cauliflower pilaf. Maybe India would like it, too. She added it to her basket. Maybe she'd cook it for them next time she came over. Look at Gina, thinking like someone in a relationship.

That her mother still didn't know about.

"It's going well. We're getting the paperwork sorted, and then hopefully, Deepak will be the perfect sleeping partner."

"He's had enough practice at the sleeping part. He was still in bed when I called him last week at 9am."

Gina's mum got up at 6.30am every day, rain or shine. Anything else she considered 'lazy.'

"Scandalous," Gina replied.

There was a pause before her mum spoke again. A man brushed past Gina and nearly knocked her basket out of her hand. She scowled at him.

"And how is your friend?"

Gina froze. "My friend?"

"India."

Her mum had never asked about one of her friends before. Then again, since coming out, Gina had been hiding her life from them, so it wasn't a surprise. Plus, she'd lost a few friends from Birmingham after she came out, after they told Gina they'd feel 'uncomfortable' being around her. Good riddance.

"She's good."

Gina's heart thumped in her chest.

Tell her.

Her pulse stuttered. She wasn't ready.

"Your dad downloaded her show. She's very good. Professional. Knows what she's talking about. Dad was saying you should get her to come up here and give a talk to the business community. I'm sure she'd be very popular."

Gina pushed down a strangled laugh. "I think she might be a bit busy to do that, Mum."

A pause. "She seemed fond of you, so she might. People do things for people they want to impress, don't they?"

Gina's pulse stopped. What was her mum saying? Did she know? Was she fishing?

"I suppose they do." Gina picked up some raspberries. "Actually, Mum, I've got something to tell you."

Deep breaths.

Take aim.

Fire!

"We're actually sort of seeing each other." Hot breath rushed out of Gina's mouth like fire.

She'd really done it now.

Another pause on the other end. "Seeing each other as in you're together?"

Gina nodded. "Uh-huh."

"Sort of, or you are?"

Gina clenched her teeth, then mustered up all the courage she possessed. "We are. Together. A couple."

Her brain buzzed inside her skull. She'd done it. Told her mum they were seeing each other. This was a monumental step forward in her life.

"Okay," her mum replied.

"Okay?" That was all she got?

"I guessed as much. Not many women have turned up on our doorstep and looked at you like that."

Gina dropped the punnet of raspberries. The plastic lid popped off, and the small red berries exploded over the shop. Gina put down her basket and looked over to the cashier. She was busy serving another customer.

"Oh shit," Gina said, still holding the phone.

"Language, Gina!" Mum said.

"Sorry, I just dropped a load of raspberries all over the shop floor." This was ridiculous. The moment she'd been dreading had casually slipped itself into her life, and it wasn't even the biggest news of the past ten minutes.

"Ask her about the talk, anyway. If she likes you, she's going to want to impress your parents."

Her mum had a point, but the thought of India going to

Birmingham to address the Asian business community wasn't something Gina's brain could compute.

"I will, Mum."

Right at that moment, a small child walked past Gina, slipped on the berries and fell on his bum. He started to bawl, and when Gina looked up, a red-faced mother was heading her way.

"I'm going to have to go. Can I call you back later?"

"Okay," her mum replied. "And Gina?"

"Yes?"

"She seemed… nice."

Gina stared at the toddler, his crying stopped. His focus now was on smearing the raspberries around the floor with his hands.

"She is," she replied.

Gina stood with her basket hanging from her arm, dazed. She'd practised that speech so many times in her head, and then it had happened in a greengrocer's? Also, did her mum just give her blessing to their relationship?

Gina needed a lie down.

Chapter Twenty-Eight

Eden was waiting in the entrance foyer of The Savoy when India walked in. She gave India a hug, before standing back and rubbing her hands together.

"You excited?"

India gave her a rapid nod, a flurry of butterflies swarming in her chest. She'd been excited to wake up in Gina's bed again this morning. Excited that Gina had told her parents. Excited they were heading in a positive direction.

But this was a different kind of excitement. Because of India and London Pride, a huge love story might be about to catch fire again. She knew she shouldn't get ahead of herself. Eunice and Joan might hate each other on sight. It could happen. However, the alternative had been giving her goosebumps all morning.

"I'm beyond that. I was saying to…" India stopped. She didn't want to jinx her and Gina so soon. She wanted to keep this to herself, not give anything away, or risk the chance for it to turn sour. They were still in a bubble. She didn't want anything to take her out of that. "To a friend recently," India continued, "that I'm so emotional about this. I don't know why. I suppose because they represent all of us, don't they?"

Eden nodded. "Couples are still driven apart by expectation and law around the world. For them, it wasn't a matter of being brave due to the time. I imagine it was a matter of surviving. But I was saying the same to Heidi last night."

India cupped the back of her neck with her right hand. "Is she coming to take photos?"

Eden nodded. "She's taken Maya trampolining this morning, one of her favourite things to do. She's coming later on, after you've chatted to them. We decided they need a little time to be with each other before they get a camera shoved in their face."

"Good point." India wasn't sure she'd ever be comfortable having a camera shoved in her face, let alone when she hadn't seen her long-lost love for 60 years. She imagined she'd just want to stare at her beloved's face. At every line, every wrinkle. To understand what each one meant. A shiver went down India's spine. Even thinking about it was a little much.

"What about your friend, Lib? Gina's coming down in a bit to meet her, too."

Eden nodded. "She's coming with Heidi. I told them both 2pm so Heidi has a chance to get her stuff ready, and Lib and Gina can have a coffee."

"I should have trusted you to have everything worked out. Organisation is your middle name."

Out of the corner of India's eye, a flash of blond hair shot across the lobby, and a figure turned a corner. India frowned. That kinda looked like Andi. She stared harder, but the woman had vanished. India shook her head. It probably wasn't Andi.

Andi had sent her a message last night again, saying she wanted to talk. She really needed to stop doing that, but India didn't want to engage with her. She hoped if she ignored her, Andi would go away. London was a big place. It was large enough for the two of them to cohabit in peace. So long as they both stuck to the same rules.

Eunice was the first into the lobby, looking gorgeous as ever. Tall and still striking, she wore flared white trousers, a blue-and-white top and a white jacket. Her royal-blue-framed glasses sat pristinely on her face, and beads adorned her neck.

She looked like she was trying to make a good impression. Like she might be going on a date. Which, of course, she was. Behind her, carrying her bags and glancing around the space, was her granddaughter, Cordy.

India stepped forward and shook both of their hands. "Lovely to see you again, Eunice, Cordy. How was your trip down?"

Eunice gripped her hand tight, her knuckles white, her skin papery. "Fine. Thank you for the first-class tickets."

India had paid for them herself. "The least we could do."

Eunice scanned the glitzy, golden foyer, before her eyes returned to India. "She's not here yet?"

Eden shook her head. "She's in a cab. Any minute now."

Eunice's face suddenly became stricken. "Do you mind if I check in and freshen up, in that case?"

India shook her head. "Of course. Big day ahead. I'll take you to the reception desk to check-in."

However, just at that second, a woman walked through the door of The Savoy. Somehow, India instinctively knew this was Joan. She had no idea why. Perhaps it was the way she walked with purpose. The way her gaze was scanning the lobby. But it was confirmed when she stopped as she saw India, then her gaze dropped to the back of Eunice.

As if having a sixth sense, Eunice turned around, too.

India heard Eunice gasp, even over the hubbub of the foyer. Then, before probably either Eunice or Joan could process their thoughts, India stood and watched as they walked towards each other, Joan silently mouthing Eunice's name, and they fell into each other's arms.

* * *

The initial meeting hadn't gone according to plan. First, India was due to shepherd them both towards a meeting room together, so they could sit down and tell her a little about their story. But having seen their emotional reunion, it was agreed to give Eunice and Joan a couple of hours to get reacquainted.

So it was that India ended up in the American Bar at The Savoy, having a coffee with Eden, her partner Heidi, and Cordy.

"I couldn't think of anyone more appropriate to take pictures of Eunice and Joan today than you, Heidi," India said. "You've done tons of weddings, so I'm guessing you know real love when you see it."

Heidi nodded. "It's all in the eyes, and the body language. Luckily, most of the weddings I do, I believe in. There have been a couple of curveballs lately, though. I did one where the bride left her groom for her bridesmaid moments before she was due to get married. She was literally in her dress and outside the church, and her bridesmaid declared her love."

India's mouth dropped open. "Wow. That's beyond brave. But also, poor guy."

Heidi snorted. "I know. He was shell-shocked. But better to know now rather than later. Like today."

"Do you two believe in one true love?" India asked them.

"I do now I've found it." Eden kissed the top of Heidi's

hand. "But I've no idea what I would think if I was confronted with someone I was once in love with decades later. I can't even comprehend that."

India glanced at Cordy. "Your gran had her reservations, didn't she?"

Cordy nodded. "But she wouldn't have been brave enough to do this without your help and prodding. Her worst nightmare was Joan turning up and rejecting her. The fact she didn't is enough for now. I know she was nervous, but she was trying to cover it up. Whatever happens from here, I know Gran is grateful for the opportunity." Cordy sat back. "Although having witnessed it first-hand, I wasn't expecting the wealth of emotion. It almost knocked me out in the foyer."

"If you're keeping something bottled up for that long, that's what happens," India replied.

Nods all round.

"Talking of that, are you loving anyone at the moment?" Eden asked. "You've said a couple of things today that made me think you might be."

India gave Eden a coy smile. "There might be someone, but it's a little early to start shouting about it." She and Gina hadn't gone totally public to anyone but family and close friends. She wasn't going to share it with the wider world without asking Gina first. Especially when Eden's best friend might be working with her.

"It's not Gina, is it?"

India hoped her makeup this morning was enough to cover the blush that worked its way onto her cheeks. She'd really slathered it on, knowing she was going to be under heavy lighting later. "All will be revealed very soon."

Eden smiled. "I didn't have you down as a woman of mystery, but the plot thickens."

India gave them all a smile. Then she checked her watch. Saved by the bell.

"Talking of plots thickening, it's nearly time to go and collect our lovers from their room for the interview." India glanced at Heidi. "Shall we get the cameras and lighting set up? Then we can get some shots before I interview them. They're going to want to look their best, and I imagine there might be tears to come."

Heidi gave her a firm nod. "Good idea. It's the function room around the corner?"

India nodded. "Right by the loo."

Heidi kissed Eden, then grabbed her stuff and left.

"Shall I go and see if Gran and Joan are ready?" Cordy stood beside India.

India nodded. It made sense. "A familiar face would be great. Do you mind bringing them down here?"

Cordy shook her head. "Consider it done."

India's phone buzzing made her grab it. It was a message from Gina.

'Just finishing up with Lib. We're walking to The Savoy in ten. Also, I might have found my new work colleague. Yay! See you soon, gorgeous. x'

The last word made India's heart swell. Gina thought she was gorgeous? The feeling was mutual.

Eden leaned over just as India was clicking out of her message app. "I'm going to find out who's making you smile like that." She gave her an amused grin.

India couldn't help her own full-beam smile. "Very soon,

believe me," she replied. "Perhaps even in the next hour." Because India didn't think she could stop herself kissing Gina when she got here, just like Heidi had kissed Eden. If that meant Eden saw them, so be it.

Fifteen minutes later and the space had noticeably filled up with Savoy theatre goers having pre-matinee drinks. India scanned the bar for a glimpse of Gina and Lib. She couldn't see them. Eden had gone to the function room to check if Eunice and Joan had arrived yet.

Minutes later, Eden sat down opposite India with a shake of her head. "No sign as yet."

India's phone buzzed again. It was Eunice. "Cordy told me to tell you we'll be down in five minutes. Joan is just fixing her hair."

From doing what? India allowed herself a small grin and put her phone on the table.

But when she glanced up and saw the woman headed towards her, that grin soon turned to a frown.

Andi.

India *had* seen her earlier. Her heart began to pump that bit harder. She straightened her spine.

Gina was due soon.

India had to get rid of Andi, and fast. She couldn't let Andi pollute her present like she had her past.

Andi was dressed head to toe in Gucci and strutting like she meant business. She was carrying a bunch of flowers, and her blond hair fell deliciously around her shoulders. She was striking, India had never doubted that. However, she also lived in her own world, and chose what she wanted to believe.

When she'd dumped India, Andi chose to believe they were at a natural end and she was being kind to sever ties. Now India wasn't dancing to her tune as she once had, Andi was intent on tracking her down. Which is why India was doubly glad she'd met Gina. Somebody real, someone with substance. The only substance Andi knew came in white lines.

However, even Andi walking across a bar meant people already had their phones out and were taking photos. Andi had that affect. India could sit fairly unnoticed. She ran a food company, and her show was on BBC2. She wasn't a household name. Andi had been on TV and radio for years. Andi most definitely was.

India got up out of her seat just as Andi arrived at her side. The floral scent of Bright Crystal perfume hit her nose.

Andi offered India the bouquet of roses. *Red roses.* Why hadn't India realised they were red roses earlier?

"These are for you. I decided to come the direct route, because you're not answering my texts."

Cold, icy dread slipped down India from head to toe. What the fuck was Andi saying or doing, giving her red roses?

She turned to Eden, whose eyes were wide.

"You'll find out in the next hour," India had said.

Oh god.

Eden would think she'd been talking about Andi. That she and Andi were back on. Which is what everyone in this room who'd ever read any gossip page would think, too.

That was a whole lot of people.

India began to shake her head as Andi thrust the roses into her hand. She wanted to throw them to the floor and scream at Andi, ask her what she was doing. But when she went to do just that, to say just that, nothing happened. She froze. All the while, India's heart slowed almost to a stop.

She had to get rid of Andi. To regain the power of speech.

She cleared her throat and gathered her strength.

"What the hell are you doing here? And why are you giving me red roses?"

Andi looked at her like she couldn't quite understand anything India said. "I'm giving you these to say sorry for everything, India. I treated you badly. I hurt you. I get that. But if you'll let me, I want to make it all up to you. I could tell how hurt you still were when we met in the Sea Containers restaurant in February. I'm a little slow on the uptake, and I apologise. But I'm here now." She grabbed India's free hand, the one not holding the flowers.

India's eyes widened.

Andi continued. "I'm finally on the same page as you, and it's about time. We're destined to be together. You know that. I know that. What do you say?"

The room began to pulse in India's ears. Around her, phone cameras snapped. A low hum of anticipation filled the air. Meanwhile, a slow roll of fear unfurled in her stomach, spiking every nerve ending she possessed.

Andi thought they were destined? She was about nine months too late.

However, India's fear exploded into technicolour when Andi dropped her hand, produced a ring box and sank to one knee.

India could hardly breathe.

What the hell was happening?

How in the hell was this happening?

"India Contelli, I've been a fool."

Andi could say that again. This was insane. But it was insanity that India could not take her eyes off. Just like everyone else in the bar.

Someone let out a low whistle.

India's brain thumped in her skull.

"But I don't want to be a fool anymore." Andi stuck the ring under India's horrified gaze. It sparkled under the bar lights just as India knew it would. "I want to make it all up to you. Put everything right. India, will you marry me?"

India was caught in Andi's manic stare.

She opened her mouth to say something, but nothing came out. Her heart was beating so fast, she thought she might collapse.

But it was nothing compared to what it did when she looked up and saw Gina standing mere feet away, staring at her open-mouthed as, all around, strangers began to applaud.

The last thing India saw as Andi stood up and embraced her was Gina turning on her heel and running out of the bar.

Chapter Twenty-Nine

Gina had always liked The Savoy, but she already knew she'd never be able to come back to the famous London hotel again. It would always remind her of the time when India said yes to marrying Andi Patten.

Had she said yes? Gina hadn't actually heard the words fall from India's lips, but why would Andi be on one knee if India hadn't encouraged it? Andi wouldn't just turn up out of the blue with a ring.

Gina's brain flared red hot. She still couldn't quite compute what she'd just seen. How could she have got it so very wrong? Maybe her mum had been right when she'd told Gina "that sort of love never sticks." Maybe she knew something Gina didn't.

She stumbled out of the foyer and ran up through the crowds milling outside to get into the neighbouring Savoy Theatre. She elbowed her way through, wanting to get away from people, especially India. They'd woken up together this morning. Shared incredible sex. India had told her she was in this with her.

How could she have fallen for such a player? How was Gina's radar for such behaviour so off the mark? Sure, she knew it happened, but she'd believed India when she'd told her the messages from Andi were all one-way. But then, there were all the nights she had to spend away for work. Now Gina thought about it, India could easily have been leading a double life. You read about it in the papers all the time, didn't you? But you never thought it would happen to you.

Well, it had happened to her. Just after she'd told her parents she was seeing India. Now, India was choosing a household name over her. Someone famous. Someone more on India's level to enjoy rooftop liaisons with. Gina had been such a fool.

Tears began to form behind her eyes, but Gina blinked them back in. She wasn't going to crumble over a woman she'd known for just a few months.

Only, she had a feeling that when she really stopped to analyse it, she *would* fall apart completely. Because the time she'd known India might not have been long, but the effect she'd had on her was deep. India Contelli had worked her way into Gina's heart and mind.

Yet, all the while, had she been sleeping with someone else? Gina didn't want to believe it. Still didn't truly believe it. But the evidence was staring her in the face.

Gina stumbled into a couple around her age, knocking theatre tickets from the woman's hands. Gina trod on them, not stopping to pick them up.

"Hey!" the man shouted after her.

"Gina!"

Gina ignored the man, turning to see India above the crowds.

Even seeing her face made Gina feel sick. She had nothing to say to her.

At the top of The Savoy's grand drive was the Strand,

stuffed with theatres, pubs and shops, cars and buses rumbling left and right. Gina took a deep breath, her system filling with diesel fumes and the smell of biscuits from a nearby bakery.

Biscuits = India.

Gina glared at the bakery and turned right. Shoppers swarmed towards her, and drinkers spilled out of pubs. Why were there people *everywhere*? Gina didn't dare look back as she dodged down a side road. She slalomed down the concrete path, tall townhouses rising up on either side. At the bottom, the Thames loomed large. She cut left and approached a tall set of concrete steps up to Waterloo Bridge.

Then her name was called again.

Gina turned. India was running down the street, her longer legs gaining with every step. She had her heels in one hand, and was running barefoot.

Gina turned and tripped, falling forward and banging her knees on the concrete steps. She swore as pain seared up through her body. She was glad of it. She wanted physical pain. It was easier to deal with than thinking about the mental pain of losing something she'd been so close to obtaining finally. Something she wasn't even going to name, because what was the point? It wasn't going to be hers now, or possibly ever. Maybe love just wasn't meant for her.

Gina shook her head and balled her heart. From now on, she was going to protect herself better. She began climbing the steps, trying to pick up speed, ignoring the pain in her knee. She was going to keep walking even if her leg was broken. The one thing she didn't want was to be caught by India, only for her to tell Gina more lies.

Gina reached the top of the bridge, just as three red buses

trundled by. She swayed in the sunshine, looking down at her knee. Her trousers were ripped. They were her new ones, too. She'd been trying to impress India. Entice her. So much for that.

"Gina, stop!"

India was nearly at the top. *Fuck*.

Gina began to run, her legs carrying her faster than she ever thought they would. Her arms pumped as cars raced across the bridge in the opposite direction. Wind whistled past Gina's ears, and sunshine dappled her face as the Thames reared up below, Waterloo Bridge stretching out before her. She dodged one tourist in a French football top, then a couple laughing at something the woman said.

Gina looked back to check if India was still following. She was.

When she turned back, she ran straight into two men consulting a huge tourist map. Who the hell still used those in the age of smartphones?

Gina stumbled again, and the men caught her, exclaiming in German as they did.

Gina held up both hands, apologising. But by the time she'd untangled herself from them, she knew India was nearby. She could smell her intoxicating perfume. The one she'd loved waking up to all too briefly.

She turned, her heart vaulting in her chest.

Ba-doom. Ba-doom. Ba-doom.

Gina was almost floored by her own reaction. Could she have loved India?

Oh yes, without a doubt.

Did she already?

Perhaps.

"Are you okay? I saw you trip up the steps."

Gina narrowed her eyes. "I'm fine," she lied.

India blinked, then continued. "I'm so glad you stopped. That really wasn't what it looked like." India's words flew out of her mouth at speed. "Andi just showed up out of the blue, I had no idea she was coming."

Gina was already shaking her head. First Bernie had betrayed her with Sara. Now India had done the same with Andi. "Why would someone just turn up and propose out of the blue, India? Listen to yourself. It makes absolutely no sense at all."

"I know it doesn't, and I know what this looks like, but you have to believe me!"

Gina held up a finger, shaking her head. She desperately wanted it to make sense. She'd been slicing and dicing it in her head to try to make it work out. But whichever way she looked at it, it wasn't good.

"You know what, I don't have to believe anything that comes out of your mouth ever again. Andi has been a constant feature during the time we've been together, and I swallowed everything you told me about her. But I don't want to hear anything else. Even if half of what you say is true, she clearly had enough signals from you to propose." Gina gave a resigned shrug. "So please, go back to your privileged, famous life. With your famous girlfriend. Leave me to live the life I want to lead, which involves none of that."

Then she turned and took off over the bridge.

"Gina!" India called one more time.

But Gina wasn't caving.

She didn't look back.

Chapter Thirty

India stared after Gina, having no idea what to do next. Fuck her life. How could this have happened? How could Gina think she'd marry Andi, after everything they'd shared? She couldn't comprehend it. Andi had wrecked her life. Again.

Seeing it from Gina's point of view, it hadn't looked good. India should have said something, done something to stop Andi, but it had been like it was happening to someone else. It hadn't been her life. Until reality had come sharply into view when Gina appeared.

India straightened up. There was no point running after Gina now. Plus, her feet were smarting. She looked down. There was blood on the underside of one foot, she could see the traces on the edge. Now she'd stopped running and was allowing her senses to reset, the pin-pricks of pain began to dance on her foot. She started to walk, hobbling slightly.

Thank goodness nobody was taking notice of her on Waterloo Bridge today. If they did, they'd be able to see her bloodied feet, her wild eyes. But they couldn't see her broken heart.

India dropped her head just in case and walked back the way she'd come, pushing any thoughts from her mind. Her body was like lead, but she had to carry on. She had an interview to do. Eunice and Joan were probably in the function room now, wondering where she was. Hopefully Eden and Heidi were managing the situation. Goodness knows what Eden made of what she'd just seen. It was hard enough for India to fathom.

She glanced up as some whooping tourists walked by. To her right, the majestic Somerset House rose up on the side of the Thames, its regal white walls gorgeous in the early summer sun. India took a deep breath. Bright white wasn't a colour she was feeling right now. She glanced down at the dirty pavement underfoot, the fag butts and paving slabs. That was more an accurate colour representation of her mood. Grey and fractured.

She got to the top of the concrete steps and began to climb down gingerly, her right foot smarting now. She was going to need a first aid kit when she got back to the hotel.

"India!"

She looked up.

Andi.

For fuck's sake, this was the last thing she needed. At least she was flowerless and alone. But India had no doubt there were a thousand photos and videos of what had gone on in the cocktail bar being uploaded to social media and beyond. It was how the world worked now. Particularly because she was a semi-celebrity. Just the kind of person Gina hadn't wanted to get involved with.

Gina. Just the thought of her was enough to make India stop and clutch the concrete rail running down the steps. Her chest heaved as she tried to catch her breath. It was no use. It was like someone had put a bullet clean through it.

She'd fallen for Gina, hadn't she? Up until now, she'd kept herself busy running around with work and Pride and her new flat, and she hadn't stopped to truly think. Neither of them had. But she'd fallen for Gina. And now she'd blown it, big style.

Or rather, Andi had blown it for her.

She got to the bottom of the stairs, where Andi was waiting for her. At least she wasn't wearing her smug smile anymore. That was something India had achieved.

"Why did you run off? I thought you were happy I arrived."

She was so clueless, it was almost not worth explaining anything to her. Was she a sociopath? A narcissist? All of the above?

"Fuck off, Andi. We're over. You got engaged to someone else!" India couldn't quite believe she was having to explain things to her, but she was.

"That was a mistake. It's you I love."

India shook her head. "I have to get back to the hotel, I have a job to do. But let's be in no doubt about this." She pressed her index finger to Andi's chest. "The only person you truly love is you."

Chapter Thirty-One

Gina made it to the other side of the bridge and walked along the Thames Path on autopilot. She ended up at her office half an hour later. Her knees were still smarting, along with her pride, and she was hoping to clean herself up.

Gina glanced up. The office window was open. She was sure she'd closed it when she'd left on Friday night. She got her keys from her bag and walked up the stairs, her body heavy with sadness. She still couldn't quite believe her new dreams had just disappeared. No more rooftops with India. No hot tub sex at India's new flat. Gina was going to give rooftops a miss from now on.

When she got to her office door, however, it was ajar.

Gina's stomach lurched. What now? How much more could she take today? Had they been burgled? She reached into her bag and pulled out her bunch of keys to use as a weapon. Her heart began to thump loudly in her chest. She clutched the keys and held them out in front of her, then kicked the door with her right foot. It swung open as she pounced forward.

There was someone in there. She raised her keys and heard a growl come out of her mouth, just as the figure turned around.

It was Sara.

Gina's mind flickered with the thought that maybe she should carry through with the keys. She didn't. When she looked left, Bernie was in the corner with a box of stuff. Perhaps she *was* being burgled. But she was well acquainted with the burglar, and Gina had caught them in the act.

Gina dropped her keys on her desk, along with her bag. Then she turned to Bernie. "What's going on?"

Bernie shrugged. "What does it look like?"

"It looks like you're robbing the office."

Bernie laughed. "Take a closer look. We're getting what's rightfully ours."

"You're selling. Or at least, that's what you told me."

Bernie put a hand on her hip. "After you got your heavies to lean on me."

Gina wasn't in the mood today. "I was just doing exactly what you would have done in my shoes. You should be proud of me." She shook her head. "I don't have time for this today. Give me the keys and get out." She'd thought that perhaps, in time, she and Bernie could become friends again. Now, she didn't give a single shit about that. "And put down that fucking print!"

Gina marched over and ripped the print that Bernie had taken from the wall out of her hand. "We bought that together for the office, and it's staying in the office!" Yes, her voice was elevated. Gina didn't care.

Bernie stepped back, giving her a startled look. "Who rattled your cage?"

"You," Gina replied, "her," she said, pointing at Sara. "The world! Now take Connie, your pens, your pads and get out. I've had enough of being polite. Don't fuck with me today."

Bernie put her hands up, then walked backwards around Gina, picking up her beloved cheese plant with two hands.

"What about all the other stuff?" Sara asked her.

Bernie shook her head. "Leave it. Let's go."

Gina didn't say another word as they left. She simply closed the door, then walked around her desk and sat in her chair. Her mind was spinning so much, it felt like it was making a noise. What was she going to do now?

She turned on her computer and an email came up about India's house sale. She wouldn't normally be so heavily involved. She'd made an exception. She should have known better. She clicked off it, then clicked over to the flat still for rent, where they'd first met up with Eunice. She hoped Eunice and Joan fared better than she and India had. The photo of the rooftop, the flat's main selling point, filled the screen.

Gina pressed her head back to her chair and spun around and around, just like Bernie used to do all the time. It was kinda therapeutic. She could see the appeal.

She glanced back at her screen. Back to the rooftop. Where she and India had first had a proper chat. Their first deep laughs. Their first sex. *Their* rooftop.

It was going to be someone else's rooftop soon as Gina had three viewings next week.

It was probably for the best, seeing as there was no 'them' anymore. India had betrayed her. She still couldn't quite get over it.

Her phone buzzed. She picked it up. A message from India. She put it down. Didn't even read it.

She pressed Neeta's number. It went to voicemail. Of course it did. She scrolled through all her old friends who she wasn't really in touch with anymore. Who would she talk to about this? It was Neeta, Bernie or India. All three ruled out in one go. She was alone. Very alone.

Her phone began to ring and Gina raised her head. It was from an unknown number.

She ground her teeth together. Should she answer it? Would it be India trying to get to her using someone else's phone? Maybe.

She answered it anyway. She wasn't sure what that said.

"Hello?" Gina's voice was weary.

"Gina? It's Frankie."

Frankie? Gina used to have her number after they did business together. Maybe Frankie had got a new one. "Let me guess, India asked you to ring me."

"No, she doesn't know I'm doing this. If I know India, she's probably interviewing Eunice and Joan right now, because she's a professional. Even though her life's just blown up."

Gina frowned. "If you haven't spoken to India, how do you know?"

"It's all over social media. Andi proposing. India looking shellshocked. I just spoke to Eden, who told me what happened and how you saw it all and assumed the worst."

"I don't think there's a lot to assume. It was all there laid out in front of my eyes." Gina pinched the bridge of her nose with her thumb and forefinger. She was getting another headache. She wasn't surprised.

"I understand what you're saying, but think about India and what's been happening between you over the past few months."

"She's been leading a double life?" But even as she said

it, there was a hint of doubt in her voice. Gina didn't want to believe it. But when something was so clear, it was generally wise to believe what you saw.

"She hasn't been leading a double life. Andi is deluded. She believes what she wants to believe. Today, she believed she could get India back, so she strolled into that hotel with one intention."

Frankie paused. "The reason I'm calling is because I feel responsible. Someone from my team told her India was going to be there today. She used her fame to tease the information from this person, saying she was interested on a professional level. She wasn't. She just wanted to get India back. But the fact is, India doesn't want Andi back. Andi might be famous, but she's a nightmare. Plus, there's also the fact India's pretty smitten with you."

Those words lodged in Gina's heart. "She told you that?" She really wanted to believe it. Could what Frankie was saying be true?

"She doesn't need to. I know her. She likes you, Gina. Don't let Andi's antics ruin things. What does your gut tell you?"

Gina paused. "I don't know. It's been churning too much ever since all this happened."

"Instinct, then?"

"That India's a genuine person." It was out before she had a chance to think about it. It was what she thought. She didn't think India was a villain, but there were too many puzzle pieces that didn't fit.

"That's the truth. India's only fault was letting Andi into her life. But hopefully, you can see past that. I hope you can. Because India's worth it."

Gina chewed on her bottom lip. "There's really nothing going on with her and Andi?"

"I think you know the answer to that already," Frankie said. "If India calls, which she will, talk to her, okay?"

Chapter Thirty-Two

When India hobbled into the hotel ten minutes later, Eden and Heidi were doing a terrific job of smoothing over the day with Eunice and Joan, making them comfortable in the room and getting their photos done before India interviewed them. Eden relayed this to India outside the function room, and India almost fell into her arms with gratitude. Eden had always been brilliant, but this was going above and beyond her job description.

"How are they?" India peered over Eden's shoulder through the slight crack in the door where it wasn't quite closed. When she caught sight of the couple, she pressed her back against the outer wall of the corridor. "I don't want them to see me, I need to go to the loo and sort myself out. I probably look a right state."

Eden shook her head. "You actually look fine, which is more than you feel, I imagine." She furrowed her brow. "I take it, from the way you took off after Gina, that you weren't expecting Andi to turn up today and propose?"

India spluttered. No, that was just about the last thing she'd imagined. "It's a very long story, mainly composed in Andi's head, but no, I was not expecting that. *At all*. Andi and I split up months ago. She decided to make a grand gesture.

Not brilliant timing when I've just started seeing Gina. Suffice to say, Gina did not take it well."

Eden winced. "I can imagine." She paused. "Did you catch up with her?"

India nodded. "But she didn't want to hear what I had to say, and who could blame her?" She glanced down at her feet. They were still bleeding and smarting. "Let me go sort out my feet and my face, then I'll be with you." India had some flats in her bag. Hopefully the hotel had some plasters.

Her bag. *Oh fuck.*

Doom rattled through India like a freight train. "Did you pick up my bag?" Sweat broke out all over her body. If someone had her laptop, phone and wallet, so much damage could be done.

This was all Andi's fault. She was going to strangle her with her bare hands next time she saw her.

Eden put a hand on her arm. "I have it. When you took off, I gathered up all your stuff and put it in the room."

"Oh, thank fuck." This time, India did hug Eden, professional protocols be damned. Eden had saved her bacon.

Eden hugged her back, as if she could sense that India needed support.

It was only when they broke apart that a blush worked its way onto India's cheeks. "Sorry, that was spontaneous. But after the day I've had so far, losing my bag would have been the last straw."

Eden shook her head. "Go and sort yourself out. We'll carry on with some set-up shots and fade-outs for the filming, so take your time. Have a coffee if you need to." She checked her watch. "You've got half an hour."

Relief flooded India. "Thanks. You're a lifesaver."

* * *

India decided to walk home after the interview, her spirits still slumped. Gina wasn't picking up her calls and she hadn't replied to any of her messages, even though some of them had the tell-tale two blue ticks. She ground her teeth together and fought the urge to throw herself on the floor and wail. She'd already received enough unwanted attention today thanks to Andi. She didn't need any more to get out into the world.

She crossed Waterloo Bridge, concentrating hard on not replaying the scene with Gina from earlier, then dragged herself down the main road towards her Southwark flat. She wouldn't be there much longer, thanks to Gina and her flat-finding skills. Gina had so many skills India wanted to hold on to.

Her phone buzzed when she was five minutes from home. She stopped walking and stared at the screen, willing it to be Gina. But also terrified it was going to be Andi.

It was neither.

It was her brother, Luca.

India blew out a breath and steadied her nerve. "Hey." She wasn't able to muster up much enthusiasm in her voice.

"You sound exactly as I expected you to sound," Luca replied. "What the fuck is this shit I'm seeing on social media? Why is Andi down on one knee proposing to you?"

India's heart dropped so low, it almost touched the floor. "Because Andi is a sociopath who wants what she wants."

Luca clicked his tongue. "I don't get it, though. What happened? You're not still seeing her, are you? I know she was in the cafe that day we got our baby news, but last time we spoke, you were giddy about your estate agent."

India shook her head. What hope was there for anybody else when the person who knew her best, her brother, wasn't quite sure what to believe? India kicked the pavement in frustration.

"Of course I haven't. I've been busy starting something with Gina, as you know. Although seeing as she walked into the bar today just as Andi was on one knee, who knows where that's at right now. She's not answering my calls and she didn't believe me when I told her there was nothing going on. Not that I can blame her. Why would she?"

Luca paused. "Fuck."

"You can say that again," India said. "Nothing's been going on with Andi. We're through. She got engaged to someone else. But now they've broken up, Andi decided she wants me back. What better way to tell me than to propose in public?"

"She always was a little out there."

India punched in the code for her building on the keypad, then shouldered the door as she snorted into the phone. "Yeah well, now we're both a lot out there and everybody will think we're back on. Including Gina. It's a fucking mess, and I don't know what to do about it."

"What did you do at the time? And why did you let Andi hug you afterwards? It looks like you said yes."

India took the stairs to her flat two at a time. "It all seemed to happen so quickly. One minute Andi appeared and the next she was down on one knee, proposing. I was gobsmacked. I tried to tell her no, but I was frozen to the spot. I couldn't get any words out. I was too busy trying to think of a way to explain this to Gina. Andi took my silence as a yes – because nobody ever tells her no. She hugged *me*. As soon as I could shake her off, I did. Then I ran after Gina and tried to tell her what had happened. You can guess how that went."

"Not well."

India unlocked her flat and dumped her bag in the hallway, then walked through to the lounge and slumped on the sofa, putting her palm to her forehead. "No."

"What are you going to do now?"

She sighed. "I don't know. Gina doesn't want to speak to me. I guess my Sunday night might involve a pity pizza, a bottle of wine and a film that will make me cry. If I'm miserable, I might as well go the whole hog."

Luca snorted down the phone. "You will not. You like Gina. Last time we spoke, you were lit up about her. You're not walking away from this, India."

"I'm not! But I can't walk away from something that doesn't exist anymore."

"You're being ridiculous. Gina needs time to calm down. However, she also needs to know that you care."

"She doesn't want to know, though." India pouted as she spoke.

"So you make her. Do you think she's thinking about anything else tonight?"

India shook her head. "If she's anything like me, she's not."

"What's the point of both of you spending the evening miserable, when you could take action. Go over to hers and tell her that you love her."

India's body went rigid at his words. "Love? She just

watched someone else propose to me. You think that might be too much for one day?"

Luca snorted. "On the contrary, it's *because* someone else proposed to you today that you need to make a grand gesture to her. Otherwise, she'll just be replaying the proposal over and over. You need to change up her mental images, and one way to do that is to give her something else to think about. Go over there and tell her how you feel. It's called communicating. You're good at it."

India sat forward, then clutched her chin with her free hand. Was Luca right? Should she press the issue tonight and let Gina know how she felt? The more she thought about it, the more she realised it was a bold move, but it could work.

"You do love her, right?"

India hesitated for a second before replying. "I do." There. She'd said it. She loved Gina.

Suddenly, a light turned on inside her. Luca was right. She *had* to talk to Gina.

"What if she won't talk to me, though?"

"What if she does? You won't know until you try. Wouldn't it be better to know where you stand and not leave things to fester? Take it from me, as one who knows, it's better to face issues head on than ignore them."

India pursed her lips. "Does Ricardo know you give out such wise relationship advice over the phone?"

Her brother laughed again. "I learnt it all from him," he replied. "Ricardo has made me a better human. I think Gina might do the same for you. You don't want to pass up that opportunity, do you?"

India smiled. "When you put it like that."

Chapter Thirty-Three

"Where the hell have you been?" Gina stood at the door of Neeta's apartment, even though the answer to her question was staring her in the face. Neeta was dressed in her work gear. "My life has been imploding and you've been at work!"

Gina brushed past her sister and stomped through to the lounge. On the sofa was Neil. Gina stopped. She couldn't recall the last time she'd seen him. It had to be at least a month ago.

Gina took a breath, then another deeper one. "Hi, Neil." She kept her voice as steady as she could. She'd been about to berate her sister for no reason other than she needed to vent at someone. Neil had tempered her mood.

"Hey, favourite sister-in-law!" Neil got up and gave her a hug. He was very much a hugger. He was also exceedingly tall, so when he did so, his limbs seemed to ensnare you in a trap.

Today, Gina needed it. She hugged him tight right back.

When Neil let her go, he stepped back, eyeing her suspiciously. "Everything okay?"

"Gina's life is apparently imploding so I would say everything is definitely not okay, am I right?" Neeta raised an eyebrow Gina's way.

Neil took that as his cue. "Right. I wanted to go for a run

anyhow." He brushed Gina's arm on the way out. "I hope things aren't as bad as your face says they are."

Gina sighed and waited for the front door to click shut. Then she sat on the spot where Neil had been, and put her head in her hands.

"What's happened?" Neeta sat beside her sister. "You left an agonised message on my phone. Now you're rocking on my sofa. *You*. *Gina*. She who does not get involved with people. Who's never been in love." Neeta paused. "Ooooh, fuuuuuuck! I get it now! That's why you're swearing, stomping and generally acting like a maniac. You've fallen for India! I mean, I assumed you had, but this confirms it."

Gina brought her head back up. It was what she'd thought on the bridge. That she *could* fall for her. But had she already? Perhaps. It would make sense. The way her stomach was curling up inside. The way her brain was on fire. The way she couldn't process a single thought without an image of India, her feet bleeding, pleading with her on the bridge. She shook her head.

Gina loved India.

This was what love felt like.

If this was love, then fuck it all to hell.

"Although I have to say, I am enjoying this new Gina a bit. I mean, I'm sorry for whatever's happened, but you're *alive*. I'm half expecting you to pick up our TV and lob it out the window." Neeta gave her a look. "Don't though. I'd be sad. I love that telly."

Neeta sat next to her and put an arm around her. "Go on then, tell me what happened."

Gina did.

By the end, Neeta's mouth was hanging open.

"Wow, that is some afternoon. Andi Patten proposed to your girlfriend in public?" Neeta grabbed her phone and checked Twitter. She winced. "It's trending, so I think maybe you shouldn't check your social media today, no matter how tempting."

Gina shrugged. "It was bad enough seeing it live. I have no desire to see it again." Gina wriggled free of her sister's grasp and leaned back on the sofa. "But it's not that easy, is it? I introduced her to you. To Mum and Dad. To my life." She shook her head. Perhaps she and love just weren't compatible. "I opened myself up to her. Now what?"

Neeta gave Gina a sad smile and put a hand on her knee. "Now, you have to talk to her to see *her* side of the story."

"I already know it."

"Do you? She said it was nothing."

"Andi Patten is a national treasure and India's ex."

"She seemed pretty into you when she was here. You've slept together, and that's not something people do lightly. People I know at least." Neeta paused. "Do you think she did it lightly?"

Gina wanted to believe India hadn't done it lightly. But right now, she had no idea.

Neeta's door buzzer interrupted their chat. She jumped up and went into the hallway to answer.

She was back in seconds. "That was India. She's outside. I told her to give you five minutes to get upstairs, then to buzz your door."

Gina's heart wheezed in her chest. She couldn't see India now! "What did you do that for?"

"Because you need to sort this out. You're in love with this woman. She's come over here, so she must think something of you, too. You're not giving up at the first hurdle. Love isn't like that. It's messy and it hurts. But it can also bring the best kind of pleasure." She grabbed Gina by the shoulders and marched her down her hallway before opening the front door. "Put one foot in front of the other, go back to your flat and speak to India."

Chapter Thirty-Four

India was thinking about Eunice and Joan as Gina's lift whisked her up to floor 17. When they were done with filming, she'd told them to get whatever they wanted from the hotel restaurant and bar, that she'd pick up the tab. She hoped they were making up for lost time right now, living it up. Being in the same space as them had felt like she was intruding. Disturbing their delicately poised universe. The force between them was bigger than anyone else in the room, and it was magical to experience. India was thrilled she'd played a part in bringing them back together and she'd told them so. They'd both blushed. She hoped with all her heart they were still smiling for years to come.

More than that, hearing Eunice and Joan's story had given her hope for this moment. After all, Joan had forgiven Eunice for leaving her 60 years ago.

"There's nothing to forgive," Joan had said, her eyes never leaving Eunice.

India wasn't expecting Gina's forgiveness right away, but she hoped she could convince her she wasn't a player. That what they had was real. Because it *was* real. India could feel it in every breath she took along the corridor to Gina's flat.

She knocked on the door, but it was already opening.

Gina was on the other side, her face spelling caution.

"Thanks for letting me up."

"Neeta told me I didn't have a choice."

"Remind me to ship more biscuits to Neeta." India paused, stuffing a hand in the pocket of her jeans. "I thought about trying to shimmy up your drainpipes in a bid to be romantic. But then I remembered you lived on the 17th floor, and I figured maybe it would be more foolhardy than romantic."

"Woman dies in a bid to show romance. A proper Shakespearian plot. No matter what I think of you, I don't want you to die."

"A good start." India shifted her weight from one foot to the other. "Can I come in?"

Gina stood back, her face stoic.

India walked past her, careful not to touch her on the way. She didn't want to put a foot wrong now she was in the door.

Everything that had gone before had been erased. Now, India had to show Gina just what she meant to her from scratch. Plus, she had to airbrush Andi out of the picture. She flexed her pitching muscles. India had given the closing speech in countless business meetings throughout her career. She was good at public speaking. Pressure situations were nothing new. However, none had ever had pressure like this. None had ever been this important.

This was her heart on the line.

More than that, her life.

She walked to the window, stepping carefully to ensure nothing was a surprise. She'd already had more than enough of those today.

But Gina didn't sit for India's performance. Instead, she stood at the kitchen counter, her arms folded. "You're not saying much for someone who's come all the way here to talk to me."

India stared out at the Canary Wharf waterway, before turning and facing the prettiest vista of all. Gina.

"You're right, I'm not. Probably because this is the biggest speech of my life to date." India ran both hands up and down her sides, then began to talk. "I was going to rehearse this, but I didn't have time. Today's been a busy day."

"I know." Gina's stare was detached, cold.

"All I can say about what happened earlier is that I'm sorry." India held up a hand. "And before you say anything, I know what it looks like. Andi is my ex. She's been messaging me and turning up to see me. Then she arrives and asks me to marry her." India stepped towards Gina. "But I did *nothing* to encourage that. Nothing at all. All I've told her is to go away, that we're over. She's a bit deluded, and I'm sorry you got caught up in it. But it was a show for Andi, and she thrives on the attention. She wants what she can't have. If I said I'd marry her, she'd disappear pretty sharpish."

India took another step towards Gina.

Gina didn't back away.

She took a deep breath and continued. "But the other key takeaway is that I don't want to marry her. She's in the past, a mistake. Plus, over the past few months, I've met someone new. Someone unexpected. But someone who's changed my life for the better, and someone I've fallen for completely."

Three more steps, and India stood in front of Gina.

Gina's stare softened, but her face was still unsure. "Are

you positive nothing's going on? People generally don't ask people to marry them without some prior consultation." There was a wobble in Gina's voice.

India hated that she was responsible. She took a chance. She took Gina's hands in hers and kissed them, one at a time.

Gina's shiver was so strong, it resonated through India.

India allowed a ray of optimism to break through her clouds. Maybe this speech was working better than she ever thought possible.

"Normal people don't propose when there's nothing going on. I agree. Andi's not normal. I'm not going to tell you she'll never bother me again, because I can't be sure of that. Our paths might cross. But me and her are done. We were done a long time ago."

India raised one of Gina's hands to her lips once more. "If you're willing to take a chance on me, I'm not playing games." She looked into Gina's eyes. She hoped she was communicating all that she needed to. Because when India was this close to Gina, it was impossible not to want the world.

For India, the world started with Gina.

"What do you say? Can we start again?"

India pressed pause on her life while she waited for an answer.

Gina took a deep breath and gave India a fixed stare that told her nothing. Then she took India's hand and pulled her towards the front door.

"Where are we going?" India frowned as Gina swung it open.

Gina turned, giving India a look that almost made her stop breathing.

India shut up.

"I've got a surprise for you. It somehow seems right. If we're going to try again, you might like it."

Gina was on board and willing to give her a second chance? India's heart burst, but she kept quiet. She didn't want to fuck this up. Today had already done a number on her.

They got in the lift and Gina pressed the button marked RT. She didn't look at India, but she didn't need to. Tension licked up the sides of the enclosed space. When the lift announced it was at Rooftop Level, India caved, a smile creeping onto her face. "You have a rooftop?"

Gina finally looked at her. "It's shared, and it's normally so windy you might take off, but I was going to show you. Tonight, it seems more than appropriate."

Gina was showing off her rooftop. This was significant. India was going with it.

She was also not wrong — it was windy. However, they were the only ones up there, and the sun was still to set. Looking out over the rooftops of Canary Wharf was far different to town: this was a more high-level view. The whole of London was laid out before them. But the only piece of London India was currently interested in was standing in front of her, giving her a tired, wary look.

She took hold of Gina's hand again. "You still haven't answered my question. Are you giving us another go?"

Gina narrowed her eyes, then gave India a reluctant nod. "I want to. I've been a wreck all day long. So long as you promise me no more Andi."

India shook her head. "We're completely done and have been for months. I know Andi turning up pressed some cheating buttons on your part, after what happened with Bernie and Sara."

Gina nodded. "It really did. I've had my share of people lying to me. Gaslighting me. I don't need that in my life anymore."

"I swear, I'll never do that to you." India pressed her hand to her chest. "I had nothing to do with it. I don't even know how she knew I was there. I didn't tell her. Do you believe me?" India's heart lurched as she waited for the answer.

Gina gave her another nod. "I do. Frankie told me it was one of the Pride committee, and Andi used her fame to wheedle the information out of them." She paused. "But just so we're clear, nobody else that you know of is likely to ask you to marry them in a very public place?"

Now it was India's turn to shake her head. "Nobody. Just one crazed ex. All the others are amateurs compared to her."

Gina's scorched gaze caught hers. "Good. There's only so much humiliation a girl can take."

"I promise, no more public scenes. We can stay in for the rest of our lives if that's what it takes."

They stared at each other for a good few moments, India's breath catching in her chest. They still hadn't kissed. She desperately wanted to. India leaned forward and took a chance, pressing her lips to Gina's. The crackle of electricity that sparked between them made her shudder. She snaked an arm around Gina's waist and pulled her close. When their lips parted, their bodies stayed glued together as the sun beat down on them.

"When you were shouting at me on the bridge earlier, I wasn't sure this would be the outcome tonight."

"Neither was I." Gina pressed her lips back to India's.

India was happy to call it quits and stay there forever. "How come relationships are so hard sometimes? I've never figured it out."

"My sister says you need the hard bits to appreciate the good. Deferred gratification means you appreciate them more." Gina paused. "I told her I was happy with just the good, but apparently that's not how it works."

"Apparently not." India licked her lips, running a finger down Gina's cheek. "But Eunice and Joan showed me today that some things are worth fighting for. I didn't want to wait 60 years, so here we are."

Gina blinked. "How did that go? I never even saw them, what with everything else."

India squeezed her hand. "They're smitten. Almost like they've never been apart. Sometimes, you just know." She could say more, but she was too nervous to chance it. She'd only just got back into Gina's good books. "What changed your mind, after you told me to go back to my famous life, to Andi?"

Gina sighed. "A little bit of time to assess. Plus, I spoke to Frankie, to my sister, and I shouted at Bernie and Sara, too."

"You saw them today as well?"

Gina let out a guttural laugh. "The more the merrier, why not?" She shook her head. "But mostly, it was knowing how I felt when I left you. It's a feeling that's never happened to me before. Something raw." She pressed her palm to India's chest. "I felt like something had fractured inside me." She flicked her gaze to India. "I know that's a big statement, but it's true." Gina dipped her head.

But India tipped it back up with the tip of her index finger, making sure she had Gina's attention. "I don't scare easily. I'm glad you don't either. And if you're worried about telling me you have feelings for me, I have them for you, too. Just so we're clear, I don't make a habit of sleeping with my estate agents."

"Do you have more than one?"

India smiled, shaking her head. "I only need one, she's perfect. I don't sleep with someone unless there's something there." She stared deep into Gina's eyes. "There's been something there since the start with us. The rooftop dates. The hotel kiss. The delicious sex. I'd be an absolute fool to bugger up a connection like we have, which is why I don't intend to. I'm falling for you, Gina. In fact, it's already happened. I don't want to let this go. It feels too important in here." She tapped her chest. "Inside."

Gina's eyes misted over. "I feel it, too."

"I'm glad." Another scorching kiss left India breathless. She eyed Gina again. She had no idea how she'd got so lucky, but she wasn't going to let go. "I do have just one other big question to ask you, one that kept bugging me today after you left."

Gina frowned. "What's that?"

"Are you still coming on the Pride bus with me? Because after the dust on today has settled, I want to show the world who I'm going out with — and it's definitely not Andi Patten."

India steadied herself. She was going to say it, wasn't she? They were on a rooftop, after all. Was there anywhere more perfect?

"I've fallen in love with you, Nagina Gupta. I don't see that changing anytime soon."

Gina's mouth dropped open.

A few seconds ticked past, India's heartbeat marking every one of them.

Then, Gina's face softened. "I've fallen in love with you, too," she replied.

Chapter Thirty-Five

The Saturday morning of London Pride broke with glorious sunshine streaming in through India's new windows. Gina had secured India the keys at the start of Pride month, but now it was June 21st, and she'd moved in three days ago. India had taken her time, having a hot tub installed on her terrace this week, as well as getting decorators in to paint the place so it was box-fresh. Hence, waking up in India's bedroom on Pride morning was like waking up inside a celestial white cloud. When Gina cracked open her eyes, she half-expected some bony finger to reach down and anoint her. Especially after what they'd been up to half the night.

If some higher being was giving out scores for sex, Gina was certain they were in line for an award. Last night's session had been epic.

India was keen to make up for any perceived wrongs she might have done.

Gina was keen for her to be keen.

They were truly a match made in heaven.

India rolled over, then sat up, wincing. "Who turned up the sun so early?" She eyed Gina, then collapsed at her side, kissing her shoulder. "Morning, sexpot."

"Morning to you, too." Gina kissed India's shoulder,

then her lips. Far from being scary, telling India her feelings had actually been freeing. Gina was far more open with her affection now their relationship was on solid ground. She'd even talked about India with her parents again, and invited them on the Pride bus. They'd turned her down, but at least they were talking without too many pauses in the conversation. It was a start.

Her relationship with her parents would be slow to change, but so long as it was in motion, Gina was happy. She had to get out of her own way and be okay with letting them in, too. For now, it was enough. Plus, Gina had enough of her family to contend with today, because Neeta, Neil and Deepak were coming on the bus.

Gina pushed herself onto her elbows, eyeing India who was still half asleep. India had got a haircut yesterday, and was now sporting a pixie style. It suited her. Gina had no doubt any cut would look good on India Contelli. If anything, she looked even more beautiful than before. Gina had a thing for short hair, so when India had appeared last night, she'd been delighted.

"You know, if I were looking at the parade from the outside and seeing the great India Contelli all dolled up with her Pride biscuits, I'd never have guessed you started the day being grumpy and gorgeous in bed."

That drew a smile to India's lips as she opened her eyes. "Is that your new name for me? The Great India Contelli? I could get used to it."

Gina gave her a languid smile, before crawling on top of her. "No, but I have some other names for you."

India quirked the side of her mouth. "Like what?"

Gina squinted into the rays of sunshine hitting the wall through the slats in the wooden blinds. "I dunno." She tilted her head. "Maybe, something like Screamer?"

India opened her mouth in mock shock, then grabbed Gina's sides and pulled her close. "I would try to deny it, but I know it's true. But it's your fault." She glanced over at her phone. "Do we have time for a repeat performance before we head to the parade?"

Gina grinned. "Not if you want Frankie to kill us both with her bare hands; 8am sharp she told you last night."

"Bloody Frankie." India kissed her. "The good thing about going out with you, though, is you're not going anywhere. It can wait. We have a big day to get through."

Gina nodded. A big day. Where some people might still think India was engaged to Andi. The tabloids had died down on the subject, but there was still some interest. India's tactic had been to ignore the story and hope it would go away. It was working.

Plus, Gina hadn't wanted to be the subject of tabloid gossip, so they'd kept things quiet over the couple of weeks since The Savoy incident. However, Gina didn't want any more mishaps. Her parents and friends knew the truth. Now, Gina wanted it to be clear to everyone else, too.

"What's that face for?" India asked.

Gina shook her head. "Nothing. I was just thinking about Andi."

India tensed up. "It's old news, I promise."

Gina sucked on the inside of her cheek. "I just want it to be clear that *we're* together. But I also don't want to make a song and dance about it."

"How about this." India sat up, turning to Gina. "I'll say something to everyone on the bus. Then they'll say something to everyone they know. It means those around us know the truth. Which most of them already do, but there will be some curious people. If today is what's bothering you, I'm happy to tell all of them, okay?"

Relief pulsed through Gina. She blew out a long breath. "I think that's what I need. I don't want people looking at me like I'm a fool."

"Nobody thinks you're a fool. I think you're brilliant and beautiful."

Gina raised an eyebrow, then jumped off the bed and rummaged in her bag.

"What are you doing?"

Gina found what she was looking for. She put the rainbow head-boppers on, then moved her head side to side. The rainbow balls on the end of metal springs wiggled right back. Gina was taken right back to Birmingham, when her life had seemed far less sorted. She crawled back onto the bed and landed on her knees in front of India.

"What do you think? Still brilliant and beautiful?"

India nodded. "You couldn't look more beautiful. Or Pride-ready."

* * *

Pride was two weeks earlier than usual this year due to clashing events in the city, and the weather was shining on it. What's more, the Stable Foods open-top bus was the gayest Gina had ever seen. It was pink, with rainbow garlands all over it, a massive boa on the front, and the Rainbow Rings biscuit logo slapped on both sides. It was also the first bus in the Pride parade, set to lead the convoy of floats, buses and organisations that stretched back as far as Gina's eye could make out behind.

In front of her, Frankie and her team of helpers were busy running around with clipboards and loudspeakers, lanyards wafting in the sunshine. The mayor of London, the aptly named Maxine Love, was chatting with Eunice and Joan. The couple of the moment, who'd truly caught the public's imagination with their love story, were going to be walking the first part of the parade alongside Maxine, with the mayor's bodyguard close by. After that, Eunice and Joan were being put in a love chariot, and were then set to be wheeled the rest of the parade by six butch lesbians in leather. If they were anything other than thrilled at the prospect, they were doing a grand job of hiding it.

Gina was still pinching herself she was here, with a front-row seat to one of the biggest Pride parades in the world. She'd met Eunice and Joan earlier, and her heart had melted. The entire time they were together, they held hands. Sixty years later, their love was still burning strong. It was enough to fuel the hardest of hearts.

As the Pride banners proclaimed, 'It's Never Too Late!' Gina was 41, and she'd only just fallen in love for real. Meeting India was one of the luckiest breaks she'd ever had — professionally and personally. Gina had only been to Birmingham Pride before, and that was with an ex. It had been a disaster. She hoped exes were now in the past, for both her and India. If Andi or Sara tried anything today, she had an army of helpers to make sure they buggered off. Plus, nothing could shake Gina's certainty about India now. Not after the past few weeks they'd shared.

To either side of her, whistles were already being blown even though the parade was yet to start. To Gina, they sounded like a welcoming klaxon for her London Pride experience. Every time she heard one, she couldn't help but smile.

Gina's phone beeped. The message was from her sister, telling her they were walking up Oxford Street and should be with her in five minutes.

A bristle of anticipation fizzed through her.

This was it: Gina's lives merging together. Family, friends, sexuality. She'd always imagined when that happened, she'd be apprehensive. However, all she felt today was love and pride. Especially when she glanced down the road, to the back of the bus, where India was instructing her biscuit crew.

India was so involved in her business, so hands-on with her team. Gina had never expected that, but India was full of surprises. The biggest one of all being that she'd fallen for Gina. It was still something she was getting used to.

Arms encircled her from behind, and she screamed.

"I heard there was an A-star lesbian around these parts. Have you seen her?"

Deepak.

Gina turned and moved her head. One of her head-bopper rainbow balls punched Deepak in the face. "You nearly gave me a heart attack!" Gina said.

In response, Deepak clutched his face. "Nobody told me Pride was this violent!" Then he peeked out from behind his fingers, picked Gina up and whirled her around. Deepak had never learned the art of subtlety. It was another reason Gina loved him.

Gina hugged Neeta and Neil, too, only clocking belatedly

they were all wearing T-shirts with rainbow love hearts on them. Something welled up inside her and she had to tamp down the urge to cry. Maybe she wasn't ready for her worlds to collide if she was going to burst into tears.

"You're wearing rainbows! I love it!" She looked down at her black shirt. "I feel a little lacking, but I do have them on my head." She pointed to her rainbow head-boppers, just in case her family hadn't noticed them.

India walked up behind her and draped a rainbow garland around her neck. "You can never have too many rainbows." She kissed Gina's cheek. Then she shook hands with all Gina's family. Gina took a snapshot of the moment. It was one for the memory bank.

"I love the new hair," Neeta told India.

India gave her a coy smile, then patted her hair to make sure it was still there. "Thanks. I'm still getting used to it, but Gina approves and that's the main thing." India gave Gina a smile that made her heart crumble.

"Glad you could all make it, I hope you're ready to make some noise!" India handed out rainbow garlands, whistles and bags of biscuits to Gina's family. "Gina told you I was making you work today, right? That bus is full of biscuits, so please hand them out to as many people as you can."

Deepak peered inside the bag. "Can we eat some, too?"

"I'd be offended if you didn't." India grinned. "When you need a break, the bus has a loo downstairs, plus a DJ and an open-air bar upstairs, so make use of that, too." She glanced over Gina's shoulder where Frankie beckoned her. "Excuse me a minute." India gave Gina the rest of the biscuit bags and disappeared.

Her family watched her go, then turned to Gina. "An open-top bus with a bar and free biscuits on tap?" Neil snorted. "I'd say you've landed on your feet with that one."

* * *

The noise was insane as the bus crawled along Oxford Street, rainbow flags and glitter everywhere Gina looked. The sky was the brightest blue she'd ever seen, the sun giving off a glamorous, accommodating glow. Gina had spent the first half hour giving out biscuits, but now she was taking time to soak up the atmosphere on the top deck, waving at the crowds. Was this what it was like being famous? Somewhat, perhaps. But nobody was asking Gina for a selfie. She was going to have to get used to sharing India with the public.

A glass of bubbles appeared at her eye level.

Gina accepted it from Deepak, as he swigged his beer and waved to the crowds. Unlike Gina, Deepak was a natural born extrovert.

"Where have your rainbow head-boppers gone?" Deepak pointed to Gina's head.

"The hairband cut into my head after a while." Gina held up her feather boa. "This is easier and doesn't make me bleed."

"A better option," Deepak agreed. He bumped his hip to Gina's. "I could easily get used to this. How do you think your mum would react if we jumped off the bus and got a photo next to one of those blokes wearing nothing but leather straps?" His grin told Gina the answer.

"You're a bad brother, you know that?"

"Your mum would say the same."

Behind them at the bar, the volume increased as the group of women who'd come onboard earlier came back from biscuit duties. Gina recognised some of them from lesbian events she'd been to, and she made a note to introduce herself. You never knew who might want a hot London property. If any one of them did, she was the estate agent to talk to. Had she remembered to pack business cards? She hoped so.

Gina turned her attention back to Deepak. "Did you get the paperwork through for the business?"

He gave her a look. "No business chat today." He waved an arm. "I just want to feel the love all around me."

"Are you coming out to me, Deepak?"

He grinned. "Never say never. Life's for living, Gina!"

She clutched the bus rail. "If you come out, please tell Mum it wasn't my fault."

Deepak laughed. "But it was. I was just an innocent boy from the Midlands before you brought me to the big bad city, put me on a bus and corrupted me." He gestured out to the screaming crowds. "Look at it. It would be easy to be seduced." He bent down and kissed her cheek. "Thanks, by the way. For letting me use your flat, and for this amazing experience, too. I'm glad you're not hiding away anymore."

Gina put an arm around his waist and squeezed. "I am, too."

"Although I hear from Neeta that your lady has a flash pad in the city, so you're not exactly slumming it."

Gina tilted her head back, soaking up the sun. "I'm definitely not slumming it." She squinted at him. "Life is good, uncle." She'd never said a truer sentence in her life. She extended her arms, turned and planted her arse on the bus railing, then leaned back. "I'm out, I'm in love, I'm proud." She raised her voice. "I'm fucking proud!" Gina shouted.

Whoops could be heard from the women on the top deck at her declaration.

Gina gave them a wide grin.

"And I'm a proud uncle," Deepak replied, in a rare serious tone. "I tried to get your mum and dad to come, but a parade was a bit soon for them."

Gina shook her head. "Truth be told, it would have made me nervous. I'm happy how it is. You being here is perfect, same for Neeta and Neil."

"Hey Gina, sorry to interrupt."

"Hey," Gina said to Lib. "Deepak, this is Lib, Eden and Heidi." She turned to them. "This is my Uncle Deepak. He's investing in Hot London Properties." She inclined her head to Lib. "This is Lib, she's going to be working with me."

They all shook hands.

"Just Deepak," he told them. "Less of the uncle."

"Got it," Eden replied. "Have you met the rest of our crew?" She pointed towards the bunch of women in the centre of the top deck who Gina had spotted earlier. Eden beckoned her friends over.

Gina scanned the crowd drifting towards them. "Some. I think I've met that woman before?" She pointed at the tall woman wearing a red-and-white striped top.

Eden beckoned her over. "This is Tanya. Tanya, this is—"

"Gina Gupta, nice to see you again." Tanya shook her hand, a firm grip and a confident smile. "I know we met at a networking event. Just don't ask me to narrow down which one."

"Glad it's not just me," Gina replied. "Lovely to see you again."

"How did you make it onto the bus? We're all mates with Heidi and Eden, so that's how we squeaked on."

"I'm…" She cleared her throat and puffed out her chest. "I'm dating India Contelli."

Gina had never told anyone that before. Her pride level shot up a little more, just as she saw India's newly cropped dark hair emerge at the top of the stairwell, closely followed by her brother, Luca, and his husband Ricardo, who Gina had met earlier. Now, when she looked up, she saw two pairs of the same piercing blue eyes staring back at her.

"Talk of the devil." Gina gave India a wave.

Their eyes met, and the noise dimmed. Then, it was just the two of them.

She was dating India Contelli.

Those words tasted delicious on her tongue.

Her girlfriend sidled up, greeting the guests, introducing her brother and Ricardo, before installing an arm around Gina's shoulders. "Everyone having a good time and rinsing the bar, I hope?"

Nods and smiles from everyone in the group.

"Great." India leaned down to Gina. "You look gorgeous, by the way," she whispered in her ear.

Gina rolled her shoulders and strained her neck, shyness hugging her. Being loved like this was going to take some getting used to, but she was prepared to put in the work.

India accepted a glass of fizz from Eden. "Eden thinks she's still on the clock." India gave her a grin. "I appreciate it."

"You looked thirsty. Plus, it is your bar." Eden paused.

"Also, the LGBT+ business bursary recipients are coming onboard when we finish the parade, just to let you know."

"Okay. I'll save some energy for them, too."

Luca waved at Gina and India to move together, holding up his camera. "We should take a photo of the happy couple, shouldn't we?"

India glanced at Gina, then pulled her closer.

Luca made approving noises, then snapped a few shots.

Gina smiled, but she could feel the weight of everyone's stare on her. They still weren't totally out in the open. She glanced at India, hoping she understood.

India gave Gina a nod, then clapped her hands.

The crowd turned.

India cleared her throat. "I just wanted to say a few words while most of the bus is onboard. I'm going to shout over the music, so bear with me."

As if vying for attention, the DJ chose that moment to drop 'It's Raining Men' and the crowd whooped louder.

"You'd better shout," Gina said.

India gave her a nod and did just that. "Just to say, thank you for coming, thanks for helping spread the Rainbow Rings around. I want you to drink, dance, eat and have a fab time. We've got the bus until 5pm, so fill your boots." She paused. "Also, in case some of you were wondering, I am not engaged to Andi Patten, despite what the tabloids have been speculating." She put an arm around Gina. "Rather, I'm very much in love with the gorgeous Gina Gupta. If you haven't met her, come and say hi!"

The whole top deck broke into applause as India kissed Gina, this time, long and slow. If Gina had any doubts about

India and Andi, they were washed away in that moment. India loved her. She'd sprinted away from Andi. Now, India Contelli was kissing her in front of everyone.

When the Pride crowds saw it, they cheered, too.

Eventually, they broke apart, India shaking her head, a smile on her face. "I love you," she repeated.

"I love you, too," Gina replied.

Because she did.

They were the truest three words she'd ever spoken.

The moment was broken as the DJ started to play Diana Ross's 'I'm Coming Out', and the air around them seemed to gather speed as if they were in a movie.

It kinda felt like they were.

India and Gina leaned over the front of the top deck with Gina's family and India's friends, and Gina wasn't sure she'd ever had such a perfect moment.

She was loved.

There was sunshine.

She wanted to bottle today and live it forever more.

In front of them, the leather-clad lesbians were doing a dance routine in front of Eunice and Joan, and the crowd were lapping it up. The couple waved from the love chariot, like they'd done this their whole lives. They were finally the leading ladies in the movie of their own lives.

"Do you think Eunice and Joan were ever entertained like that when they were courting in the fifties?" Tanya asked next to India.

"I'll ask them later," India replied. "I hope they're enjoying it. I promised they could come on the bus afterwards. They seem to be coping with the spotlight pretty well."

"Amazingly well," the woman next to Tanya replied. She leaned over and offered a hand. "I'm Sophie, Tanya's girlfriend."

Gina and India shook her hand, and they all turned around. Sophie introduced Gina to Jess and Lucy, Kate and Meg, and Rachel and Alice.

"I'll never remember all of your names, so excuse me if I forget you."

"You're fine," Lucy told her. She had a haircut similar to India's, and it looked just as good on her. "Also, thank you for stepping in on the Birmingham trip to meet Eunice and Joan. I know India was grateful to have company." She gave India a look. "Now I know just *how* grateful."

India laughed, but also blushed. "It might have been the start of something, so sorry you weren't there. But also, not sorry."

Lucy laughed. "Glad to be of service."

"Where's Cleo and Becca?" Jess asked Rachel. "Becca is Rachel's sister, and Cleo is her partner," she added to Gina by way of explanation.

Rachel shrugged. "On holiday or in Boston. I lose track. They were back here for a bit. Heidi might know, she speaks to Cleo more than my little sister speaks to me." Rachel cupped her mouth. "Heidi!" she shouted.

Heidi turned at the bar.

"Where's Becca and Cleo?"

"Boston!" came the reply.

"Cleo works there," Rachel told Gina. "Not that this is very interesting to you, seeing as you don't know them. But you will. Now you know us, there's no getting away from us."

She indicated the group of women on the top deck surrounding Gina with beaming smiles.

"That's fabulous. I could do with some new faces in my life."

Rachel grabbed Gina's arm. "You should come to my restaurant in Woolwich. I opened last year. It's doing okay."

"It's doing more than okay," Alice intervened. "Rachel's too modest."

Rachel rolled her eyes. "India's been before."

India nodded. "Rachel is a fantastic chef and her restaurant is brilliant. In fact, I wanted to speak to you about catering my house-warming next month. I have a rooftop now. I want to use it. Can we chat another time soon?"

Rachel nodded. "I'd love to."

Heidi returned with two bottles of champagne, to great cheers from everyone.

"Spot the woman who's farmed her child out for the weekend!" Eden said, laughing.

"Too right," Heidi replied, waving the booze in the air. "Who needs a top-up?"

Every hand on the top deck went up.

Gina laughed. London laughed with her.

India caught her eye.

Today was a good day.

Chapter Thirty-Six

"What's this?" India sat on her terrace, holding up a present Gina had just given to her. It was long and cylindrical. "If this is a weird sex toy, I think we should have talked about it first."

Gina grinned. "Does it look like a sex toy? It's the length of my torso."

"That's what's worrying me," India replied.

Gina gave her a look, then leaned over and kissed India's lips. "Open it."

India did, then she smiled. "Isn't that perfect?" She pressed the button and the umbrella shot up, nearly flying out of her hand. "That nearly took me with it." India stood up and hastily put the umbrella down.

"Flying off your *Mary Poppins* rooftop with your Mary Poppins umbrella would certainly have been a look. You might have made it into the papers."

India snorted. "I think we've had enough public attention for a little while, don't you?" She put the umbrella on the wooden table. "But I love it, thank you."

"You're welcome."

To their right, the hot tub was lit up and bubbling against the night sky.

"But now, shall we get in the hot tub?"

Gina glanced down at her clothes. She hadn't changed since they'd got in from Pride half an hour ago. "Are you putting on a swimsuit?"

India shook her head with a grin. "Nah." She flipped off her sandals, then pushed down her jeans and took off her T-shirt. "I've been boiling all day, and it's still warm." She reached out her hand and smoothed some air between her fingers. "It's very much a hot London night." She fluttered her eyelids at Gina. "Made hotter because you're going to be naked in a hot tub with me soon, am I right?"

Gina blinked, then nodded. "Right. I just need to stop staring at my sexy girlfriend and get undressed."

India climbed into the bubbling water. "Come on in, the water's lovely." She settled on the first underwater seat, closing her eyes as the bubbling water cloaked her body. Suddenly, she was weightless. All the stress of today seeped out of her body, and now she was in her new happy place. With Gina, on a rooftop, naked, in a hot tub. All her dreams had come true.

India glanced over to where Gina was stripping off. She licked her lips as her heart fluttered anew. She loved this woman. She should tell her again, just in case there was any confusion.

"Gina," India said. The bubbles stopped. She leaned across, resting her arms on the hot tub lip.

Gina shed her pants, then climbed into the hot tub, settling beside India. Before she could say anything, Gina's lips were on hers, her tongue inside her mouth.

All thoughts but happiness left India's mind.

When they pulled apart, Gina sat beside her, holding hands under the water, staring out at the London skyline.

"This is a pretty special view, especially at night. I love that I can come here anytime to see it."

India brought Gina's hand up from underwater and kissed it. "Anytime you like. My hot tub is your hot tub."

"You had me at hot tub." Gina kissed India's lips, then settled as India put an arm around her.

"Today was okay in the end? My speech? Meeting my brother? Having your family there?" India had thought so, but she'd left Gina to her own devices for long periods while she'd overseen her biscuit army.

Gina nodded. "It was, surprisingly. I've always been worried about my worlds colliding, but when it happened, it was like it was meant to be." She paused, turning her face to India. "Now I just have to worry about meeting your mum and dad at lunch tomorrow."

India shook her head. "They're excited to meet you. I'm more nervous, as it's the first Sunday lunch I'm hosting. Luca and Ricardo have done a couple, but it's normally at my parents'. This means I'm a grown-up now." She made a funny face at Gina.

Gina bumped her with her hip. "It comes to us all. You've got a flat, a company to run, and a girlfriend. It's about time you cooked a roast, Contelli. Plus, you have a very sexy and willing sous chef." Gina paused. "By the way, when I spoke to my mum this week, she reminded me to ask you a question." She winced. "They want you to come and speak to the Asian business community in Birmingham. She thinks it would give them a boost. I think it's my mum showing off, but I said I'd ask."

India hated the hesitation in Gina's voice. She pulled Gina

tighter to her. "If it mends any fences with your parents, of course I'll do it."

Gina shook her head. "Forget I asked. You don't have to."

"Stop." India stroked Gina's arm and waited for her to still. "Your family is important. You're meeting mine tomorrow, and if we're a couple, it's what couples do, right? They do things for each other. I'm happy to do this for you."

Gina stared at her. "I'm not sure how I found you, but I'm happy I did."

"The feeling's mutual." She gazed at Gina, then shook her head. India brought a hand out of the water, drops and spray scattering as she swept her arm through the air. "This is everything I ever dreamed of. A place to call my own where nobody else has a key but me. My family might be coming tomorrow, but they have to ring a doorbell. That's a big difference." She turned to Gina. "And then there's you. You're way beyond what I dreamed of."

Gina rolled her eyes. "Stop it, you're going to make me blush or barf, I can't decide which."

But India was serious. "I don't care if I'm being sentimental or over the top. I've never felt like this before." She rolled her shoulders, trying to convey her emotions. "It feels like…"

The world stopped for a few seconds as India tried to finish her sentence.

Instead, Gina finished it for her. "Like you're finally living the correct life?"

"Yes." *That was it*. Meeting Gina had turned India's life from mottled to gold. "I feel like my life is on an even keel, rather than listing."

Gina gave a slight nod of her head. "Me, too."

India pulled Gina into her lap, so Gina was straddling her. "I think today was the most perfect day."

Gina gulped, eyeing India's lips. "I agree." She moved so their mouths were inches apart.

India's heart hammered in her chest. "Whatever comes next, promise me we'll handle it together? Even the Birmingham Asian business community."

Gina let out a howl of laughter. "I promise. Just you and me."

India leaned in and pressed her lips to Gina's, and her whole world lit up. Kissing Gina was life. Being with Gina was life.

She believed in them, and she believed Gina's words. Whatever was next, they were going to face the world together.

Living their lives. Just one heartbeat at a time.

THE END

Want more from me? Sign up to join my VIP Readers'
Group and get a FREE lesbian romance,
It Had To Be You! *Claim your free book here:*
www.clarelydon.co.uk/it-had-to-be-you

Would You Leave Me A Review?

 If you enjoyed this slice of sapphic London life, I wonder if you'd consider leaving me a review wherever you bought it. Just a line or two is fine, and could really make the difference for someone else when they're wondering whether or not to take a chance on me and my writing. If you enjoyed the book and tell them why, it's possible your words will make them click the buy button, too! Just hop on over to wherever you bought this book — Amazon, Apple Books, Kobo, Bella Books, Barnes & Noble or any of the other digital outlets — and say what's in your heart. I always appreciate honest reviews.

Thank you, you're the best.

Love,
Clare x

Also By Clare Lydon

London Romance Series
London Calling (Book One)
This London Love (Book Two)
A Girl Called London (Book Three)
The London Of Us (Book Four)
London, Actually (Book Five)
Made In London (Book Six)
Hot London Nights (Book Seven)
Big London Dreams (Book Eight)
London Ever After (Book Nine)

Standalone Novels
A Taste Of Love
Before You Say I Do
Change Of Heart
Christmas In Mistletoe
Hotshot
It Started With A Kiss
Nothing To Lose: A Lesbian Romance
Once Upon A Princess
One Golden Summer
The Christmas Catch
The Long Weekend
Twice In A Lifetime
You're My Kind

All I Want Series
Two novels and four novellas chart the course
of one relationship over two years.

Boxsets
Available for both the London Romance series and the
All I Want series for ultimate value. Check out my
website for more: www.clarelydon.co.uk/books

Printed in Great Britain
by Amazon

40556429R00169